instances of the number 3

Salley Vickers' novel *Miss Garnet's Angel* attracted wide critical acclaim. A former university lecturer in Literature, she also works as a psychologist. She divides her time between London, Venice and the West Country.

For more information on Salley Vickers' *Instances of the Number 3* and to download a reading guide, visit www.4thestate.com/salleyvickers or visit the author's website at www.salleyvickers.com

instances of the number 3

SALLEY VICKERS

FOURTH ESTATE • London

This paperback edition first published in 2002
First published in Great Britain in 2001 by
Fourth Estate
A Division of HarperCollins*Publishers*
77–85 Fulham Palace Road,
London W6 8JB
www.4thestate.com
www.salleyvickers.com

A catalogue record for this book is available from the
British Library.

ISBN 1-84115-659-0

Typeset by Rowland Phototypesetting Limited,
Bury St Edmunds, Suffolk.
Printed in Great Britain by
Clays Ltd, St Ives plc

For Rupert Kingfisher,
whose play *The Prisoner's Dilemma* first
suggested to me the creative possibilities in
the number 3

It must have required many ages to discover that a brace of pheasants and a couple of days were both instances of the number 2: the degree of abstraction involved is far from easy . . .

BERTRAND RUSSELL

Preface

It is said there were ancient schools of thought which held that the number 3 is unstable. If the reasons for this belief were ever known they are lost in time. A three-legged stool refutes the claim, as – less prosaically – we are told does the Christian trinity. Whatever the case, it is a fact that three is a protean number: under certain conditions it will tend to collapse into two – or expand into four . . .

I

After Peter Hansome died, people were surprised that his widow seemed to be spending so much time with his mistress. Bridget Hansome was not the kind of woman who could have failed to notice her husband's discreet, but regular, visits to the flat in Turnham Green where Frances Slater lived. And, indeed, anyone married to Peter Hansome would have needed to learn the art of turning a blind eye. Had the various friends and acquaintances of the Hansomes' been asked to bet on how the wife might deal with a mistress discovered in the aftermath of the husband's death (were it the thing to gamble on the likely effects on a widow of the discovery of a long-established infidelity), the odds would probably have been on Bridget allowing Frances to attend the funeral, but with an unspoken provision that no mention be made of the reason for her being there.

In the event the punters would have lost their bets for this is not what occurred. In spite of the fact that she lived nearby – the cremation was conducted at a cemetery off the Lower Richmond Road – Frances did not attend the funeral ceremony. She had a still lively recollection of a warm evening, on which the same cemetery had been the scene of one of Peter's more flamboyant acts of lovemaking. Whether it was this, and the fact that she could not, therefore, easily reconcile herself to it as the place from which she must make a final farewell to the body that – flanked by marble angels and other funerary pieces – had lately enjoyed her own, must rest as one of those matters into which we shall not, for the moment, enquire. What is known is that on the day of the funeral, Frances took the Eurostar to Paris, where she concluded a walk by the Seine with a visit to Notre-Dame – stopping, before entering the cathedral, to buy a bunch of anemones from a flower seller.

Bridget Hansome was well aware that she was not the only woman to enjoy her husband's affections. 'Handsome is as handsome does!' she had been in the habit of saying, making a small pun on her husband's name. This observation was generally accompanied by one of her little ironic smiles. These smiles might have been described as affectionate, but they might equally have been described as sly. Whatever the truth of the matter (and it is also a truth that human emotion tends to be made up of different, and often competing, strands), Peter took the smiles in good part. He was a physically vain man and, not quite understanding the point of the saying – more accurately, for he was not stupid either, not really troubling to comprehend it – was mildly pleased to have a wife who appreciated his looks enough to joke about them, despite the fact that they brought with them certain consequences.

One of these 'consequences' was Frances. There had

been others – not too many – over the years, but Frances was the only one who could be said to have stuck. In fact it was Bridget herself who had been the cause of the introduction, during one of her trips abroad.

Early on in her marriage Bridget had discovered that her husband disliked her being away from home. It is unlikely that Peter himself was aware that his extramarital escapades had more to do with an incapability with his own loneliness than the outward appearance he was quietly proud of – women tending, perversely perhaps, to be more susceptible to marks of inward frailty than rugged good looks. It is a fact, however, that it is easier to be tender towards a failing when it is not part of one's daily dealings. Bridget had been first alarmed, then concerned and finally increasingly impatient when she found that Peter became fractious, and prone to what she privately termed 'sillinesses', when she made one of her regular trips abroad.

Bridget sold old French bric-à-brac. She had started with a stall on the Portobello Road but now ran a thriving shop in Fulham, which traded in garden furniture, aged linen, enamel pans, lace curtains, parasols – items of faded beauty from a French pastoral past for which she had a particular eye. In these days of shabby chic such shops are commonplace. But Bridget, in perceiving that something worn and traditional might be what was missing from modern lives, had been in the vanguard of contemporary taste. It was she who pioneered the belief that the venerable might be more stylish than the smart – the glass and steel designs which were once the height of interior fashion for the well heeled. Ahead of her imitators, she became established as a 'name', of sorts; the 'Living' pages of newspapers and magazines deferred to her for hints on the newest 'old' styles.

Bridget was also blessed with sources of supply for the items she sold in her shop – still-secret places in the heart of rural France which her later competitors had neither the luck nor the stamina to discover. The stamina was required for the combination of long drive and longer conversations in vernacular French, accompanied by large quantities of coffee or wine or, as the day went on, spirits drawn from complicated bottles. These tête-à-têtes would be conducted with elderly men or women in minor decaying châteaux, who were pleased to offload the mouldering relics of a bygone way of life to the blonde *Anglaise* who seemed sincere in her love of their country and its artefacts.

And there was no doubt that Bridget was sincere. One of her hallmarks was that she was a person who lacked 'side' – too much so for some, who found her blunt. This did not mean, however, that she necessarily revealed all that she thought. Indeed, the years of living with Peter had taught her to keep many of her observations to herself, full revelation, she couldn't help feeling, being something which was a virtue only among the reckless or the cruel. So that finally – for her rather late in the day – perceiving that her husband missed her, she did not voice this realisation directly but instead asked Mickey, who lived next door, if she would 'keep an eye' on Peter.

Mickey had lived in their terraced street since long before Peter and Bridget had married and bought their house. Although the house had not been fashionable when they bought it, they had had to scrape around to find the deposit as these were the days when Bridget was just starting her Fulham shop and Peter had another wife and another establishment – one with children in it – to keep. The area had 'come up' since, but Mickey was a survivor of its more modest past, having inherited the house from her mother whom she had womanfully looked after till the day the old lady died.

'It's my pride my mum never saw the inside of a hospital,' Mickey had said to Bridget when the latter had called asking to borrow sugar for the removal men's tea, thus setting the tone for a relationship in which Mickey had continued, on and off, to supply sugar for twenty years. Mickey loved to chat and as Peter liked, in a certain mood, to chat himself – chatting being something which Bridget was conscious of not always sufficiently supplying either for her husband or her neighbour – the hope had been that Mickey might go some way to fill the gap made by Bridget's periodic 'French leaves'.

Mickey also liked her drink. Driving through the quiet countryside of mid France, observing the boles of mistletoe silhouetted in the columns of poplars against a wide azure sky, Bridget would think of her husband and Mickey sipping whiskies together; it was easier to feel fond of them both when she was away.

It was on just such an occasion, when Bridget was off in Normandy for a pre-Easter run, that Mickey invited Peter round. The weather was unseasonably fine, the sun quite searching for March, and they sat outside admiring the smart ranks of colour-coordinated daffodils in Mickey's garden.

'This is my friend Frances,' Mickey had said, indicating a thin, dark woman, considerably younger than her hostess, but with what Peter was later to describe as 'old'

5

eyes. It was not exactly the case that Frances was a 'friend'. Mickey was liberal in her friendships and Frances turned out to be someone Mickey had met casually at the estate agents where she worked part-time on Wednesdays and Saturdays.

Frances was looking for a house in the area and Mickey, who liked to be of help (it was also to soak up some of that liking to help – where she was conscious of giving disappointment – that Bridget had made the suggestion about Peter), had asked Frances back for a drink to 'give her an idea of what these are like', since Frances had indicated it was such a house that she was hoping to buy.

In the end Frances bought a flat in Turnham Green, the prices of the Fulham houses having risen beyond her pocket, where, after a suitable lapse of time, Peter visited her during one of Bridget's summer trips to the Vichy area.

'I love my wife,' he had declared, this being the gesture of fidelity to Bridget he was in the habit of making on such occasions. 'If we are going to do this you must understand I will never leave her.'

And in saying he 'loved' Bridget Peter was not, as it happens, speaking to deceive. His liking for chat was not, as is sometimes supposed, a sign of superficiality, any more than a tendency to silence necessarily indicates depth. 'Chatting' was one of Peter's means of helping himself to stay alive.

Frances, who had closed down an affair when the man was foolish enough to suggest that he was 'misunderstood', was not displeased to hear a man speak unashamedly of love for his wife. Although Frances was not prone to introspection, unconsciously she was aware that as a man speaks so he is: a declaration of conjugal love was a sign of an affectionate nature – and a loyal one, of a kind. At least Peter was not going to 'explain' any entanglement with her as a product of ill treatment meted out to him elsewhere. Frances did not care to be seen as some sort of therapist – sexual or otherwise. She liked – as most of us do – to be liked for her own inherent qualities, good and bad, and not as a reaction to qualities in another person.

Frances was thirty-six when she first met Peter – an age when women often suffer degrees of anxiety about 'settling down'. Whether her liking for Peter was as innocent of a reactive component as his was for her is another question entirely.

2

Peter was sixty-two when he died. A truck driver, in an October fog, leaning to adjust the volume on his tape of *Elton John's Greatest Hits*, took his eye from the road, failed to see a car coming up on the run into the Hogarth roundabout, swerved to avoid the car and, instead, hit Peter's BMW, broadside. This, not fatal in itself, had the result that the BMW was swung around in the path of a speeding Mercedes. The driver of the truck was shaken, the driver of the Mercedes damaged his arm, but Peter's neck was broken in the ensuing crash.

The Hogarth roundabout happened to be the spot where if he had been going to visit Frances Peter would have swung off to the left. The roundabout was also the final stage of the normal route home to Fulham. What no one could know was that Peter was intending to make his way to neither of these destinations, but instead to a discreetly-fronted house in Shepherd's Bush where unusual tastes of all kinds were catered for. Although neither woman had any knowledge of this other destination, it is true to say that of the two Bridget would have best tolerated the knowledge.

For weeks after Peter's death Bridget was unable to do anything about his things. Reluctant to move so much as a paper clip from his desk, she walked about the house playing old records, opening and putting down books, eating cold baked beans, keeping unusual hours. Sometimes she moved in a slow, stately dance to the voices of Nat King Cole, Johnny Mathis, Eartha Kitt – tunes she and Peter had known when they were younger: 'walking out', as she herself had called it; in particular she became addicted to a song entitled 'Love for Sale'.

Because Bridget was older than Peter she had always imagined to herself that she would be the one to die first. This had mildly bothered her: past form suggested that she would better be able than her husband to cope with a permanent absence. From time to time she had allowed herself the luxury of making vivid how, in the event of her own death, she would be missed by Peter. She had not quite defined in her mind the form this 'missing' would take, but it might have included a new-found impatience on her husband's part with an alternative source of feminine comfort.

What Bridget found she disliked most, in the weeks after Peter's death, was having to talk about him. There were numerous phone calls; the letters were not such a pressure – these she could reply to in the familiar-smelling comfort of their double bed, where she wore Peter's shirts and sometimes, because her feet had grown unaccountably cold, his woolly socks. But the *talking* . . . how she loathed it! And yet, how kind people wanted to appear – really, it made one take against 'kindness'. Yet for all Bridget's indifference to appearances it seemed wrong to her to leave the answerphone on. She must not be stingy with her loss – she felt it should be shared, available to all, like the torrential rains they were having this autumn.

And it was the case that the skies seemed to have some secret sympathy for her dead husband: they wept and howled impressively, highlighting her own lack of tears.

Bridget found she could not cry for Peter. Indeed, when she was obliged to participate in the conversations she so detested, she was conscious of a note in her voice which she knew must sound at odds with her situation. She was aware that this was disconcerting to those who had called to condole.

To call this note 'gleeful' would be inaccurate. It was not glee in Bridget's voice, but it might have been mistaken for it; so that Frances, when she plucked up the courage to call the Fulham number, thought for a moment, as Bridget peremptorily answered the phone: Oh, she doesn't mind!

'It's Frances Slater,' she said. And waited.

Bridget knew, of course, who Frances was. Peter, with unusual foresight, had once said, 'If anything happens to me there's someone who might get in touch,' and Bridget, with perfect understanding – though not, as it turned out, perfect prescience – had replied, 'Nothing's going to happen to you – don't be melodramatic.' But had added, less briskly, 'Of course I would speak to anyone who mattered.'

However, when she took Frances's call, she simply said, 'Ah yes!' which Frances found discouraging.

'I knew Peter,' Frances had continued, and just in time prevented herself adding 'a little'. She did not want, by implying the connexion with Peter was less than it had been, to slide into appeasing Peter's wife.

Bridget had never been one for appeasement. 'I know,' she said. 'I expect you're feeling odd, aren't you?' which was a surprise to Frances after the discouragement.

The two women met first in the café at John Lewis. This was Bridget's idea – she was keen to avoid anything which hinted at the scent of camellias. And it was convenient for Frances, who worked in Soho nearby.

'I've bought a night light,' Bridget announced after Frances had found her ('You'll know me, I expect, I'm big and blonde and I'll be wearing green'). A conical transparent light with coloured seahorses bobbing around in it sat, slightly absurdly, on the pale teak-effect table between the two women. 'The seahorses rise and fall when the light is on.'

'Are you sleeping OK?' Frances asked. It had sounded like a cue.

'Moderately,' said Bridget. 'And when you switch it off there's a mermaid at the bottom, combing her hair and admiring herself in a looking glass. See!' She pointed out a small but perfectly formed maiden with a curvaceous green plastic fishtail.

Frances, who was quick, got the drift: there was to be no demonstration of emotion. 'I had something like that once,' she offered. 'It was in one of those globe things children get given – you shook it and bits flew around.' The remark felt like a shot in the dark.

Happily it hit home. 'Usually snow,' Bridget agreed.

'Do you want tea? If so we'll have to get another pot – I've drunk nearly all this already.'

Outside the weather rained down tears. Bridget thought: She's not too bad, and felt it was not impossible that she might, one day, drop tears too.

'You don't look like the kind of woman who "needs to talk",' Bridget said. 'I'd better say, frankly, from the outset, that "talking" is not part of my plan. However –' she went on, as if there had been an attempt to interrupt, which was not the case, for Frances was listening in silent fascination – 'it seems discourteous, somehow, to Peter if we don't meet, though I hardly know how we should conduct ourselves.'

What Frances thought was: Why does she have to be so *different*? Aloud, she said, 'I don't know that I want so terribly to "talk" either – though there are things I could probably only say to you.'

'That's true,' conceded Bridget, and lapsed into morose silence.

Frances tipped tea around the cup and watched a couple across the way having a row. 'You've always fancied her – don't bother to deny it!' she heard the woman say – a woman with badly applied make-up and backcombed hair. At least, Frances thought, we are spared scenes like that. For the first time it crossed her mind that they were a threesome – herself, Peter and Bridget. *Were* a threesome, she supposed she must think of it now.

'There's a concert on at the Wigmore Hall –' Bridget said, suddenly coming to – 'Schubert – which I like – and Mahler – which I don't, but we could sneak out after the interval – unless you like Mahler, that is?'

Frances said that she had no particular view on Mahler. As it happened, she had no particular view on Schubert either.

3

'The point is,' Bridget said, sucking noisily at a bone from the remains of her *coq au vin*, 'Schubert is never bogus – but Mahler can be.'

They were eating, after the concert, at a restaurant which each woman had visited with Peter. Neither made even oblique reference to this. Tactfully, they commented on the decor, the stylish young waiters and waitresses, with no suggestion that they might have shared opinions on such matters with the dead man who had brought them together.

Frances said, 'I'm ignorant about music – but I suppose like it better when it isn't too loud.'

'Quite right,' Bridget agreed. 'Symphonies are over-rated.' She tapped a cigarette from a blue *Gauloise*s packet. 'Do you mind?'

Too late if I do! thought Frances. 'Not at all.'

'You never know these days.'

Frances thought: She must have been pretty once with that colouring.

Bridget thought: I wouldn't have minded a nose like that, beaky and aristocratic.

The waiter came and flirted idly with the two women, but more with Bridget because of her French. Bridget asked which part of France he was from and there followed an animated conversation on Arlesian sausage.

'How did you learn?' Frances asked.

'Practice. I learned most haggling. The French respect you more if you bargain hard – but you need the slang to keep up.'

'I'm not good at languages,' said Frances. 'That's two things you're better at – languages and music.'

'It's not a competition!' Bridget remarked coldly.

Frances always travelled to work by tube so Bridget drove her home. Passing Turnham Green Bridget said, 'It's where they turned 'em back, isn't it?'

'Back?'

'The Civil War,' Bridget explained. 'The Roundhead apprentices turned back the Royalists here – hence "Turn 'em Green" – it was the site of a battle.'

'Oh, yes.' Frances was not really listening. Bothered over what she should do about asking Bridget in when they reached the flat, she preferred not to be lectured to about her own neighbourhood. She wanted to dispel the annoyance by saying, 'That's three things then you know more about than me: music, languages and local history.' It was the kind of remark she might have made to Peter and it would have made him laugh. That she could no longer say such things suddenly depressed her. She decided she wouldn't ask Bridget in after all.

'Would you like to come in for a drink?' she heard herself saying and was doubly angry when Bridget accepted. I am managing this badly, she thought, ushering

15

Bridget into the flat where she had been used to receiving Bridget's husband.

Frances's flat was like Frances. Drifting round the room Bridget noticed the books were all in alphabetical order. Few ornaments, but three very good paintings on the sunflower-yellow walls.

'That's a Kavanagh, isn't it?' Bridget peered at a picture of a nude in high heels, reading in a striped deckchair. (Peter, in fact, had bought it for Frances's thirty-seventh birthday. 'I thought she was like you,' he had said, removing all her clothes but her shoes.)

'Yes,' said Frances, shortly, glad she had her back to Bridget and was occupied with pouring whisky and water.

Bridget, who had her country's usual measure of tele-pathic powers, smiled rather nastily at the back. The nude's resemblance to Frances had not escaped her; Peter liked that sort of statement: he had once given Bridget a small, powerful bronze of a woman naked on a horse.

She lay back, deliberately sprawling across the clean lines of the sofa, imagining her husband here. He would have drunk whisky and water too. Frances had poured Jameson for her, the whisky Peter had liked. Frances herself, she noticed, was drinking brandy.

'It's funny,' Bridget said, conversationally, 'I can't believe he's dead. Do you weep at all, yourself?'

'Not at all,' Frances lied. She didn't want this. 'I've been too busy,' she added, unnecessarily. It wasn't true; time had hung about her like a moody adolescent.

'You see,' said Bridget, ignoring Frances's efforts at camouflage, 'a person – I expect you know this – isn't only flesh and blood. A person exists inside one, informing one's state of mind. There were whole weeks when Peter and I were apart – of course, you know that too! – so my system hasn't got the habit of the difference. I keep expecting to come home and find him there. And when I don't, when I walk in and everything's as I left it, my system just thinks: Oh well, he'll be along later, what's all the fuss about?'

Frances, who had noted the parenthetical 'of course you know that too', was partially reassured. 'I haven't got used to it, either,' she agreed. 'But then I saw him in patches anyway.' She felt better with the matter of her arrangements with Peter broached.

'A thing of something and patches,' said Bridget, lazily. 'What's that . . . ?'

But Frances didn't know. She was thinking it mightn't be so hard for Peter to have been in love with his wife. This thought only faintly troubled her: Peter had needed her too, needed her orderliness. Bridget had the air of something frightening about her: she might be amused by, even entertain, perturbation.

'*Hamlet*,' Bridget said suddenly. 'Of course, it's *Hamlet*, I'll forget my own name next. It's "*king*" not "thing" – "a king of shreds and patches".' She fell backwards on the pale sofa, triumphant.

'We did *Hamlet* at school,' said Frances, determined this time not to be outdone. 'I played Gertrude; I didn't like her.'

'Hmm,' said Bridget, unconvinced. She had some sympathy for the queen who had married her husband's killer. '*Hamlet*'s a case in point.' she said darkly. 'Look what happens when Hamlet's father dies – he doesn't go

17

away. Quite the reverse. He comes back and rants like all get out!'

'I do hope Peter won't come back and rant,' said Frances, feeling it was safe now to risk humour.

4

It seemed obvious that Frances should be the first to be told.

'I'm buying a house in Shropshire,' Bridget had said.

'But you're not leaving Fulham altogether, are you?' Frances had asked, with an odd sense of being abandoned.

By now Frances and Bridget had met several times. More regularly, Frances suggested, trying somewhat to mollify Bridget, than she had met with Peter. Bridget, however, had not been mollified. She was quite able to like Frances without liking what Frances had meant to Peter.

Most women in Bridget's shoes as a matter of course would have detested Frances. But this is not an account of feminine jealousy, or even revenge, and not all human beings (not even women) conform to the attitudes generally expected of them. Bridget was interested in Frances because Peter had been. She did not enjoy the fact that Frances had been her husband's mistress, but she was aware that her thoughts or feelings could now have little impact – if they ever had – on the hard facts of Peter's liking for another woman.

Frances, equally, might have disliked Bridget, except that in Frances's case, with Peter gone, it was almost as if Bridget was a point of contact with him.

It was also interesting to Bridget that she and Frances talked on the phone, because Bridget was not, as she liked to say, a 'phone person'. 'I prefer letters,' she had explained to Peter when, still married to someone else, he had reproved her for being brusque with him when he rang unexpectedly from a coin box. 'With letters you can be sure you are not interrupting someone.' 'I'm sorry if I was interrupting,' he had declared, slightly huffily.

Bridget had found the house when she had gone away for a weekend to a country hotel. The hotel was a reward for having finally steeled herself to go through Peter's bureau drawers – an exercise to which she had not been looking forward. She had never been what Peter had referred to as a 'rummager'. Whatever Peter kept in his drawers was his own affair: Bridget had never had the faintest temptation to pry.

This lack of temptation proved unhelpful when it survived her husband's death. Certain forms of intimacy seemed out of place to Bridget within the cool depths of her union with Peter. She did not warm to the kind of relationship which shares bathrooms, just as she felt there were other matters which should be kept private. On several occasions she had opened the desk, taken out a few papers and felt a strong inclination to make a bonfire of them. As it happened, she had just braved the first pile of bank statements when Frances made her introductory phone call and it was relief at this distraction which had prompted Bridget's suggestion that they meet. Maybe it was the stimulus of meeting Frances, but after that long, peculiar day – the tea at John Lewis's followed by the Wigmore Hall and ending with the whisky at Frances's flat – Bridget set to work, 'like a Trojan!', and polished off the contents of the oak bureau with surprising speed. It was after this that she had gone to stay in Shropshire.

The hotel had been shabby, with chestnut-wood fires and wild duck on the lake – also on the menu. It was in the hollow of time before Christmas and the hotel was empty except for herself and a couple conducting an illicit affair.

Bridget scrutinised the couple with more-than-usual intensity. They seemed much too merry for her, with none of the easy familiarity which she had known with Peter. Possibly Peter had been 'merry' with Frances? One day, she speculated, she might ask.

On the Saturday morning Bridget had set out to follow a footpath across a ploughed field, bare but for a grounded flock of strutting lapwing. '*O green-crested lapwing, thy-eye screaming forebear-air,*' sang Bridget at the top of her voice. '*I-eye charge thee disturb not my-eye slumbering fair,*' passing, at the first stile, the young woman from the hotel alone, and in visible tears. Well, if that was going to be the penalty of merriment! Not wanting to be dogged by this picture of woe, Bridget had turned off the footpath and followed along a hawthorn hedge to a lane.

The lane resolved into a red-brick house with four chimneys and a 'For Sale' sign stuck on a post in the garden. Hearing footsteps, and fearing pursuit from the tear-stained young woman, Bridget veered into the porch.

'I'm sorry to disturb you,' she apologised to the man who answered the door. 'But I saw the sign.'

The oak bureau had lately yielded up the news that Bridget would be £250,000 better off from a life-insurance policy. It seemed fitting that this should turn out to be the figure quoted for the Shropshire house, which Bridget bought at the asking price without even benefit of survey.

'There was no need for one,' she explained to Frances when she telephoned her. 'It smelled dry, there are fire-places and there's a view.' Of hills – remote, misty. There was also a rookery in the elm tree at the bottom of the garden but that she kept to herself.

What Bridget found she wanted, once she had begun to assimilate the fact that Peter would never return, was a place where there were no associations. It was not so much Peter himself that she needed the rest from, but the effect of his dying. The dying had eaten into her reserves: the people, the pitiless paperwork, the exhausting failure to weep. The house where they had spent their married life seemed filled with bewildering and demanding tur-moil. She resented the expense of trying to meet all this – that was why she wanted to get away – among the rooks.

'It'll only be for weekends,' she reassured Mickey.

Bridget had decided to give Mickey something from Peter's alleged will. In fact, everything had been left, in her lifetime, to Bridget, but this did not hinder Bridget from interpreting the will in her own way. Mickey had stood in for Peter's wife in her absences; it was appropri-ate Mickey should be rewarded. A thousand pounds seemed the right sort of sum.

Mickey had taken the money with a lack of resistance which made Bridget wonder if the apocryphal legacy should have been rather more; nor had Mickey been reassured by Bridget's account of the house in Shropshire.

'If it's weekends you're thinking of going there and you away all that time abroad, I shan't hardly see you, then.'

'Not every weekend.' Bridget had tried to be placating. She had, in fact, hired an assistant to serve in the shop at weekends so theoretically she could be away every one if she wished.

'I'd say it was dangerous, leaving your house with no one there like that. Course I'm next door but I'm only an old woman – no match for any burglar or whoever chooses to call!' her neighbour had said with unconsoled relish.

5

Mickey's words stuck in Bridget's mind. Perhaps it was foolish to leave a London house regularly unattended? How she wanted to get away, though, and be by herself. It seemed as if she had never been by herself, not since she married Peter. So when the boy turned up it was almost like an answer to a prayer.

The doorbell rang one Saturday morning when, dressed only in one of Peter's Vyella shirts, she was trying to steel herself to face Peter's papers and was tempted not to answer. She had found Peter's dressing gown and had it clutched about her when she got to the door and saw the boy walking back down the path. Thanks to the many occasions she had crept home from trips abroad in the small hours, the hinge of the door had been worked on to open quietly, so he did not hear her and she could have let him go altogether and resumed her vague sortings of the papers into toppling piles. It was the sight of the sharp little protruding shoulder blades, almost like wings, she thought, which made her call out, 'Did you want something?'

The boy turned at her voice and she saw a young face which was, as she phrased it later to Frances, 'as beautiful as the day – quite breathtaking!' Frances, who had so far encountered only the firmer of Bridget's surfaces, was momentarily surprised and then amused at the hyperbole. (That this was not hyperbole but the straightest report became clear only much later when Frances also met Zahin and described him, in turn, as like a 'dark Apollo'. By then the 'Apollo' was staying in Bridget's house – but this is to anticipate.)

The boy hesitated, then moved back up the path towards her. Bridget noticed that he had plucked a soft green frond of the rosemary which grew in an aromatic bush by the front door. He was neatly dressed, the boy, in a white shirt, navy sweater and grey trousers. The trousers gave the impression of having been pressed for the occasion.

Moved by the sight of the tender spear of rosemary twisting in his hand Bridget thawed. 'Hello?'

The boy did not smile but bowed his head a little. When he looked up she saw that despite his dark hair and complexion he had eyes of the deepest blue. 'Excuse me please.'

'Can I help you?' He had a small gold earring in his right ear.

'I was looking for Mr Hansome.'

'Ah,' said Bridget, 'in that case you'd better come inside.'

He stood in the middle of the kitchen in an attitude of respect so that Bridget felt she had almost to push him down into a chair. 'Would you like coffee?' He shook his head. 'Tea?' Another shake. 'What can I offer you to drink then?' If this young man was unacquainted with Peter's death he might need to be fortified against the news – or she, at least, needed to be fortified against telling it.

'Please, a glass of milk?'

Grateful for this temporary relief Bridget took down one of her glasses that she had brought back from Limoges and filled it to the brim; the white milk glowed green behind the thick glass. She poured herself coffee and sat down opposite the boy across the kitchen table. 'I am Mrs Hansome,' she said. 'I'm sorry if this is a shock to you but Mr Hansome, my husband, is dead. He was killed in a car crash some weeks ago.' It would soon be Christmas; almost two months since she herself had received the news from the policewoman with the guarded face.

An expression of intense surprise flickered across the blue eyes. 'But he is married . . . ?' It was as if the other news had passed quite over him.

'Yes,' said Bridget amused. 'He is, or was married. I am his wife,' she repeated, 'or his widow, I suppose now.' And indeed this was the first time she had consciously applied the word to herself.

The boy put his head upon the table and began to cry. The crying made big searing sobs so that Bridget hearing them was filled with something like admiration. To be able to weep like that – it was remarkable!

She leaned across the table and patted his shoulder. 'He felt nothing,' she said. 'Don't worry – he was not in pain.' Against such a torrential display she felt she must provide some consolation.

The boy lifted his head and looked at her with tragic

26

eyes. 'I did not know. He was my friend and I did not know.'

'Yes,' said Bridget, taxed by her ignorance of the identity of this young person, 'I agree. It is terrible not to know.'

The boy began to drink the milk. He took big noisy gulps, draining the glass. Then he licked around his upper lip where a soft vestigial moustache was barely showing. 'I am called Zahin,' he said.

'And I am Bridget.'

'You are Mrs Hansome?'

'Yes,' said Bridget. The penny seemed at last to have dropped. 'I am Mrs Hansome.'

'Then,' said the boy, 'you will help me.'

'And he just sat there and asked you, straight out?' Frances asked.

'Not so much "asked" – more like told.'

They were eating together in Bridget's kitchen. On the wall, behind Bridget from where she was sitting, Frances could see the plate she had given Peter for his fifty-sixth birthday. A pale green glazed plate – Chinese; the kitchen wall was not where she would have hung it.

'But who is he?'

Supper was eggs and tomatoes which Bridget had fried in the virgin olive oil she brought from France in unlabelled bottles, only produced for special guests. Mopping her plate with a corner of baguette, Bridget checked an automatic inward response of: Mind your own business! 'He seems to have met Peter at a sponsorship do – his firm sponsored kids through school from

27

various parts of the world they were dealing with.'

From Iran. The boy had told her. 'My father's family were good friends with the Shah – when he died my family became outcast – it is dangerous for the men in our family. So, two years ago I come to England.'

Frances did not say, as another woman might have done, I wonder why Peter never mentioned it? She knew as well as Bridget that Peter was a man whose life ran to compartments. Instead she said, 'But where has he been living until now?'

A sensible question, Bridget thought, approving Frances's practicality. 'With another Iranian family, but now they are moving to the States. Apparently, Peter knew this and promised, when the time came, to help the boy find a new berth. But the time came for Peter first,' she concluded, making one of her slightly morbid jokes.

Frances, whose failure to respond to the joke didn't mean she didn't get it, said, 'Is he a nice boy? Did you like him?'

'I liked him, I think,' said Bridget. 'As to whether he's "nice" I wouldn't care to say.'

And it was the case, she thought later, washing up after Frances had left – having declined Frances's help – she couldn't say whether the boy was 'nice', 'niceness' being a quality which did not have much meaning for her. The mechanical business of washing and drying dishes was calming before bed. As to 'liking' people, that was a different matter. Did she like the boy? It was too soon to say. But there must have been something or she would not have come out with her bold suggestion.

Climbing into bed in Peter's shirt it came to her that

the boy had had some effect: he had been enlivening, quickening something which had lain fallow in her since Peter's unexpected departure.

6

Bridget called to deliver Mickey's Christmas present, a blanket made up from coloured knitted squares. Bridget was aware that this might not find favour: Mickey, who was a traditionalist, would have preferred something on more conventional lines – a set of bath luxuries, a frilly nightdress, port. But Bridget could never bring herself to give to others what she herself would not enjoy.

'I have found a lodger,' she said, as much as anything to fill in the silence with which Mickey was contemplating the cheerful squares. 'He will be here when I am away so I have said to him that if there's any problem he can ask you.'

'My mother had one like this. Where d'you get it? Wouldn't be surprised if it wasn't hers come back to me.'

Bridget, who had bought the blanket from a colleague in Southend in exchange for a stuffed tapir, said she had bought it in a Chelsea sale.

'There you are – could easy be mother's, she got rid of all her stuff when she come to live with me.' With an air of one who knew how to do things properly Mickey presented Bridget with an oblong package wrapped in red and gold ribbon and holly paper. A strong smell of violets confirmed the identity of the gift. 'Coty bath cubes – same as I always give you.' No surprises there.

Mickey, at first pleased to have news that there was to be company next door, was dismayed to find that the lodger Bridget was planning to install was what, among her friends, she still referred to as 'dusky'.

'He's a nice enough boy, I'm sure,' she confided to Jean Clancey, over a pre-Christmas drink at the Top and Whistle, 'and pretty as a picture, I'll say that for him. But it's not the same!'

What, for Mickey, was 'not the same' was left to the sympathetic imaginings of her friend. For Bridget, certainly, it was different having Zahin in the house.

In her adult life, Bridget had lived for any space of time with no one other than Peter. She had graduated early from shared flats and had gone without the things other people find essential in order to be able to afford a place on her own. The early days with Peter had sometimes ragged Bridget's nerves. She had found it tiresome when Peter would ask questions when she was engrossed in her book, or demand immediate help in searching out missing socks or journals; or, on one occasion, an old copy of *Wisden* in which he wanted to look up some ancient cricket score. This last had tried Bridget's patience too far and she had remarked, rather acidly, that she hoped he was not going to make use of their relationship to become 'infantile'. Peter had sulked for several days until by a mixture, on her part, of unvarying good temper and ignoring his ill one, harmony had been restored.

It was eight weeks to the day from Peter's death that

Zahin had appeared. In those eight weeks Bridget had found that on the occasions when she was not either missing Peter, or, as she had intimated to Frances, had been unable to believe that his absence was to be permanent, she had failed to recover her old pleasure in her own company. It was true that it was theoretically pleasant to be able to do as you liked; but what she liked was compromised by an awful, lowering sense of futility which had insinuated itself into everything. Without quite recognising that she was doing so, she had turned the beam of her attention towards her husband, whose regular little demands had first irritated, then amused and finally made up much of the regular substance of her life. Now, without spectacles and missing papers to find, calls to make, tickets to order, diets to cook for – Peter had been prone to hypochondria, which had expressed itself in various and often conflicting culinary regimes – she felt dry as dust. The tears the boy had wept so bitterly in her kitchen had somehow fallen upon that 'dried-up' feeling, so that when he spoke of his being at a loss where to live it was not merely sympathy for his plight which had led her to say, 'You can come and stay with me, if you like,' – though caution made her add, 'until you find something more settled.'

Zahin had given an impression which had reminded her of the occasion when she had bestowed Peter's 'bequest' on Mickey: he accepted her suggestion without protest, as if it were his due. Mr Hansome, he told her, had also said that if necessary he could stay at his house with him. The news of this offer, and the fact that Peter had evidently neglected to mention that there was also a Mrs Hansome who might need to be consulted on such a matter, had neither surprised nor angered Bridget. She was used to Peter's quixotic moods: had the boy actually turned up while Peter was alive, he might easily have denied the fact that any such suggestion had been made by him. 'Nonsense, the lad's making it up,' he quite likely would have exclaimed – and Bridget would have had to suggest that in the circumstances it would not inconvenience them greatly if the boy stayed a night or two.

In a sense, then, she was doing no more than she might have done anyway, in proposing that Zahin bring his things over from the flat where he had been living in St John's Wood in time for Christmas Day. I might as well have someone to cook Christmas dinner for, she thought, conscious that this was solving a problem for her which she had not looked forward to having to face.

Frances, who was accustomed to making her Christmas arrangements in time to avoid the sense of aloneness which Bridget was experiencing for the first time, spent the festival with her brother's family. Her brother was a judge on one of the northern circuits and lived in a large house in Northumberland. James's family was large too – also his wife. She and the five girls were good-hearted and energetic – 'excellent people' a friend had once called them.

It is a sad fact that 'excellent people' are often dull. Frances, who began her visits to her brother's home with a pang of envy, usually left the substantial household with a stab of relief: the peace and quiet, if loneliness, of Turnham Green was at least air she could breathe freely.

What with the Northumberland visit and the recovery

from it, it was some days into the new year before Frances finally called by with a present for Bridget.

'I'm sorry,' she said frankly, 'I was too busy to call by sooner. It'll have to be a New Year's gift.' There was a particular reason why she had felt reluctant to see Bridget before Christmas: for the last five years Peter had found time to visit Frances on Christmas Eve.

Bridget, who had already worked out that it must have been Frances over whom Peter had made up the Christmas Eve excuses, had bought her nothing for Christmas. Unwrapping the gift, a glazed dish, which she recognised as bearing a likeness to a dish which Peter had been 'given by a customer at work' one previous Christmas, Bridget surmised that what was being presented to her had been originally bought for Peter. Frances looked the type to plan ahead for Christmas.

'How nice,' she said, without enthusiasm, 'a bowl.' Then, catching sight of Frances's hand clenching the back of a chair, 'Peter would have liked this – it's the sort of thing he often brought home.'

Frances flushed: the frosty jibe didn't escape her. She said, rather strained, 'Did your Christmas go well? How was it with the boy?'

'You can meet him.' Bridget called out, 'Zahin! Come and meet a friend of Mr Hansome's.' Her voice was surprisingly guttural; Frances wondered if Peter had found it sexy.

When the boy came through the door she almost gasped aloud at his beauty. 'Heavens,' she couldn't help exclaiming, 'where ever did you get those eyes, child?'

Zahin, to whom nothing, Bridget had observed, was a compliment said only, 'My mother's people come from near the Caspian Sea. They have blue eyes. Mrs Hansome, may I have some milk?'

'Help yourself.'

In his white shirt, pouring milk, he looked, Frances thought, like some cool-toned modern painting – maybe Hockney?

'Frances knew Mr Hansome, Zahin.'

Intrigued that Peter seemed to have become 'Mister', Frances asked, 'How did you know – er, Mr Hansome, Zahin?'

'It was through his work,' said Bridget, smoothly. 'Remember, I told you – Zahin was one of the families the firm sponsored.'

Peter had confessed to Frances that being confined to England made him restless. Frances, conscious of – indeed, benefiting from – Bridget's own trips abroad, had sometimes wondered why Peter's wife had not noticed that he, too, might have done with a more regular change of scene. Now she said, 'Where is the Caspian Sea? My geography's hopeless.'

The boy was swilling his milk in the glass, watching the viscous surface slew round the side. His blue eyes stared at Frances for a second. Then he said, placidly, 'The part my mother came from is now Iran. My mother is from the old Median people.' It was as if he were speaking of someone known to him long ago.

'The Medians are very ancient,' Bridget said. As usual, Frances thought, she seemed to know all about it.

Noticing that Bridget had plonked the bowl down on the dresser and was carelessly brushing crumbs from the surface around it, Frances suddenly burst out with, 'You needn't keep the bowl if you don't want it,

Bridget. It was silly of me to think of giving it to you. Mistake.'

There was a silence during which the three people in the room all looked at the bowl.

Bridget had been correct in her hunch that Frances had planned to give the Chinese bowl to Peter. Taking it down from the wardrobe shelf, where she amassed her Christmas gifts, she had debated what to do with it: to keep it seemed ghoulish; also, it would be a gesture to give something to Bridget: the thought had given substance to Frances's wish to be generous to Peter's widow.

'It is beautiful.' The boy's words spoken into the charged atmosphere had the quality of some bell – whose authority was no less for its comparative softness – rung as part of some obscure but picturesque ritual. 'I would like to have it in my room. May I, please?'

Bridget was rummaging in a drawer. She said without looking at Frances, 'If Miss Slater doesn't mind . . .'

'Frances,' said Frances firmly – she had had enough of this 'Miss', 'Mrs' business. 'Please, Zahin, do call me Frances. Of course I don't "mind" – it was intended as a present. I just thought maybe Bridget had enough dishes . . .'

Bridget had found Mickey's bath cubes. 'Here you are, present for you.'

Zahin had finished his milk. He walked round the table to the bowl and picked it up, turning it over with delicate fingers. 'The colour is blue – like heaven.'

He looked at Frances and she saw how his eyes had the same blue opacity.

Bridget said suddenly, 'Well now, I'll leave you two to sort it out,' and left the kitchen.

Zahin gently put the bowl down on the table. The silver-bell-like voice spoke again. 'You and Mr Hansome, you were sweethearts . . . ?'

7

Frances and Peter had been away together only a few times. Twice she had travelled with him to Scotland, where Peter had gone for business reasons. On those two occasions they had stayed in the Edinburgh flat of an old school friend of Peter's, a bachelor who travelled abroad, and was grateful to have the flat occupied during his frequent absences. Nor was he fussy about the moral conduct of his guests. Another occasion had been when they had gone to Paris.

The visit to Paris had remained to Frances a kind of touchstone of what people meant by being 'happy'. They had stayed on the Left Bank, in a cramped, almost drab hotel – so dim was its lighting, so very ancient its thread-bare furnishings.

It was in Paris that Peter had begun to call her 'France' the diminutive which he alone was allowed – all other, and previous, attempts, such as 'Francie', or 'Fran', or, once – quite frightfully – 'Frannie', having been instantly squashed by one of her looks – the 'basilisk look' Peter called it. There had been only one other to whom any abbreviated form of address had been permitted: her brother – not James, the judge, but her younger-by-two-years brother Hugh, who had been killed on his motorbike when she was nineteen.

Hugh had driven the bike full tilt into the stone gatepost of the country house of a friend, whose family was grand enough to own a drive down which one could drive at 70 mph. Hugh had also called her 'France'; that there had existed certain resemblances between Hugh and Peter was a secret which was now known only to Frances.

Perhaps it was that likeness to her younger brother which had prompted a kind of playfulness with Peter. In Paris they had been like children: it was cold, and Frances had taught him how to keep warm by skipping, and hand in hand they had skipped along by the Seine looking, as Peter had said, 'like geriatric kids!' But they had had their moments as lovers too.

It was on a morning after a night of lovemaking that she had wakened to find Peter, in his socks, about to tiptoe from the room. The lovemaking had been of the kind which routs paranoia, so her first thought was not, as it might have been: He is leaving me! Instead she said, still half asleep, 'Where in the world are you off to at this hour?' and he, slightly embarrassed, had murmured, 'Mass. Go back to sleep.'

Frances had submissively rolled down the dip in the aged mattress. When Peter returned she was propped up against an unyielding bolster reading about Matisse.

'It's nice when one's prejudices are confirmed,' she said, noticing his slight awkwardness. 'I always suspected Picasso was a bastard. He encouraged his toadies to throw darts at poor Matisse's paintings.' Then, seeing he was still fiddling with the change in his pocket, 'I waited breakfast for you – I must love you a whole lot because, frankly, my dear, after last night I'm ravenous!'

At that, Matisse was tipped to the floor and it had been some time, after all, before breakfast was ordered.

She had not enquired about the Mass, sensing that this was a subject which, if it was to be raised at all, must be so by him. And two nights later, over dinner in a restaurant in Montmartre, he did himself bring it up. 'When I was in Notre-Dame,' he dropped the name casually, 'there was a beggar woman some rows in front of me – pretty tatty and quite niffy, I should think. When it came to the Sign of Peace everyone kissed her or shook her hand most courteously.' They were discussing declining standards of manners in Britain.

'But mightn't that be true also at an English service?' She was shy of speaking the word 'Mass'.

'Maybe. But afterwards she was looking a bit unsteady on her pins and a young man, a very well-dressed young man – good clothes – took her arm and helped her down the aisles outside. He wasn't a relative, or anything to do with her – I was watching: he went off afterwards in a quite different direction.'

'Do you think it's their being French or being Catholic that makes the difference?' she had said, feeling bold enough to broach the topic.

And he had replied, quite casually, 'I'm a Catholic, if it comes to that, but I'm not sure I have their manners – really, it does seem to be a different culture here.'

That Bridget was unaware of her husband's faith was something which Frances had suspected before Peter's death. Just as well, as it turned out, for otherwise, she could have put her foot in it. Peter could never have guessed that the two would become such intimates – if that was what they were, for 'friends' did not quite capture it – no, 'friends' wasn't it at all, Frances thought, leaving the house that afternoon when the young man had so disarmingly referred to her and Peter as 'sweethearts'.

'Sweethearts, we are sweethearts,' Peter had said to her. In the 'childlike' spirit he had bought her a bag of coloured sugar hearts. How *could* that young Iranian have known? Frances, nostalgically remembering the sagging French bed and the hard usage they had put it to, wondered again if it was the lovemaking which had occasioned that early-morning visit Peter had made to Notre-Dame . . .

Bridget, as it happens, had found a rosary hidden in one of the small interior drawers of the oak desk but she had thought little about it: Peter was a man who collected talismans – worry beads from Greece, Maori carvings from New Zealand, fragments of lichen-covered marble from abandoned Turkish temples. Rosary beads were merely one among the many superstitious fetishes which had accumulated at the close of Peter's truncated life.

To the end of that life Bridget remained ignorant of her husband's faith and her own role in his observance of it. Without other information to go on Bridget had chosen the cremation service for Peter on the basis of her own preferences. It would suit her to become ashes – 'ashes' was what she, herself, felt like; to have her husband rendered into an ashy condition seemed perfectly acceptable. She enjoyed shocking the cremation officials by asking scientific questions about what the post-cremation remains were actually composed of. 'What about the coffin?' she had asked, when solemnly presented with the casket. 'Solid oak – I paid through the nose for it. How can I tell which of the cinders is expensive coffin and which dead husband?'

In fact Peter's attendance at the Paris Mass had not arisen, except in an indirect sense, from the night's abandonment with Frances. Mistresses fill many needs, not exclusively sexual, and if truth were told Peter had often found more satisfaction in making love to Bridget than to Frances. This was not due to any deficit in Frances, other than a sensitivity in her which Peter sometimes found daunting. If Bridget's wordless and robust responses suited him better, it was because they relieved him of the requirement to worry about how she was finding things. Not that he would ever think of revealing this to Frances – he was not without sensitivity himself, and it was alive to him that it was as a desirable lover that she gained part of her self-esteem. Nor was it something he could say that the morning visit to Notre-Dame had nothing to do with their unusually satisfactory time in bed.

On the whole, Peter restricted his extramarital activities to those times when his wife was away – her absence, he might have argued, legitimising any steps he took to make time pass without her less disturbing. As he had frankly told his mistress, he loved his wife and made his own efforts to behave honourably to her. But honour is not a commodity you can ration: almost by definition there is a place for honour towards one's mistress as well.

Honour, however, is not the only engine of erotic escapades; and perhaps this is as well since history suggests actions performed for lofty motives are more likely to be dangerous than those performed for selfish ones. Peter may not have noticed this himself but he took his mistress to France after a period during which his wife had visited that same country three times in as many months. Bridget, busy buying for an international antiques fair, had made more than her usual quota of trips abroad: there was a current craze for rural French cribs and she had tracked down a number of possible sources; then there was the old lace she had been partly responsible for making fashionable – and wicker garden furniture was making a comeback. She set off on these trips, often in the small hours of the morning, leaving Peter to the ostensible care of Mickey. So, Peter might have argued to himself, if he chose to take Frances, who was looking peaky after a bout of flu, to Paris, it could be said that his wife had left the door fairly open to that possibility.

Yet, waking in the musty erotic aftermath in the Paris hotel, beside Frances's warm body, Peter had felt the painful lance of remorse; it was this which had taken him out into the pearl-quiet morning and along by the placidly flowing Seine to the service in the cathedral where the light, filtering the amethyst and blue of the great north rose window, hinted, he reflected as he bent his knees, at some oblique promise of a life to come.

Perhaps it was the effect of that sincere blue light which had prompted him to tell Frances, over the intimate Montmartre dinner, the tale of the young man's courtesy to the beggar woman, the story which had harbingered the admission of his faith. The next day they had passed a flower seller, where Frances had pointed to some brilliantly coloured flowers – pink, red and the lambent blue and purple of the stained glass in Notre-Dame. 'Look, lilies of the field! Did you know they were anemones?' Happy that, for the moment, his faith had lain down like a lamb with his worldlier self, he listened as his lover explained that this was the flower in the parable which, arrayed like 'Solomon in all his glory', had no need to toil or spin.

On that misty October morning when the journalist friend telephoned with news of the fatal accident, the biblical flowers came into Frances's mind. Peter had said, 'They're awfully merry,' and he had bought her a bunch, adding casually, 'when I die, you can send me some of these.'

In the split second before he died Peter remembered these words, and remembered that, unlike Bridget, Frances had not disputed the likelihood of his death.

8

'Does Zahin know about me and Peter?' Frances asked.

They had been shifting furniture for hours. The coolness over the Christmas bowl had been patched up – or, more accurately, had been passed over, since neither woman wished to be thought undignified. It was Bridget, though, who had made the peacemaking gesture, asking Frances if she was free for a weekend at Farings, the Shropshire house.

The cynical part of Frances had suggested, when she arrived at the slightly austere brick house, that she had maybe been invited as a useful pair of hands. Bridget had piled a whole lot of furniture into the downstairs rooms with no apparent plan as to where it was to end up. Frances had hauled and dragged, pushed and shifted until her back and ribs protested. Finally she sat down on a roll of carpet. 'Where am I sleeping, as a matter of interest?'

'Hell!' said Bridget. 'I forgot. No bed.'

'What?'

45

'There's only one bed – I was planning to bring one of the ones from the shop – it's a sweetheart bed, with intertwined hearts on the head and foot. But I never picked it up.'

'Uh-huh,' said Frances. 'Sweetheart' made her think of the boy's odd, telepathic comment. Which was when she asked, 'Does Zahin know about me and Peter?'

But Bridget was preoccupied with the sleeping arrangements. 'There's the sofa but I don't even think I've brought enough bedding – damn.'

'Don't bother,' said Frances, coolly, 'I can stay at the hotel.' She suspected the forgotten bed and bedding were a ploy and that Bridget preferred her not to sleep in the house after all.

Bridget, sensing this, said, 'The hotel's closed down – I noticed as we were passing – the nearest other one's miles away. But if you didn't mind we could always share – I mean, it's a big bed, it was Peter's and mine!'

Looking at Frances she started to laugh, and Frances, seated on the dust-filled Indian carpet, caught the mood and began to laugh too. Helplessly, the two women wheezed and Bridget all but rolled about the room.

'Oh dear,' said Frances, wiping tears from her eyes – brought on as much by the dusty carpet as the laughter. 'We'll be able to tell no one – people will think – I don't know what they'd think!'

'Who cares?' Bridget was soberer now.

'What would Peter think?' Frances asked as a while later together they made the bed upstairs.

Bridget reflected a moment. Outside, through the west-facing window, the far hills were turning indigo – 'blue remembered', she thought, like Housman's.

46

'He'd have been sorry not to be joining us,' she finally announced.

It was not that Bridget had failed to hear Frances's question about Zahin but that she had decided to ignore it. She hadn't yet assembled her impressions of the boy. Christmas had been . . . she needed time to ponder . . .

Except in the first years of their marriage, Christmas with Peter had never been a tranquil event. Bridget's consciousness of a regular Christmas Eve assignation, long before she met the object of it, caused her bridled indignation. To say she was without ill feelings towards Peter's other 'associations' – as it was her habit to call them – would have been stretching a point. Possibly there are people large-hearted enough to offer perfect charity towards those with whom they are asked to share the person of their beloved; but purity must be its own reward: while commendable it is hardly interesting, and anyhow Bridget was not among this angelic band. On the other hand, she had learned the dangers of bearing grudges.

Bridget had been born and bred in Limerick, in the south-west of Ireland. Her father had been tricked by a phantom pregnancy into an ill-matched wedding. When, in time, a child was eventually born, she received the brunt of a resentment which had had five years in which to accrue. Among families, resentment is often expressed indirectly. To Joseph Dwyer's fear of his wife was added an even greater fear of her brother, Father Eamonn, priest to the neighbouring parish and spoken of as 'episcopal' – even 'cardinal' – material. Unhappily for Bridget, her father kept his interior rage for the family who had

47

curtailed his snappy-bachelor freedom, while he vented it more openly upon his daughter.

Bridget was born curious. She questioned her mother, her grandparents – who lived a village away – her uncle the priest, her teachers – most of all she questioned her father, to the point where her mother finally abetted her daughter's flight from home, lest, as Moira Dwyer confessed to her brother, 'there be a murder in the house'.

That there was not a murder was due to Bridget's early discovery that life tends to be unyielding to our desires. She was unusual in perceiving so soon the gap between what we want and what is possible; more remarkable still, in time she came to recognise the distinction between what she felt was her due and what was actually on offer – a distinction which stood her in good stead when, years later, on Christmas mornings, having returned late from Turnham Green, her husband would say, in varying accents of agitation, 'I'm *sure* I did buy you something – no, hang on, I *know* I did – let me think a moment while I remember where I put it . . .' or 'Good God, have I left it behind in the shop . . . ?'

All this might have been easier to accommodate had not Bridget, not meaning to pry, once come across a small box, which curiosity had made her open and which had shockingly revealed a costly looking square-cut sapphire ring, a particularly brilliant blue. It was, in fact, the sight of this ring on Frances's finger, which had sparked the moment of tension over the Christmas bowl. Seeing it, Bridget had felt a return of the nauseous rush of jealousy which had accompanied the original discovery of the ring in its expensive leather hiding place.

Christmas with Zahin could hardly have been more

different. He had arrived, with his things from St John's Wood, late in the day on Christmas Eve. How in that short space of time he had managed so to infer her tastes and buy accordingly, Bridget could never fathom. She had popped out and bought him a rather dull shirt, feeling that to do more on such a short acquaintance would be overdoing it. But no such reserve had apparently constrained Zahin.

Bridget had woken on Christmas morning to find a pile of glitteringly wrapped gifts at the foot of her bed. Wonder vying with a sense of slight fear – caused by the appearance of something at once so long desired and so unexpected – she had gathered up the colourful, gleaming parcels and returned, like a child, with them to bed. Here she undid swathes of tissue paper with the astonishment of one schooled in deprivation. Silk scarves, silver bangles, a stole, scent, a gilt peacock, a leather-bound diary, a pair of velvet slippers – it was like produce from some fabulous dream, or bazaar in the *Arabian Nights*.

Downstairs in her kitchen she found Zahin had also been at work. The table was laid with a length of some old lace he must have found in the linen cupboard and adorned with scarlet poinsettias, pink azaleas, golden roses. The smell of superior coffee mingled with the scent of roses to perfume the room, like incense from some exotic temple.

'Zahin?'

'O Mrs Hansome,' the boy had cried. 'How pretty you look! It suits you – look how it suits your colouring!'

Bridget, who had strung the scarves round her neck and wound the stole round her shoulders, glanced over to where he had gestured towards the long glass which hung by the kitchen door. It was a glass which Peter had used to scrutinise his carefully accoutred frame, before meeting the world.

Handsome is as handsome does – her own mocking words came back to her,

'Zahin – I am overwhelmed. There was no need for all this.'

'But I like to.' The boy spoke with an odd note of authority. 'Now, I make you coffee, and toast. You like jam, honey? See, I have also made pancakes.'

Bridget had not noticed the sapphire ring again until Frances took it off and placed it in a saucer beside the bed at Farings before visiting the bathroom. Bridget waited until Frances had left the bedroom and then examined the ring under the bedside light. No doubt about it – it was the same. She considered stealing it and then denying all knowledge. But what would she do then – throw it away? She could hardly wear it herself! Or she could raise the matter with Frances and they could have a tremendous row. That might be satisfying but in the end she felt she couldn't be bothered.

'Turn out the light when you're ready,' she said when Frances came back, steamy, from the bathroom, and surprisingly middle-aged in a washed-out candlewick dressing gown. 'I've put a bolster between us in case one of us kicks.'

'I don't kick.' Frances was not looking forward to a night spent with Bridget.

'Well, I can.'

Peter had said so. But Bridget kept this from Frances. Turning her back to her bed companion, she had a sudden

50

flash of Peter's face, should he see them there – his mistress and his wife – tucked up together in his bed.

That night Peter Hansome did indeed come to the room where the two women lay side by side in the bed which had once been his. For some while he remained looking down at their sleeping forms. Then, when a cock crowed, and the green dawn light began to seep through the curtains, he vanished back whence he had come.

9

Frances had wondered whether it was wise to wear the sapphire ring to Farings. Apart from other considerations it hardly seemed polite. But she was also apprehensive, staying in Bridget's house, and glimpses of the blue square offered little oases of reassurance.

Peter had given Frances the sapphire the Christmas after Paris. Opening the compact leather box she had exclaimed, 'Notre-Dame blue!' which made Peter, who had worried, pleased he had bought it after all.

It might have surprised Bridget to learn that her husband was aware that, in matters such as this, he might be said to favour his mistress over his wife. Yet, essentially, he was not an unfair man.

No one has ever fully explained why humankind so resists a sense of requirement. Perhaps it is this very propensity which constitutes what it means to be 'human' – certainly it seems to have been at the bottom of the debacle in the Garden of Eden, or so the story goes. In Peter Hansome's case the tendency expressed itself towards Bridget because she was his wife: within the convention he was reared to she came with perceived obligations. He did not allow his inability to be demonstrative when it was expected of him to trouble him much of the time; but times of celebration, especially Christmas, had the effect of exposing a moral nerve.

Peter would not normally have risked his conscience so far by making such a one-sided gesture as the gift of the sapphire ring. It was the extraordinary colour of the stone which had drawn him – that ethereal blue – the colour of Paris. Perhaps – he didn't know – it was the colour of his soul? If he had a soul . . .

Neither woman knew this but Peter's hatred of Christmas began when his father had deserted his family on Christmas Eve. His mother had made the best of things – but 'the best of things', even when executed with genuine selflessness, often turns out to be worse than selfish protest.

From an early age Peter had monitored his mother's face. That Christmas, undeceived by a not-too-convincing story about 'Daddy's business' calling him away, Peter had watched his mother's expressions more closely than usual. There had been a horrible moment between the turkey and the Christmas cake – decorated that year with a superfluity of snowmen and hard little silver balls, which Peter afterwards always hated – when he had sleuthed his mother to her bedroom and, through the keyhole, had spied her lying on the bed, her face pressed into a pillow to stifle any sound.

Six-year-old Peter had been tactful enough to remove his presence from this private grief, and to hurl himself, with unusual energy, into a distractingly boisterous game with his elder brother, Marcus. He had also been unusually conciliatory with his little sister, Clare, and had played doll's-house tea with unwonted sweetness which had raised – unfairly in the circumstances – maternal questions later about his state of health.

There had been other, happier, Christmases when his mother's smiles had been less forced, and, later still, his mother's smiles had become genuine, for a time, when his stepfather, the MP, had first appeared on the scene. But the early loss had fractured for good the young Peter's capacities for enjoying the 'season of goodwill'. The pillow which had stifled the mother's anguish acted as a more permanent block upon the son's capacity to rejoice. From that time on Peter grew to think of Christmas, and its attendant duties, as dangerous, an ordeal rather than a blessing – one of many – to be 'got through'.

Bridget woke in the bed she had once shared with Peter, left Frances sleeping and went barefoot downstairs to make herself a cup of tea. Outside the kitchen window a flock of goldfinches made a vivid zigzag across the pale wintry field. Bridget stretched and yawned noisily. There were advantages to living alone – Peter, who could be prim, would have grimaced at the sound. What was the collective noun for goldfinches?

She had dreamed of Peter – the first time since he had died. She couldn't bring the dream back but she knew from the feeling in her limbs it was Peter all right.

Bridget filled a kettle and looked appraisingly round the kitchen where Frances had hung on nails bags of Italian pasta and some of the large copper French pans. The paint work wasn't right – too shiny – but with the old brocade curtains she'd been waiting to find a use for, and a lick of distemper, the place would do up fine.

She made tea in a big mug, stirring the tea bag to give the brew strength, and stuck her bare feet into boots. Outside, she surveyed the field where the striking looking finches with their gold-flashed wings and crimson fore-heads had flown. The bare soil, fringed by bleached grasses, stretched in gleaming furrows where the light struck the early-morning moisture.

Frances appeared and began opening cupboard doors. 'There's some coffee in that cardboard box.' From the doorway Bridget pointed. 'Otherwise there's tea and some rather mouldy bread in that bag. It must be damp here.'

Maybe she could grow mushrooms? Suddenly she remembered: 'Charm', that was it! The term for a flock of goldfinches was a charm. 'Why do Renaissance paintings of the Virgin have goldfinches in them?' she asked Frances.

Frances wrinkled up her forehead. In the morning light and with her pointed nose she looked quite witchy. 'The red spot at the top of their heads, isn't it? The goldfinch fed from the crown of thorns and Christ's blood anointed its head; I think that's the story.'

Frances, who had dreamed of Peter too, was also trying to remember the dream. Had he said anything to her? There was something but it was more a mood or a flavour – like the lingering scent left by an interesting visitor.

Bridget noticed Frances was not wearing the sapphire. 'Don't forget your ring's upstairs,' she threw over her shoulder, going back out into the garden.

*　　*　　*

55

The two women had worked hard all day.

'That looks better,' Frances said, looking round the parlour with satisfaction. She had polished the wooden furniture with some beeswax which she had found under the sink, left behind by the house's former occupants.

The doorbell startled them. 'I'll get it,' and Bridget opening the door saw a man with a big slack face and high colouring. Only then did she see the collar.

'Bill Dark,' said the man holding out a hand. 'Rector of St Anselm's. Called to introduce myself.'

Bridget found a bottle of sherry in one of the boxes they had not yet unpacked and Frances kindled a fire.

'Mrs Nettles is your nearest neighbour,' their visitor ('Call me "Rector Bill"') said. 'She's pushing eighty but spry as anything.' He pushed his empty glass vaguely in Bridget's direction.

'Another?' Bridget tried not to sound ironic – this was his fifth – sixth? She had lost count.

'Don't mind if I do, since you ask.'

Frances, catching the lift of Bridget's eyebrows, and practised in shifting people from gallery dos, said, 'My friend is staying here until the morning but I have to get off tonight. Which is the best route, would you say, to the M50?'

'Forgive me! Time flies when you're having fun! I'll wend my weary way, then, ladies.'

'God help us!' Bridget said, 'or me, rather, you're safe. But thanks for that. Look, he's as good as polished off the bottle – the old bugger!' She indicated an inch of sherry.

'Not a "bugger" anyway – he was looking at your bosom pretty lecherously. Look, I'm going to have to

56

grab a slice of bread and cheese and scoot.' Frances was genuinely regretful. She had been looking forward to talking to Bridget in the parlour she herself had polished. Now there was no chance to enjoy her own virtue.

Bridget pointed the way down the drive with her torch. 'Goodbye,' she yelled. 'And thanks again. I'll ring you!'

'Take care!' Frances called back. She declutched and drove carefully down the sticky lane.

Peter monitored Frances's departure then hurried back into the house to hover over Bridget as she finished off the sherry. This business of watching over his consorts was proving a responsibility . . .

10

Journeys offer opportunity for reflection. Driving back to London, Frances allowed the night's events to seep into her mind. She eyed the square blue gem on the fourth finger of her right hand – the ring finger of the unattached – as it grasped the wheel. Well, there were worse things than unattachment. It had been less of an ordeal than she had expected to share a bed with Peter's widow . . . 'Widow' – what a word! Bridget wouldn't thank her for it! How funny she should have spent the night dreaming of passionate sexual congress with Peter. The dream reminded her of Paris – perhaps it was because she had been wearing the sapphire . . . ?

Back at Farings, Bridget was also considering the insubstantial. She had found, and opened, a second bottle of sherry which she was downing, with bread and cheese, by the fire. The dream she had had in the bed with Frances was also filtering back: in this case there had been no vigorous coupling; rather, a walk – down a lane where purple flowers were growing – near Farings, she felt it was . . . ?

Bridget was not the sort to analyse her dreams but she wondered if this one had some message for her. Perhaps it meant she should settle here? Give up the shop and the house next door to Mickey and up sticks altogether now she was, more or less, alone.

If she was alone. There was Frances, and Mickey, too, of course – and then there was the boy.

Bridget had never wanted children so she was relieved rather than disappointed when it became clear that Peter was a far from paternal man. His children – a boy and girl – by his former wife seemed to embarrass him. They came to stay at weekends during which everyone behaved with unnatural stiffness and Bridget was thankful when the time came for them to be returned to their mother's house in Barnes: she could hardly bear the sight of Peter trying so hard – with so little aptitude – to be jolly.

Peter's first wife had remarried – a solicitor in a City firm – and she was now buffered by demonstrable prosperity. Nevertheless, she continued to receive Peter – still more Bridget, should Bridget happen to be the one to chauffeur the children home – in the manner of a mendicant, whose impoverishment should be laid at the door of her former husband. Hopeless to try and suggest – as Bridget did – that his children's mother's attitude was injurious, not only to relations with their father but also to the children themselves. As Bridget came to see, Peter did not greatly care what his children felt or thought about him. She suspected they irked him; and that he was glad when the regular visits tailed off and he was released from the pressures of family obligation.

The children, now adults, had appeared at the funeral

and the girl had cried, mildly obedient to some atavistic sense of her loss – while the young man, a stockbroker in the City, in his new dark suit had hung his head sheepishly. Bridget had felt sorry for them: they had no language with which to mourn their father.

Their mother, Peter's former wife, had sent a massy wreath of ostentatious whiteness, and a card with sentiments on it which had left Bridget particularly cold.

No, there was little enough love lost between Peter and his children which is why it was mildly surprising to discover his attachment to Zahin.

Back in London Mickey said to Jean, 'It doesn't seem right that boy having a girl round there like that with Bridget not at home. I don't know if I should say anything.'

'Perhaps she said he could?' Jean was more phlegmatic than her friend.

'What if she didn't?'

'Girlfriends aren't any harm, are they?' Jean didn't think Bridget seemed the type to lay down draconian rules.

'She looked a forward little thing if you ask me. All tarted up in them platform heels, with what you could see of her BTM – which wasn't much of one anyway – stuck out. And plastered all over in make-up. A young girl does better showing off her own skin, in my view.'

'It's the way with modern girls . . .' Jean's more charitable nature suggested.

'Better say nothing this time,' Mickey decided. 'But if

it's going to keep on happening, I'll have to. My conscience wouldn't let me off otherwise,' she concluded with stark satisfaction.

11

Bridget had not started back to London as early as she had planned. The chimney had smoked and she had taken time to ring round the *Yellow Pages* in search of a sweep. A Mr Godwin was found who promised to visit when she returned in a fortnight. And she lingered on after the matter of the chimney had been resolved, dawdling and watching the rooks, reluctant to have to make the effort of the drive.

Zahin was at the gate when Bridget arrived and took the holdall from her.

'Zahin! How did you know I was back?'

'Instinct, Mrs Hansome.' She had tried, and failed, to get him to call her 'Bridget'.

'I didn't even know myself when I would get here.'

'The traffic was heavy.' He had a way, she noticed, of making questions statements.

'As life!'

'You are tired. Come in, please, and relax.'

Sitting with a glass of Jameson, Bridget thought: If only Peter could see this! Chaotic himself, he had the obsessional nature which sees chaos in others' mess but not his own. Bridget was no housewife and Peter's fussy comments had been a source of ruffled feelings. Yet now, with Peter gone and unable to appreciate it, the house gleamed with the patina of dedicated care. Upstairs a bath was running and a scent drifted down to her.

'Zahin, what is that you have put in my bath?' she called upstairs.

'I bought it in the King's Road, Mrs Hansome. Meadow flowers – it is very you!'

Flowers had been in the dream of Peter. Or had they? The mind played tricks – she was aware of the human tendency to weave 'reality' out of wishes.

'You are too kind,' she called again. Zahin's politeness was catching.

'Oh, but it is not kind to look after one who is beautiful!'

Zahin had appeared at the top of the stairs which, in the Hansomes' house, descended to the sitting room. Bridget had taken time to persuade Peter that the removal of a wall, and the inclusion of the space which had been the hall and stairway into the living area, would give an added dimension and light, but it took Zahin, standing like a model or a film star, to show off the alteration. He was dressed in a vivid blue silk shirt which Bridget had not noticed when he appeared so miraculously at the gate, and which brought out the colour of his eyes.

'Zahin,' she said, 'that is called hyperbole.'

But she was not displeased. She was not beautiful, nor had ever been – but it was a long while since anyone had even pretended that she might be.

'Oh, but you are.' The boy was down the stairs now

and plumping cushions. Bridget could make out the shoulder blades which she had fancied resembled incipient wings. 'Beautiful in your spirit. I see it.' He stared at her and to her chagrin she found she was blushing.

'Get away, child!' she said, and his voice followed her as she hurried up the stairs,

'I know what hyperbole is, Mrs Hansome – and it isn't you!'

No, indeed, she thought, lying in the bath, where she had brought up the tumbler of golden whisky, she was not much given to exaggeration. Peter had, one had to admit it, embroidered – improved on life, as he might, if challenged, have put it. But she herself did not wish such improvements. Not for reasons of greater honesty than her husband (about human honesty, even her own, Bridget was firmly sceptical) but because it wasn't safe, she felt, to polish things up, or dim them down. Not to name things as you found them put you more at their mercy . . .

If Peter Hansome had not named things quite as he found them it was because he had problems discerning them clearly in the first place. Reality may be singular but the sense of it is not, and 'one man's meat is another man's poison' refers to more than simple taste. 'A fool sees not the same tree that a wise man sees' perhaps puts it better. Many conflicts of opinion can be explained by the fact that perceptual systems depend on the personalities of the perceivers.

In Peter's case, behind all his responses lurked a chronic panic, which coloured – or obscured – his apprehension of reality. Although he would never have owned to it he could not forget that day when half his known world walked away and left him. From this moment, he had constructed a personality upon which such a loss had made no obvious dent; but this did not mean that the dent had not been planted. As a child the knock had made for a wary caution. In time, and with training, the wariness had become overlaid with an acceptable veneer, one in which a kind of genial sociability acted as a polished surface which deflected intimacy; but the most significant feature of his character was that at bottom he was frightened of people.

It takes a rare man to know he is afraid – and why. Peter was not aware that he was fearful of other people's power to remove themselves, nor that he had chosen Bridget because although she exuded a power which did not always make him feel comfortable, it did not, at least, feel as if it might desert him. And in this he was correct. That he was capable of being harmed, perhaps mortally, through loss of another's love, was a secret, even from himself. Dormant and lethal, it lay hidden at the centre of Peter's universe, until the October day when the truck driver adjusted his cassette and exploded Peter's former reality.

It is part of nature's way to meet threat with superfluity: toads puff up their skin, snakes rear, peacocks rattle and spread their tails; the habit of hyperbole is but another version of this florid system of defence. Lying in her bath, inhaling the scent of meadow flowers, Bridget remembered Peter, late one Christmas Eve, returning, as she now understood, from seeing Frances. She heard again the familiar accent of anxiety, concerned to account for time which could not be accounted for except by honesty or omission – 'I would have been home earlier but there was an accident on the M4 – terrible catastrophe – I shouldn't be surprised if someone got killed!' – and wept for the way life had apparently taken him at his word.

12

The Soho gallery which Frances managed, dealt, among other contemporary artists, in the works of Patrick Painter. Although Frances did not own the gallery she was indispensable to its running: it was understood that without her skills Gambit Galleries would never have hung on to its most prestigious name.

There were rules for dealing with Patrick Painter: you did not call him before noon; you never enquired about his health, or his financial affairs, and no one was permitted to comment on his name. A journalist from a respected broadsheet had lost a promised interview because he had been unable to refrain from audibly murmuring, 'Painter by name . . .' Frances, who arrived too late to prevent this outrage, explained, 'It is not his own name, you see. It was his stepfather's – they didn't get on.' 'Why for Christ's sake didn't he change it then, if it offends him so much?' the aggrieved young journalist had asked, conscious of the hole in the copy this upset would make, and doubly conscious of his editor's displeasure.

Painter lived in Isleworth with his mother and his

tortoises. Frances had sometimes speculated that the mother and the tortoises occupied interchangeable places in the artist's mind. It was to visit Painter that Monday morning that Frances had returned the previous evening from Shropshire.

When Painter asked to see Frances, it was generally to seek her view on some painting on which he was stuck. As with everything to do with him these meetings involved a certain amount of ritual before a hint of anything to do with work-in-hand could be broached.

'So you've deigned to come and see me, have you?' Painter said, meeting her at the front door and indicating she should go ahead into the front room. 'About bloody time, too!' He swept a chair free of a pile of unsorted magazines and papers.

Paradoxically, the house, although apparently a tremendous muddle, always had an ordering effect on Frances, a product, she supposed, of the fact that the house itself made up much of the subject matter of the artist's orderly paintings. There was some to-do about the biscuits – the tin could not be found. 'Jesus, Mary and Joseph, the ginger nuts. What has the bloody bitch done with them?'

Frances was used to this. 'If by that you mean Mrs Hicks, I think it most unlikely she has done anything. I expect you've eaten them.' She looked about the Formica-covered kitchen until she found a tin with a picture of the Queen with her corgis on it. 'These shortbread, will they do?'

'At a pinch – but you would prefer ginger nuts . . . ?'

Frances said she'd prefer not to have a biscuit at all lest she grew fat.

'Rubbish, you have no arse to speak of.'

'Well, I hope to keep things that way.'

'Nonsense, a woman should have a decent arse.'

Other than the nude models he must have drawn from in his pre-abstract days, Frances doubted Painter had ever had anything to do with a woman's bottom. Nevertheless, because he seemed to like it, she kept up the myth of his erotic interests.

'Where are the tortoises? Are they out of hibernation?'

'Fred is – Ginger is still comatose, lazy cow.'

'Can one call a tortoise "cow"?'

Frances was not deceived by Painter's habits of speech: she knew him to be a man of warm, if secret, sensibility. After Peter was killed she had found herself ringing the artist in need of the kindness which lay beneath the superficial savageness. Also, he was from Cork and she liked an Irish accent. Maybe that was why she got on with Bridget . . . ?

Painter had got round to his current fix. 'It's this effing catastrophe,' he complained, indicating a canvas composed of tiny delicately painted squares of lilac – recognisably a mutation of the hall wallpaper. 'Look at it, will you just – I'll have to destroy the whole bollocking thing.'

'Maybe it just needs some balance,' said Frances carefully. She had decided long ago that it didn't much matter what one said to Painter about his pictures – all that was required was to sound as if what was said made sense. What was important was that Painter felt safe in showing her uncompleted work. It was like being the stooge to a highly strung comic – he relied on her to feed him the right lines.

'No, no, no, no,' said Painter, falling into the familiar patter, 'it's vile, vile – I'll have to ditch it.'

'Hmm,' said Frances, 'I see what you mean – but it would be a pity.'

They stood side by side and stared at the canvas. Frances had noticed before that Patrick was nice to be near: he gave one space; there was no crowding in – or pulling away.

A tortoise, presumably Fred, ambled through the door and rested where a patch of sun lit up the pattern of the carpet.

'"Gaming in a gap of sunlight",' said Painter resting his foot on the tortoise's back. 'I'll scrap it then, shall I?'

This was the crucial moment. Frances gambled, 'Maybe you're right . . .'

'Or maybe I could do something with it,' said Painter, quickly. 'What do you think?'

'I think you generally know.'

'That's all right then,' said Painter relieved. 'Glad we sorted that out. Damn that tart – I could do with a ginger nut.'

Frances walked down to the corner shop with Painter where he bought Typhoo tea, 'Extra strength', and two packets of biscuits. The woman in the shop said, 'You still want the *Sunday Sport*, Mr Pinter?'

'*Pinter*?' asked Frances outside. 'What's this?'

A sly smile spread over Painter's face. 'Their mistake, not my doing. She thinks I'm Harold Pinter. Writes plays,' he added helpfully.

'I know he's a playwright – a highly civilised one. What's going on?'

'It's an identity swap,' said Painter, slightly sheepish.

'When the silly cow took over from the Patels they told her I was famous – and she read the name as Pinter. She's got a daughter doing Media Arts at Luton. I can't help it if the woman's a star-fucker.'

'Is that why you're ordering the *Sunday Sport*?' asked Frances, light dawning. 'Honestly, Patrick, how infantile!'

13

If an impression has been given that Peter Hansome was not a particularly brave man it would be misleading. At boarding school he passed through the ordeal of separation from home and familiars without even the sharpest-eyed, and most malicious, of his peers noticing that the experience left him feeling he was bleeding alive. More heroic still, he resisted the urge to find relief from his own despair by joining in with tormenting those less successful at concealment. He became popular, up to a point, never reaching that pinnacle of popularity which, from the start, attends the lucky – if luck is what it is. And 'luck' made up no conspicuous part of Peter Hansome's history.

Once we are in the way of losing things, life seems to determine that other goods shall go: having lost his father Peter went on to lose his mother, to a Member of Parliament who chose Peter's siblings, Marcus and Clare, as the foci of his step-parental care.

There is a kind of person who, if aware that an affection is not directed towards them, will set out to destroy it. With the acuity of the sadistic, Evelyn Hansome's second husband recognised the deep link between his wife and her second son. Such bonds between mothers and sons are not uncommon – nineteenth-century fiction depends upon them; but they should not, for that reason, be dismissed as unreal. Peter watched his mother falter in her expressions of love towards him and knew that she did so, not through any dereliction but through the desire to protect him. But understanding does not necessarily dispel reaction: as the mother became guarded, so did the son. When his stepfather died it was difficult for Peter to find a way back to any spontaneous expression of feeling.

By the time he reached Cambridge Peter presented to the world the character of a conventional public schoolboy. He was rangy and, on the surface at least, good-humoured. Differences from others he expressed in minor, socially acceptable ways, by changing subjects from history to anthropology, for example. About this time he made friends with his father who, when Peter left university, celebrated the event by taking his son to a Soho strip joint. Peter responded to the prominent breasts and buttocks with an excited fascination he later defined to himself as loathing – though whether it was the naked gleaming girls or the profusely sweating figure of his father beside him which produced this reaction he could not have said. These uneasy emotions he ascribed to feelings of loyalty to his mother. It was the last year of conscription and he was about to leave for military service.

He went to serve in Malaya, where he learned to command men and issue orders. And it was in Malaya that Peter Hansome first fell in love.

14

Zahin explained that he attended a college near the King's Road. 'I am doing physics, also maths and chemistry.' He sighed.

'But why do them if that is not what you want?' Bridget asked, and Zahin had explained that this is what his family wished for him.

'I am to be a chemical engineer. In America there are big salaries for this work.'

Long ago Bridget had recognised that not having children put her at a disadvantage in understanding parental motive. Unimaginable to her the idea of setting another human being to do anything for which they had no inherent desire. Yet a rebellion against a parent was the basis of her own escape; maybe it was necessary that the young were made to comply with uncongenial demands – to ensure a kind of survival of the fittest . . . ?

Zahin, despite his expressed reservations, appeared to take his academic obligations seriously. Each morning, already showered and neatly dressed in his sober navy or grey pullover, he woke Bridget with a tray of tea. Only occasionally, on half-days and holidays, did he break out and dress in the colourful shirts, such as the blue silk he had been wearing the evening she returned from Farings. These he ironed with a professional skill. What he seemed to like best, however, was cleaning.

It had not escaped Bridget's notice that Zahin's programme of cleaning included her bedroom. Not usually at a loss, she was unsure whether or not to take this up with the boy. On the face of it, it was an atrocious invasion – it was clear to her that he had not only tidied her dressing table, but that his domestic efforts had extended to more private areas.

Bridget's chests of drawers were full of the antique lace and cotton which she creamed off from her commercial purchases. She enjoyed the knowledge that beneath her rather serviceable clothes lay unseen knickers and bodices and petticoats, ribboned and tucked and sewn with the fine seams of French seamstresses. Peter had enjoyed them too – in particular a pair of knickers with a convenient flap, one an adroit hand could undo and make use of (without recourse to further removals), cunningly fashioned, no doubt, for some busy Frenchman's mistress.

Peter himself had sometimes taken advantage of this prudent piece of design economy while visiting his wife at her shop. Both parties had enjoyed the wordless exchange. Since her husband died, Bridget had not thought about this much enjoyed arrangement but seeing the knickers carefully folded, alongside her other underwear, it seemed right they should be put away in tissue paper – it was not likely that they would be useful again.

But what to do about the hand responsible for that neat folding?

There is some law which determines that a pronounced trait or characteristic in childhood will often tend, later in life, to turn into its opposite. Bridget's childhood had been made turbulent by her questioning mind. She pursued matters – especially with her father – which might have been better left undisturbed. After she left Ireland, Bridget had worked first in a hospital, then in a hotel. The hotel manager's second in command was a cautious kleptomaniac. Bridget, being sharp, noticed him slip a lighter from a drinks table into his pocket. But further observation suggested that he confined his thefts to those guests who treated the staff rudely, and decided, when another member of staff under suspicion for the crimes was threatened with dismissal, not to come forward with what she had seen.

The innocent staff member was dismissed. About this Bridget felt no compunction. She could have averted the injustice but . . . it was not, exactly, that she couldn't be bothered – more a sense that there was something dangerous in any tendency to meddle. Better to let the criminal go scot-free, she felt, than get involved in acts of moral denouncing. If she had pushed the thought a little further, she might have added that a touch of injustice here and there was safer than too much righteous interference. And, to be fair, she would have acknowledged that that was reasonable only if she, too, were prepared to take a pinch of injustice as part of her own measure.

This small illumination lit the way for others: Bridget, while she lost none of the quickness which so antagonised her father, dropped some of the indignation which had attended it. She became expert at letting things ride; and, indeed, it was partly this quality which had endeared her to Peter.

Sitting at her dressing table, from whose surfaces all trace of her pale French powder had been dusted, she decided to let the matter of Zahin's intrusion into her bedroom ride too. So what if Zahin had inspected her underwear? It was underwear she was proud of.

15

Bridget's plan was that she should visit Farings every fortnight. To establish her presence in London she made a point of calling in on Mickey. It was clear that Mickey had taken the hump.

'Nice, is it, your new house then?' she asked, as if enquiring about the comforts of a bordello.

'Very. There's not much to do to it, which is just as well.'

'What you going to do with yourself there then?'

Bridget guessed that Mickey hoped for an invitation. Besides the fact that her neighbour was a committed 'townie' it would be hopeless if Farings became a place where she had to invite people. She steeled herself not to be drawn. 'D'you know what, Mickey – I really want to do nothing there. That's the point.'

'Frances like it, did she?' So that was it. Mickey had discovered that Frances had visited and was jealous.

Frances, too, was conscious that there was a coolness between her and Bridget's neighbour. Her introduction to the Hansomes had, after all, come through Mickey, who was not to know that there were delicate reasons why Frances, having been introduced to Peter, had suddenly to cease to be seen near his home. In the aftermath of Peter's death she had tried to re-establish a friendly link; but Mickey, who had an elephant's memory, wasn't having any of it.

Frances and Bridget were spending Saturday together, so when Frances turned up and found Bridget out she called at Mickey's house to see if Bridget was there. The meeting didn't go well.

'She's annoyed with me,' Frances said, back in Bridget's kitchen after Mickey had made only the most perfunctory attempt at civility. 'She thinks I dumped her after she introduced me to Peter.'

'Well, you did,' said Bridget.

'Yes,' said Frances, stung, 'but there were reasons . . .'

'Yes, like sleeping with my husband!' jeered Bridget. 'Listen, don't worry about it – Mickey loves to take umbrage. I'd rather it was you than Zahin she took against – it's more convenient,' she added, then, not being quite without kindness, noticed that Frances's face had that crumpled look as if she might have been crying.

Frances had, indeed, been crying. Lacking Bridget's steelier foundations, she was, nonetheless, possessed with more than average self-control. When she wept it was generally in private. And had an impartial observer been present they would have had to report that the crying was, mostly, not of the self-indulgent kind.

Frances had not cried so thoroughly since she lost Hugh. Or rather, since she told Peter about her younger brother. It was one of the most treasured aspects of her time with Peter that he had encouraged her to cry her heart out – all over him – tears she had not been able to shed when she learned she had lost Hugh.

Frances and Hugh had shared a language, and a country – like the young Brontës, she had been told since. Only Peter had been trusted with the fictional land she and Hugh had dreamed up together, where children had the power of telepathy and were acknowledged superior to adults.

If not telepaths in the full sense, Frances and Hugh certainly shared some unspoken communication. On the day that Hugh drove into the gatepost, Frances, a hundred miles away, came down with a migraine so severe that she had to be admitted to hospital. It was in hospital that she was told of her brother's death, a fact which seemed to cause her so little surprise that the nurse who had come to tell her believed that her patient couldn't have heard and told her – in identical words – again. 'We have some very sad news for you, I'm afraid . . .'

Frances had found Peter's arms to encircle her while she cried for Hugh; but there was no one to hold her while she cried for Peter.

Driving to the Tate, Bridget felt compunction. 'Let's have lunch,' she said, as the London Eye loomed. 'My treat. I never thanked you properly for your help with Farings.'

Astonishing how strong a part food plays in our humours. Just as dyspepsia can rapidly translate into bad temper, the offer of a cup of tea, the share of a sandwich or an ice lolly will often provide more of a fillip than the most carefully chosen words. Bridget kept her thoughts to herself but the promise of a meal found its way to Frances.

'I don't think they do lunch there on a Saturday but I'd love to go somewhere else,' she said, and felt calmer.

A short while later, standing with Bridget before a Sickert of two women on a couch ('I wonder if that's how Peter saw us?' Bridget asked herself), Frances turned, and, in the room beyond, caught sight of a large painting.

A man and woman seated at a café table; even at a distance it was possible to tell that this was a couple engaged in some equivocal escapade. The woman is looking, a little too yearningly, into the face of the man, who has a bunch of flowers at his side, presumably a sop to conscience and not for the woman who is seated by him. Looming over the couple, prepared to take their order, stands the figure of a waiter, manifestly aware of the nuances of the situation his customers find themselves in.

As she gazed across at the painting, Frances, in peripheral vision, saw another figure also looking – so that after a moment she turned to Bridget to say, 'Look, over there. For a second I thought it was Peter . . .'

Peter, standing before the painting of the Edwardian threesome, felt the eyes of his mistress on him, and turned back round the corner to melt into the crowd.

16

Bridget had driven up to Farings on the Friday night to be ready for the sweep the following morning.

The front doorbell rang on the dot of 10 a.m.

'You're punctual, Mr Godwin.'

'Godwit. Like the bird – everyone makes that mistake. I used to be a psychoanalyst – a job like that you have to be punctual.'

'Good heavens! A psychoanalyst!' Bridget, who prided herself on being unsurprisable, was surprised.

'No, my joke . . .'

Bridget was relieved. She disliked anything of that sort – though the thought of a psychoanalyst sweeping chimneys was appealingly bizarre.

'My joke – my daughter's married a shrink – so I tease the son-in-law. Tell him she only married him because of her dad being like clockwork. A father complex, they call it!'

'Do you think it's true?' Bridget was intrigued. She had read that the Irish were said to be unanalysable because they couldn't distinguish external reality from their own unruly Celtic unconscious.

'About Corrie having a father complex?' asked the sweep. He was on his knees delicately fitting long wooden-handled brushes together. 'This'll be starlings' nests.'

'I meant psychoanalysis,' said Bridget, embarrassed. 'I wouldn't be so rude as to ask about your relationship with your daughter.' The sweep had nonplussed her – not at all common.

Mr Godwit was lying on his back staring up the chimney. 'Yup, starlings,' he announced. 'Little blighters. Be about half an hour doing this. All right for you?'

Bridget made tea for them both and came and watched as the sweep turned and furled his brushes with a dexterous competence. 'If you go outside you'll see the brush head coming out the chimney. My dad used to ask me, "Can you see the starling, then, sitting on top?"'

He seemed an unusually cheerful man and without the knack of being irritating which the perennially cheerful often have.

'Godwit,' she said over a second mug of tea, remembering how he had introduced himself, 'Godwits are birds, aren't they?'

'Black-tailed, Bar-tailed – you get them round Pembrokeshire. Wonderful coastline for waders.'

'I bought this house because of the rooks,' said Bridget. It was the first time she had told anyone.

'That's lucky. Rooks won't go where there's bad feeling. They building yet?'

They went outside. Bundles of nests made black raggedy marks in the elm trees against the sunlight.

'I saw a charm of goldfinches last week,' said Bridget, not noticing that she was showing off.

'It's famous for birds, Farings,' said Mr Godwit. 'Tell you what, if you like, next time I'm going to the coast I'll take you down there with me birdwatching.'

Bridget, who was unexpectedly pleased by this offer, had trouble finding her bag to pay him. In the end it was the sweep who found it, wedged behind a box of books. A red-leather-bound Shakespeare lay on the top.

'You like to read then? That's a tenner.' For all his good humour he gave the impression of being a shy man. 'Shouldn't be surprised if she did have a father complex – my daughter. Called Cordelia, she is. The wife's idea, not mine!'

It was not until supper – cheese on toast by the fire – and listening to the radio that Bridget remembered that the clocks went forward that night. Marianne, a hypochondriacal woman who painted furniture, was supposed to be delivering some chests to the Fulham house because for reasons to do with her health – which she would always go into – she could not manage deliveries during shop hours.

Bridget had asked Zahin if he could be at the house to take in the chests on the Sunday. 'But of course. It will be the utmost pleasure, Mrs Hansome.'

'Don't exaggerate, Zahin,' said Bridget, laughing.

'O Mrs Hansome . . .'

'All I need is to be sure you will be there. Marianne is a pain, if you want to know. If there is no one in she will just go off and then God alone in his mystery knows when I shall get the chests.'

'Mrs Hansome, like the Lord Himself I will be there. You can rely on me!'

But she hadn't remembered to tell him about the changed hour.

Bridget rang the London number and got the answerphone. Damn. She had no idea if Zahin listened to it. Probably he did, but better not bank on it. No good phoning Marianne either. If one tried to explain things to her there would certainly be a muddle. And she couldn't be sure of Mickey's feelings towards Zahin; it wasn't safe to ring there.

In the end she rang Frances. 'Look, this is a cheek but . . .' and she explained about the hour.

'I'll go round,' Frances said. 'It's no bother, really. I'll call at a respectable hour and tell him about the clocks.'

'You don't mind?'

'If I did I wouldn't say!'

Frances had been feeling better since her visit to the Tate. Perhaps it was that man in the crowd who had reminded her of Peter? The week which followed held fewer nights of anguish. In some way, she wasn't sure how, the lunch with Bridget had helped.

And she didn't – or she would not have joked about it – at all mind putting on her tracksuit the following morning and driving past the Fulham house on a round-about route to Richmond Park. She was, she had decided, getting fat and needed exercise.

The upstairs curtains were drawn when she rang the bell at 11.15 a.m. Perhaps a note would do? She was rummaging in her bag when the girl answered the door.

'Oh, is Zahin there?' The girl shook her head. 'Mrs Hansome asked me to call. Will he be back?'

A nod. A pretty girl, with two scarlet velour flower grips in her hair.

'Could you give him this then?'

Frances wrote: *Zahin – Mrs Hansome rang me to let you know that the clock has gone on one hour. Please be in for Marianne at 4 o'clock (what was 3 o'clock!)*

Would that do? Or would it, as was so often the case with explanations, only cause more confusion? Well, she had done her best.

Running round Penn Pond, Frances thought: I wonder who she is . . . ?

Bridget rang Zahin. 'Zahin, did they arrive?'

'Oh, of course, Mrs Hansome, and I was there on time to receive the lovely chests.'

'And Frances told you about the hour?'

'I had already moved the clocks.'

Frances had decided there was no need to worry Bridget about the girl. But Marianne had the effect of making people fuss out of character, so Bridget rang Frances to check the chests really had arrived, and then it seemed pointless to conceal the encounter.

'What was she like?' Bridget asked, more intrigued than offended.

'Very pretty. I wondered if she was his sister . . .'

When Bridget returned home the following evening she found an opportunity to say, 'Zahin, do you have any family here?' and with the perfect concordance with her thoughts which, almost eerily, he often betrayed, the boy replied, 'There is my sister, Zelda – she is staying here in England presently.'

'I see.' Pause. 'Did she visit you here, in the house this weekend? By the way, "presently" means "in a while" – not, as you used it just now, "at the moment".'

'O Mrs Hansome I was going to tell you presently, I promise . . .'

'Zahin, get up from the floor, please, there is no need for this exaggerated display . . .'

'Where does she live?' Frances asked. She was amused to have been the instrument of the uncovering of Zelda.

'With some sort of relations in St John's Wood.'

'They must be rich, this family,' Frances said. 'Zahin seems to have plenty of money. I hope you're charging him a proper rent?'

Bridget, who did not care about money – Zahin's or anyone's – had concluded that Zahin was fearful that the news he had relations in London might precipitate his departure from her house. That he was keen to stay with her – almost fantastically keen – was touchingly apparent. The discovery of Zelda's existence brought on a bout of intensive cleaning.

Bridget had considered making some demur when she saw the latest cleaning programme had reached Peter's study – she had not been able to touch it herself. But then, as with the knickers and petticoats, she thought: Why not? It was Peter who had first befriended Zahin – she must assume he would not have minded.

And why, anyway, did one bother about what a dead person might or might not 'mind'? 'You know,' she remarked to Frances, 'I still can't register that Peter doesn't exist. It's not that I can't *cope* with it, it's that it doesn't go in.'

'No,' said Frances. The nights of weeping had been exchanged for a series of erotic dreams. Most of these were more satisfying than any real-life encounter with Peter had been.

Frances had never given Peter reason to suspect that there was anything wanting in his lovemaking because it had never entered her head that there might have been; her interest in him had not been primarily physical anyway. To suggest that she pretended with him would be to overstate: she did not exactly pretend, but played, as it were, to his idea of himself. That this idea included some notion of a more than ordinary virility was something she grasped implicitly; it was tacit between them that theirs was a violent passion.

It may be the case that wherever large and romantic notions crop up in human associations they cover some corresponding lack. And it may also be true that where, in a couple, one party is straining a little, the strain will be matched somewhere in the other too. Perhaps what we like to call 'love' is, in part, the willingness to keep such strains from the other's knowledge, and mutual 'love' a reflection of the desire to protect? Just as Peter was less contrived in bed with his wife than he was with Frances, Frances, when lovemaking with Peter was successfully concluded, was often somewhat relieved – although this was something she never told Peter, nor ever made quite conscious at the time.

17

Peter had no thought of falling in love when he first saw the girl in Malaya. He had had girlfriends up at Cambridge: a trainee teacher from nearby Homerton, a nurse from Addenbrooke's, nearer still, and he had dutifully put his hand inside the brassieres of each of these girls (a disconcertingly grubby pale blue in the case of Homerton, a more stimulating black in the case of the nurse) and, as dutifully, been slapped down – for such was the custom of the times. He had not, as had the more persistent of his peers, pressed forward, ignoring these quite standard, and insincere, put-downs in pursuit of something more rewarding.

This did not mean that Peter was not endowed with a normal sexual appetite. He had been through the usual stages, being first the object, and then the instigator, of homosexual crushes at school, graduating to girls when that possibility became more available. He liked girls but he was shy – and it was the kind of shyness which lay concealed beneath a veneer.

As a result, at Cambridge he got a reputation for being

a heart-breaker, merely because when a girl responded he tended to pull back. The myriad influences of sexuality are subtle and hard to account for: it takes a very advanced person to comprehend his own sexual make-up, and if Peter himself did not quite know why he hung fire, most who have been in that boat will sympathise.

It is a stereotype that men are sexual aggressors: knights in armour, full of buck and swagger – potential rapists, no less. But in truth men – indeed most of humankind – are far more fragile than is commonly supposed. Peter was no exception. His love for his mother had left him vulnerable; the loss of her had left him fearful. And, to date, none of the girls he had met had aroused the protective tenderness that is often needed to overcome a disabling fear.

Peter met Veronica by the river where, on a free day, he had gone to swim. Tired of the company of his men, he had made an excuse and gone off on his own, feeling that slight sting of guilt which can plague the sensitive when they follow their own whim.

He had dried himself and was dressed when he observed a girl swimming with her friends and was struck by her natural grace and the sweetness of her smile. So that when he saw – or supposed he did – that she was having trouble in the strong current, he stripped off his clothes and dived, manfully, in.

Veronica – an orphan, brought up by Catholic nuns and named for the saint who wiped Christ's face – was, in reality, a strong swimmer and was merely fooling around in the water, pretending to drown to amuse her friends. She allowed herself, however, to be assisted to the bank by the tall English officer and thanked him charmingly for his intervention. (The true nature of this event was revealed much later amid much teasing and giggling.)

At the right moment, after the appropriate number of other meetings, Veronica translated her thanks into something yet more gracious. The remaining time spent in Malaya was, as a consequence, like the homecoming he never had – a miracle of happiness for Peter.

When the time came to leave Peter thought seriously of throwing over his commission and staying on; just as, a year later, the stint in the army behind him, he thought about returning to find the girl who had finally cracked the straitjacketing shyness. But upbringing sticks; he had lost the one resource – the regular contented congress with Veronica herself – which might have made such a departure from custom possible.

Thus Peter put away that small peculiar taste of paradise, believing, with the genetic optimism of youth that one day, another – more suitable – paradise would supplant it.

18

The night light Bridget had bought at John Lewis had been installed beside her bed. The purchase may have been initiated by a wish for distraction before the meeting with Frances. However, in the months which followed, Bridget had grown attached to the translucent column, with its tiny voluptuous mermaid and the bobbing coloured seahorses.

She was finding that she missed Peter at night. From the time she left home and could afford not to sleep with a knife under her pillow, she had been, with one or two ups and downs, a sound sleeper. But since Peter's death she found that sleep had become a kind of circle of hell – one in which, nightly, she was judged guilty of crimes, from which she woke into yet more terrible daylight misery. She missed not only Peter's demanding ways but – even more strongly – his sleeping form beside her.

'You are like a pig!' she had once remarked when he apologised for his snoring. 'I like it – it's reassuring.'

Without Peter's familiar porcine presence the nights had grown hostile. Incidents from her past arrived in ravening packs: the man she had slept with who turned out to have a wife who had tried to kill herself; the flat from which she had done a flit where the landlord had trusted her; letters she had pretended had never arrived she had let go unanswered; the bangle she stole from a school friend – she had had no idea that she possessed a conscience, yet here it was, a baleful, many-headed Cerberus.

During one such sleepless night Bridget, whose early exposure to Catholicism had formed in her the mental equipment, if not the spirit, to engage with such matters, read of an anthropologist who had hung the religious totem of some primitive tribe on his wall. As a form of self-experiment the anthropologist had begun to worship the totem himself. To his astonishment he had found a belief in the totem's numinous power had grown in him, as if the act of worship carried within it some invisible seed which could take root even in the most inhospitable crannies.

The article was in one of the anthropological magazines to which Peter had subscribed, and which, after his death, Bridget had somehow not got round to cancelling. Maybe, then, it influenced her when she found herself counting seahorses.

The light was constructed so that the seahorses rose and fell according to the expansion of the water, which in turn was governed by the heat emitting from the light bulb. 'When I have counted twenty-one rise-and-falls,' Bridget decided to herself one night, 'I shall fall asleep.'

Although Bridget had discarded her country's faith, it is harder to rid oneself of the superstition which is the ancestor of religion. Ireland is a country where, long before St Patrick set foot, magic reigned. Indeed, belief in religion is possibly dependent on superstitious magic and the number 21 is famous for its power to charm. The night light had seven seahorses trapped within its transparent walls; Bridget decided that the charm which would put her to sleep would consist of watching each of the seven seahorses rise and fall three times. On the other hand, she thought, she could ring the changes by watching three of the seahorses make the same motion seven times.

The elaboration of this ritual, as with countless of its primitive predecessors, was worked out over successive efforts. It was weeks before the finished form became established; and not until after Christmas that the alternative form was devised. The 'seahorse effect' was needed only in the Fulham house. Already she had established that at Farings no such soporific was required. It had to do with Peter's missing presence – other people would call it 'mourning' – but then, she never took much account of what other people called things.

So when, having got to the third seahorse, in what had become a regular ritual count, she looked up and saw Peter in the corner of the bedroom, she was startled of course, but not altogether surprised.

Months later, when trying to recover that first shimmery snatch of him – 'first' in the sense that it was the first time she had seen him since he had died – she decided that what he most resembled was the mummified starling which Mr Godwit had fetched down from inside the chimney. At the time she said, simply, 'Peter?' at which the thing-which-had-been-Peter folded back into the rooky darkness.

19

Frances had had to turn down a second invitation to Farings. There was a show on at the gallery and she had to be on hand to organise the moving in of the works of the young sculptor who was showing there. Roy, whose taste had made the gallery, was a puzzle to Frances. 'How can someone with such an aesthetic gift be so personally unpleasant?' she had once asked Peter. To Peter this was no contradiction. 'Some of the nicest people I know have the most terrible taste,' he objected, 'and vice versa. You seem to expect people to be the same all through!' 'You mean like that toothpaste –' Frances had asked – 'with mouthwash in the stripe, or jam in a Swiss roll?' 'Talking of rolls . . .' he had said (they were in bed at the time).

The sculptor arrived and fretted as the van containing his work was unloaded. Frances understood this: she knew about artists' anxiety from Painter. 'You've only yourself that really knows,' he had declared, when she had tried to reassure him after a critic had damned with faint praise his latest show. 'The arsehole thinks that just because it looks easy it isn't deep.'

Frances herself was not sure if she would recognise 'deep' but she knew the sculptor was not being grandiose when he fussed about the transport of his pieces; or how they were placed around the gallery, whether or not in the right light. 'It isn't egotism,' she had said to Peter once, of Patrick in fact. 'It's a kind of self-respect.'

Patrick, unusually, had agreed to attend the opening. It was part of Frances's value to the gallery that she had a gift for getting people along to functions; but even with her influence over Patrick it was unusual for him to put himself out for a fellow artist.

'I'll come,' he had said, 'provided I don't have to talk to anyone but you,' which wasn't so easy, Frances reflected as she steered him through to the drinks table.

Painter was wearing a bubblegum-pink waistcoat and matching socks. With his black beetling eyebrows, springy, untameable hair and the hum of fantastic energy which almost audibly came off him, it was impossible to miss the fact that here was someone who 'counted'.

The concept of those who 'count' was one which Frances had learned from her brother Hugh who had counted so much that the loss of him shattered for ever the weak ties which held the Slater family together. Neither his father nor his mother, it was understood, had ever recovered from the death of their dashing young-est child – who claimed men and women alike. And James, poor James, had had to grow insufferable as a result – his only means of combating the dead charm. She herself, she knew from the way in which her presence made so little difference to her parents' grief, had never counted. In fact, she was aware her mother often wished it was her only daughter who had been killed instead of Hugh.

Patrick, a glass of Roy's cheaper wine (a special offer at Majestic) held grimly in his fist, had, against all precedent agreed to speak to the young sculptor, who stood guarding his prize exhibit, a massive boulder within which were carved intricate and delicate fronds of fern.

'Bloody piss, this,' Painter remarked.

The young sculptor jerked round and for a moment Frances thought he was going to hit the older man. 'He means the wine,' she explained.

Painter gave a farmyard bellow. 'Don't read a word the arseholes write about you, will you!' He brought a fist down on the shoulder of the younger man – who reeled backwards as much at the unexpected compliment as at the force.

Frances, seeing Patrick into a taxi, said, 'That was kind of you – he went the colour of your socks!' at which Painter went quite pink himself.

'How's the widow?'

Frances had told Painter, when she last visisted, that she had been staying with the widow of 'an old friend'. Now she explained that she had been invited to the country with Bridget again but hadn't gone on account of the show.

'I'm an "old friend" too, aren't I? Come and visit me instead. Fred and Ginger would like to see you . . .' he yelled through the open window as the taxi pulled away.

Back home, Frances ran a bath under Peter's watchful eye. He waited, like a fussy nurse, to see that she had rubbed and patted dry all the crevices of her naked body, before he slipped back, through the hole in reality, into the windy dark.

20

It is easier to refuse an invitation if you have a guest staying. Part of Bridget's reason for asking Frances up to Farings again was a hesitation over Mr Godwit's promise to take her birdwatching. So when the offer showed no sign of being renewed she was at first relieved – then, perversely, a little annoyed. It was one thing to turn down an invitation; another to have the prospect withdrawn.

Bridget took herself into the garden and did some heavy digging; the ground was clay and she had to work hard to clear the patch of ground where she had decided to grow beans.

'"Nine bean rows will I have there,"' she intoned to herself, '". . . And live alone in the bee-loud glade."' What did the young Yeats want with *nine* bean rows? Nine bean rows would feed an army.

Bridget had never quite trusted the poetic grasp of the natural world since she had detected a confusion between 'alder' and 'elder' in the work of a contemporary poet. She had written to the poet to point out the error but, unsurprisingly, had received no reply. It was not a mistake you would find Shakespeare making even though he was sometimes shaky on his geography. Maybe it was just a matter of what one felt was important – for her, and for Shakespeare, the difference between elders and alders mattered – for other people it might be the non-existent coastline of Bohemia.

Bridget was lighting a fire when someone rapped on the window. Looking out she saw the sweep.

'Meant to call earlier – you've been gardening.'

Bridget explained about the bean rows.

'Going to put any broad beans in? They're my favourite – the first broad beans with potato and mayonnaise – a meal for a king!'

There was tea brewing in the brown pot.

'That's apple you're burning.' The man sniffed like a connoisseur. 'How are the rooks doing?'

' "The rook-delighting heaven",' said Bridget automatically. As she spoke a cloud passed across the face of the sun, darkening the room, and she shivered. A goose walking over her grave. She hoped whatever it was that had looked like Peter wasn't cast out naked.

'Ah yes, Yeats – the "injustice of the skies". I like that one. One I don't like is "Innisfree" with the "evening full of the linnet's wing". The linnet's wing is brown – it's the head that's pink, if he wanted to talk sunsets. Still, you can't have everything.'

'How funny,' said Bridget, 'I was just thinking about that, too. I was thinking that nine bean rows was far too many for a single man.'

'Unless he meant bean *poles*,' said Mr Godwit. 'Nine bean poles in a wigwam. He's a great poet – I suppose we should give him the benefit of the doubt.'

'Then he should have said so!' A poet should be accurate.

There was a pause.

'It could be he didn't mean to refer to the colour pink at all,' Bridget said, relenting. 'It might just be the wings – that peculiar whirring sound of birds' flight you get just before dusk – that he felt the evening was full of, and the pink heads get confused with sunsets . . .'

Shyness mingled in the air with the apple smoke. Mr Godwit drank his tea and they both stared at the fire as if it held some arcane secret.

'Well, I must be going.'

'Thank you for coming then,' Bridget said politely.

'Goodbye then,' said the sweep. He went out of the door and down the path.

Bridget thought: I didn't want to go anyway. I wouldn't have known what to talk to him about.

'Just thinking,' said Mr Godwit, putting his head back round the door. 'If you'd like to come to the coast with me tomorrow . . . ? There's been talk of sightings of choughs.'

The air was sharp with the scent of incipient spring and the sun on the field was laying the lightest benediction on the pale ranks of spring wheat when at 8 a.m. the sound of a diesel engine could be heard coming up the lane.

'Hope you don't mind leaving at this hour,' Mr Godwit enquired, declutching to negotiate the steep mud ruts. 'Only, by this time of year the traffic gets going early at the weekends.'

In near silence they drove through the greening Shropshire countryside. Occasionally Mr Godwit pointed out objects of local interest: the old cottage hospital, now being turned into tasteful apartments; the house where a local bigamist had lived, supposedly with a third wife under the floorboards; an oxbow bend in the river – good for frogspawn. Bridget's mind roamed back to Peter – or whatever it was that had looked like Peter in her bedroom. Speculating about the place into which she had watched her husband vanish, she hoped it might be soft and warm – like down feathers plucked from the breast of some vast night-plumaged goose. Peter – wherever he was – would need comfort. Had she given him comfort? Probably not enough; but then, maybe nothing one gave another person was ever quite enough . . . ?

Bridget might have been pleasantly surprised to learn that Peter himself had no complaints on this score. Had he been asked – as he might have been, for who knows the form of that measureless infinity which Bridget had been contemplating – he would have answered that his life with Bridget had been better than he could ever have expected – much more than he deserved, for deep down he was a modest man.

As we know from his early declaration to Frances, Peter loved his wife and admired her well-delineated character. If his own character was more susceptible to influence, and, as a consequence, more shifting, he accepted that as a fault on his part and a virtue on hers. Her uncompromising nature made him feel that, even if he had not found them for himself, there were certainties in the world.

For Peter the prospect of certainty was a kind of grail. His first wife – whom he married because she flattered his vanity – had delivered all certainty an almost fatal blow when she dismissed her own prenuptial declarations as, 'the sort of things people say – of course I didn't mean them!' Odd as it may sound, the idea that people might say things they didn't mean was a difficult one for Peter, though he himself could hardly be said to be always quite square with the truth. But the gap between what we are ourselves and what we want others to be is rarely measured, and a certain simplicity – naivety, almost – was part of Peter's character. In fact this was one of the traits in him which Bridget later found attractive.

Bridget and Peter met at a café in Notting Hill in the days when Bridget was still running her stall in the Portobello Road. She was sitting at a table reading when Peter entered the café in search of some refuge against the sudden sweep of nauseous dizziness with which he was occasionally afflicted. Peter noticed at once the aura of calm which surrounded Bridget and which was to make up a strand in her attraction for him. He sat down, near her table, and tried to make out what it was she was reading.

In a moment of hilarity afterwards, Bridget suggested that it was usually women who resorted to such tricks; having failed to see what it was that so absorbed the handsome blonde that she had no mind to notice him, Peter made as if to get himself another cup of coffee at the counter, staggered, grabbed at the table where Bridget was sitting, and thus, finally, succeeded in drawing her attention.

'I'm so sorry,' he had said, dramatically impersonating the giddiness he actually felt, 'let me get you another,' for in the cafuffle he had engineered, her cup of tea had spilled.

The tea had penetrated the leaves of *The Inferno* and

the discovery of the name of the engrossing book had given Peter pause: he was not sure he was up to a woman who read Dante.

'But it's not a bit "intellectual", really,' Bridget had said, on the mirthful occasion on which the subterfuge had been acknowledged. 'It's full of sense. Just what hell would be like – if there was a hell. But then I was brought up a Catholic so I'm conditioned to notions like hell and purgatory.'

At this time Peter was not a Catholic himself. When later he became one we know he never let on to his wife. The cautious part of him feared a jocular response from Bridget – and caution is often a sound guide. It is likely that though Bridget would not have openly mocked him for adopting the religion she had fought to escape, her humour might have been too rough to bear without resentment – and instinctively Peter knew that resentment is an enemy to marriage.

Bridget nearly cried out when the sweep's van came in sight of the long, low line of shining, shivering grey. She loved the sea: an ancestor had been a pirate and privately she liked to imagine that piratical blood flowed in her own veins. Perhaps, she had speculated as a child, the man had been hanged? Why, when the thought of hanging made her feel sick, was the idea of it in connexion with a relative so intoxicating?

She got out of the car rubbing her back which had seized up during the journey.

'That's the way down, there,' Stanley Godwit pointed. 'It's pretty steep, mind.'

'Damn!' Bridget said, 'I forgot to bring boots.'

But this proved no deterrent. 'What size are you? Six, I'd say. You can use Corrie's boots. She keeps them in the van – you and she'll be about the same size.'

Cordelia – King Lear's daughter – 'Choughs are those birds with red bills, aren't they?' – there were choughs in *King Lear*.

'Part of the rook family. Used to nest here common as gulls a couple of hundred years ago.'

When blind Gloucester, seeking to end his life, stands on the edge of the cliff which, even in the play's terms, isn't really there, his son, Edgar, to support the delusion, describes the dizzy heights his father imagines he stands on the verge of: *The crows and choughs that wing the midway air/ Show scarce so gross as beetles* . . . But could Shakespeare, living only in London and Warwickshire, ever have seen the sea? Bridget wondered, her ankles bending against the steepness of the descent. Her grandfather, who swore the playwright had been to Ireland and back, would have said so. And when you heard how Shakespeare wrote about the sea, it seemed incredible if he had never seen it. Was it possible that, like the cliff where the supposed choughs are sighted, Shakespeare's 'sea' was merely spun from his imagination? But then so was everything else he wrote 'spun': Hamlet, Lear, Gertrude, Cordelia – like the choughs, you could hardly say they didn't exist, they were realer than most people. What kind of existence did a character in a play have? Did Shakespeare's characters 'exist' in another world, in your mind, the way that a memory did – or a dead person, as Peter now seemed to . . . ? But where, or what, was Peter's world now? Was what she had seen real, or was it just in her mind . . . ?

But then she herself, she had often speculated, was no more than a dramatic construction, made up of fleeting feelings, idle introspections, vain wonderings – glimpses in the 'glass of fashion', she thought, taking hold of the sweep's hard hand as he helped her down the drop to the uneven, many-pebbled shore.

21

Although Frances had now met his sister, she had not seen Zahin since the day she called round with the Chinese bowl, when he had referred to her and Peter as sweethearts. The odd pronouncement – Peter's own word for them – remained for her a conundrum. She had not mentioned it to Bridget for she was well aware that, despite their quirky acquaintance, Bridget retained an understandable hostility to the affair.

Lying in bed one morning, Frances wondered how the boy could have come by his knowledge of her and Peter, and was suddenly overcome by remembrance.

What she was recalling, in particular, was the summer after they had first met at Mickey's, when she had gone regularly to the open-air baths to swim. The purpose of the exercise had been to trim the body which Peter seemed so to like, but the swims had evolved into a ritual through which, mad as it seemed even to herself, she sought to keep him.

'If I swim another seven lengths,' she used to incant, 'he will ring me tonight.' The seven would be followed by another seven – and so on. When, returning home exhausted, her hair damp and smelling of chlorine, she heard his voice on the answerphone, she tasted triumph.

It has been suggested that what we want and pursue with a whole heart we can always have. Who can tell the validity of this proposition – yet there are people whose conviction is strong enough to steer fate. It may be that without Frances's propitiating swims – or what lay behind them – Peter's interest in her might have waned. Certainly, at the simplest level, he responded to her need of him – as a man who has been abandoned always will.

The belief that we are worth loving is a blessing granted to very few and with that one blessing all others become redundant. To Peter Hansome, the idea that he might be the object of another's desire was inherently unbelievable. And yet there had been Veronica . . .

Peter was too untried at the time to perceive that the uncomplicated merging of body and emotion he had known in Malaya was one of those gifts which, through its very simplicity, gives an illusion of being commonplace. He had taken the whole experience simply, very much in the manner with which he had caught up the gold-skinned girl's body in his arms and threatened, amid squeals of delight, to 'crush it to death'. That mix of amorous sadism and erotic masochism was too fine-blent – in those days, too far below the surface of conscious thought – to be recognisable to Peter for what it was: a complete compatibility of disposition and longing, an example of natural partnership – in other words, a once-in-a-lifetime opportunity.

It has been told how, on the discharge of his commission, Peter had contemplated returning to Malaya to marry Veronica. What has not been told is how letter after letter had arrived – all in the childlike cursive handwriting taught by the Sisters of Mercy – how these had been read more and more sketchily until, finally, they had been put away, unopened, in a far recess of the oak bureau. (That these were not among the relics later found by Bridget was because, long before, during his first marriage, Peter had consigned the collection of manila envelopes, addressed in the round hand, to a purpose-built fire in the back garden, and had gone out afterwards to a nightclub in Soho where the 'waitresses' were obliging.)

It would be easy to assume that it was that lack of commitment with which women these days so often charge men, which led to Peter's seeming brutality. Veronica, back in Malaya, was first worried, then hurt, then, finally, angry when, after a few increasingly terse cards, she heard nothing back from the man who had 'died' inside her with the most unguarded expressions of ardent adoration. But guarded men do not always care to recall their unguarded moments; it was the memory of that uncollected wash of feeling which was partly responsible for shoving away to the back of Peter's mind, as well as his desk, the envelopes written by the slender hand which had so often – and so unexpectedly – brought him such exquisite delight.

But just as memory can recede more swiftly than we expect so the opposite is also true: people do not fade away inside us as easily as we sometimes hope. There came moments when, before he had consciously formulated the reason, Peter's heart would quicken and lurch, as, in the distance – perhaps walking down the street, or at the far end of a carriage on the tube – his eye was deceived by the sight of some slender, gold-skinned girl into believing his first, misprized love had returned.

The onset of significant developments in our inner lives is not easy to date: often they drift upon us casually, like snowflakes which do not announce the speed and severity with which they will become a storm. Peter could not have precisely said when it was that, in the act of making love to a woman, there began to come always a moment when she turned into Veronica.

At first he had been disgusted with himself. We know that in his fashion he was faithful, and the idea of super-imposing another on to the body of the woman he was making love to, tarnished his own picture of himself. But no one has ever found a successful counter to the anarchic forces the heart is host to – and, in the end, Peter had to accept that whenever, or however, he made love, and with whatever degree of fervour, there would always be three present: himself, the woman – and Veronica.

Some say this is what is meant by the law of karma, a stepping aside from a moment of possibility only to be for ever haunted by its unrealised spectre. If this is the case it seems hardly fair on those who have had no part in, yet suffer, the consequences of such derelictions. But here too there may be some pattern, and perhaps it is as well that whatever runs the system which is life has not found time to read the Declaration of Human Rights. By the time Peter met Bridget and Frances, both women to whom he longed to give his ardour unconfined, he found, when making love, he was impossibly and inescapably merged with the ephemeral body of a young Malayan girl, who by now if not, conceivably, dead was certainly middle-aged.

Frances was entrusted with the knowledge of her lover's faith but he never divulged to her his love for Veronica. Nor could she have borne that knowledge. Lying in bed months after her lover's death, she resolved the mystery of the young Iranian's clairvoyant insight with the consoling thought that the passion she and Peter had shared was so tremendous it had manifested itself to others, even after death.

22

Bridget, shopping in the village, bumped into Stanley Godwit in the company of a man with a ginger moustache and a cross-looking young woman.

'My daughter, Corrie.' Stanley made the introductions. 'And this is my son-in-law, Roland. Mrs Hansome.'

'Bridget,' said Bridget, staring at the moustache. The owner of it had a roly-poly look. Well named, she thought, Was he really a psychoanalyst? The humorous sweep could have been having her on.

'I took Mrs . . . er . . . Bridget birdwatching a fortnight back.'

'What did you see?'

Bridget, who had brought pebbles back from the beach, fingered them smooth and hard in her pocket. The eyes of the sweep's daughter were somewhat pebbly.

'Your father showed me some waders. Turnstones and golden plovers.' She remembered the names but did not mention that they had also seen a whimbrel – a slender, solitary, grey-plumaged bird, smaller than a curlew, with long elegant legs and an aristocratically curved beak.

There in the high street the bird suddenly reminded Bridget of Frances.

'There were said to be choughs but –'

'– we didn't manage to see any,' Bridget interrupted. She had been disappointed not to see the fabled rook-like bird with the scarlet beak and matching legs. She didn't mention that she had worn Cordelia's boots. Stanley Godwit seemed uncomfortable and, wanting to ease things for him, Bridget invited them all round for a drink. 'Your wife too, Mr Godwit, of course.'

'My wife, bless her, is in a wheelchair. She doesn't go out much.'

Hell, why hadn't he mentioned this during their trip? To her alarm Bridget found she was blushing.

The daughter furrowed her brow and said, 'We should be getting back, Dad,' and grabbed his arm, which made Bridget remember the conversation about father complexes.

'Are you really a psychoanalyst?' Bridget asked.

As if to keep her company the roly-poly flushed too. He had the kind of complexion which at best tends towards pink.

'I work at the Paddington Clinic and Day Hospital in London.'

'Heavens,' said Bridget, noticing that he was wearing bicycle clips, 'that sounds pretty terrifying!' The bicycle clips gave a rather endearing look.

'Better watch it or he'll lock you up!' said Stanley Godwit, laughing loudly.

Bridget, recognising this as the mirth of social embarrassment, let the Godwit party go. She had come to the village more to explore than to make any radical purchases. It was easy to bring stuff with her from Fulham. Nevertheless, it was useful that beside a tea shop with the legend 'Daisy's Teas' in green and white, there was a chemist, a dull-looking greengrocer's and what looked like a proper butcher's. There were pigs' trotters in the window; also tripe. Bridget did not much care for either but she liked to see that they were still in supply. Peering into the shop's interior she could see a whole pig's head, waxy-yellow with wide, red, splayed nostrils. A pork butcher's then? She decided to show goodwill by buying sausages.

But the experience was disappointing. The woman serving smiled – to disguise ill temper – and the diplomatically intended purchase did not go well. All the sausages of Shropshire, it appeared, had already been snapped up.

'You need to order in advance for the weekend. We've sold right out, I'm afraid.' The woman's voice reflected satisfaction at being unable to meet this new customer's demands.

'How fortunate for you that your business is thriving,' said Bridget and bought chump chops instead. 'Is this local lamb?' she enquired, but the woman sucked her teeth as if being required to solve a deep, theological question.

'I couldn't say. Welsh, I would think.'

So much for welcoming locals, Bridget thought. The scowling Cordelia and the pork butcher's assistant were not great adverts for the community.

She drove home, passing, on the way, the psychoanalyst, pinker than ever and pedalling hard on a state-of-the-art-looking bike. A wish not to be influenced by her unaccountable embarrassment made Bridget wind down the window and yell, 'I meant what I said – do come round and have a drink some time, any of you who feel like it . . .' and he gestured and waved back in quite a friendly way. Probably frightened of his wife, Bridget thought.

This sparked other thoughts: back at Farings one of the sudden swinging moods of listlessness, which had visited since Peter's death, swept over her – everything seemed too much trouble and pointless – there was no one who cared whether she was alive or dead, she had no child, or god, nothing to lend purpose to existence. Not even the book she was reading seemed worth the trouble – a modern book, one of those published to extravagant acclaim, none of it borne out by the experience of reading it.

Bridget had been a reader since the age of four, when she had found that, by concentrated staring, she could make sense of the magazine called *Housewife* which her mother was sent each month by a cousin who had married into the north. It was in *Housewife*, a few years on, when the habit of reading had become compulsive, that Bridget had read *The Greengage Summer*, and it was from this that she had learned about forbidden passions.

It was the kind of story which her mother's brother, Uncle Father Eamonn, would have censored had he been aware of its content. But Bridget learned self-preservation from her mother, and the clandestine affair between the older man and the young girl, which Moira Dwyer and her daughter devoured, was described to Father Eamonn by his sister as 'a great story about a fruit farmer'.

From *Housewife* Bridget had graduated to *The Famous*

Five, *White Boots*, *Treasure Island*, *Jane Eyre* (with whom she formed a certain fellow feeling) and finally, and permanently, Shakespeare. After that there was to be no equivalent love, as a disgruntled boyfriend later commented.

Bridget was introduced to Shakespeare by Sister Mary Eustasia who taught her in the first year of secondary school. Sister Mary Eustasia had a shrewd expression and the kind of voice which does not need to be raised. 'Now I want no nonsense, mind,' she would say. 'Any girl giving me any nonsense and it's extra homework and staying behind after school, make no mistake.'

Where there is true authority there is no need for punishment; there were few enough occasions when girls were made to stay behind. If Bridget was an exception it was because she preferred to remain in the company of the strict Sister Mary Eustasia than face the erratic justice of home. If her father was in when she got back, the chances were she would end up eating her supper in the yard, with Cindy the dog.

On the whole, Bridget liked animals, but Cindy, her father's pet, an ill-disciplined, bad-tempered bitch, had picked up her master's habits and would snap and snarl at Bridget, as if currying favour with the father when the daughter was in disgrace. Not only Bridget's fingers and toes but also her knees developed chilblains during the colder months, a fact which was not missed by the sharp-eyed Sister. When Bridget had attracted attention to herself yet again, by talking during a silent period for the third time in as many weeks, Sister Mary Eustasia called her over to her desk and said, with, for her, unusual mildness, 'I'll see you after school and have your English book ready to show me as well, will you?'

When the time came it was not the English book which Sister Mary Eustasia seemed concerned with. Instead she pulled from the pocket of her habit a book bound in dark red leather with a gold script.

The Works of William Shakespeare, Bridget read.

'Have you read much of him yourself?' Sister Mary Eustasia asked, and it was only many years later that Bridget realised that this severe, exact woman had dropped her usual tone and spoken to her almost as a colleague. When Bridget said she hadn't her teacher went on, 'Well now, he's the very best. People say you should start with the comedies but for myself I got to like them only later. Life isn't comic when you're young, would you agree? Start with *Hamlet*, I think is best; you won't go wrong there.'

And, slightly bewildered, Bridget had seen that the red book, with its gold italic lettering and grand binding, was meant for herself to borrow.

From there began a routine whereby Bridget stayed behind after school while Sister Mary Eustasia marked books, wrote reports, or tidied out her desk. Later, driving through the gloam-lit evening lanes, Sister Mary Eustasia's occasional post-school garrulity would lapse, and there would be moments of tranquil silence. Neither Bridget's parents, nor the girls at school, ever commented on this unusual arrangement and this was how Bridget learned that if you behaved as if your differences from other people were to be expected, they would be allowed to you.

Lying on the sofa at Farings, watching through the window a wren weave its way through the lords and ladies which grew at the foot of the hedge, Bridget recalled that first evening by the stove in the corner of the classroom, reading, with Sister Mary Eustasia passing the occasional comment.

'They say that Shakespeare was a Catholic, of course, but if so it's a damn queer ghost, coming out of Purgatory, as it tells us it does, and trying to entice young Hamlet to commit a murder! But then if it's a Protestant ghost there wouldn't be mention of Purgatory at all – the Prods don't believe in it – so it's a puzzlement, wouldn't you say?'

Bridget had heard of purgatory – of course she had; you did not grow up in Uncle Father Eamonn's ambit ignorant of the 'fires which cleanse and purge'. 'The smallest pain in Purgatory is greater than the greatest on earth,' he liked to tell his captive congregation.

For Bridget this meant the place where she might be rid of pardonable sin resembled something along the lines of a particularly horrible supper with her father. Possibly breakfast, lunch and supper lumped together – rather like the school holidays but with no time off for reading in between. Her mother – who, much later Bridget saw, used religion as a trade unionist might use statutory sick leave: as a means of taking legitimate absence from the regular bind – had taken Bridget during one such holiday to St Patrick's Purgatory. This was to be found on Station Island in Donegal, a location where Christ was popularly alleged to have revealed to St Patrick an entrance to purgatory and – presumably from there – a successful route to paradise.

The trip was not a success. The Irish summer, always unpredictable, was more than ordinarily inclement and they had had to queue up for the holy site in driving rain. A priest, in the crush to see the sacred spot, had taken the opportunity to crush himself against Bridget's thigh and in retaliation she had bitten his hand. Uncle Father Eamonn had smacked her hard on the same thigh – which Bridget had loudly asserted she greatly preferred to having 'that old priest press his old thingy there' – for which she got smacked again rather harder, this time round the head.

Thereafter, in Bridget's mind, purgatory became a kind of amalgam of that visit: an unholy mix of freezing wetness, lecherous priests, discarded cigarette packets, sweet papers and crisp bags – left by the pious pilgrims – and the sickening buzz in her ears while Uncle Father Eamonn dealt out righteous punishment upon them.

The idea, therefore, that purgatory might be a concept appropriate to a great play was intriguing. On that evening when she had first remained behind in the classroom with Sister Mary Eustasia, Bridget read the story of Prince Hamlet and his father, the old king, who had been murdered, poisoned through his ear by his ambitious brother while sleeping in an apple orchard. ('A reference to the Garden of Eden, wouldn't you say, Bridget?' Sister Mary Eustasia, in her collegiate way, had remarked.)

There was one line in particular which attracted Bridget. The murdered man had been *Cut off even in the blossoms of my sin/Unhouseled, disappointed, unaneled*.

Bridget liked the sound of 'unhouseled'. Sister Mary Eustasia explained to her that it meant that Hamlet's father had died without benefit of the 'housel' or Eucharist. 'What we call the Blessed Sacrament, Bridget. "Disappointed" is a fine, rich word, too, look. It means the old king died without having made the proper "appointments" with death – the chance to make confession and receive absolution.'

What Bridget concluded from this was that she herself must have failed to make some similar appointment. She had learned disappointment early and one consequence of an education in disappointment is that you learn not to take your own desires too seriously. Or you learn to defend them, if at all, by stealth.

So when the travelling theatre came to the city with a production of *Hamlet*, Bridget didn't even consider seeking permission to go; she embarked at once on a scheme to see the drama which had so momentously altered her mental life.

23

In the plan to see *Hamlet* as usual it was Sister Mary
Eustasia who came to Bridget's aid; more properly, the
image of her, since Sister Mary Eustasia, in person, was
away, taking her annual vacation in Galway. But invok-
ing her name was a powerful amulet against her father
and Uncle Father Eamonn, so that when Bridget said,
'Sister wants me to stay over and help her with a play she's
doing with the third years,' no one raised any objection –
though Joseph Dwyer did mutter, 'What she want to fill
them babbies' heads with that for? Where's that going
to teach them how to mend the shirts off their men's
backs?'

Truth is often the safest form of deception. Bridget
went on to explain that the play was by Shakespeare,
who was familiar to Joseph Dwyer from the legend which
claimed that the playwright had visited Youghal, Dwyer's
home town, as part of a travelling band of players invited
by Sir Walter Raleigh. The Irish, always ready to be allied
with genius, swore that the character of Shylock was

based on Youghal's Jewish mayor of the time. Had it been at all possible, they would have claimed Shakespeare too for one of their countrymen.

'It's *The Merchant of Venice*, Da,' Bridget explained, 'the one Grand-Da used to tell me about, you know?' – and in this way won her small freedom.

'You see, Bridget,' Sister Mary Eustasia had said, by the stove that first November evening, when the centre of gravity in Bridget's world shifted, 'Hamlet was a sweet prince, with a noble mind, and that old misery guts of a ghost came and corrupted it with all that talk of the torment he was suffering – how, if you were to hear about the dreadful time he had been having, it would make your hair stand on your head like the quills on the "fretful porpentine" – for Heaven's sake! And people imagining Shakespeare could possibly have endorsed such terrible self-centred nonsense! But that's "people" for you! They say the young prince dithered instead of getting down to it – but "people" don't think! It was a mortal sin he was being asked to commit – and his not the soul for it at all.'

Bridget watching the play that first time recalled her teacher's words and asked herself: Whose soul is?

Vengeance, then, and its attendant dangers, were already on her mind when she arrived home.

'Where were you then, you little whore?' her father asked knocking her down.

To give herself courage, before setting out for the play, Bridget had inexpertly applied make-up. Now she vaguely wiped her hand across her mouth, smearing the blood, which was streaming from her lower lip, into Rimmel's 'Honeykisses'.

'I'll wipe that whore's muck off your fucking face, so I will!'

Economy with lying is sometimes as important as economy with the truth.

'It's Maeve Whelan as is playing the part of Portia,' Bridget had thrown off as she was leaving, the copy of Shakespeare already tucked inside her coat, a scarf loosely draped around her face to cast a shadow over the illicit make-up. An unnecessary fiction; but Bridget was human and only sixteen, and had not had time to learn that simplicity in fiction (and lies are only one of fiction's many forms) is generally best. She had elaborated – dangerously, as it turned out when Mrs Whelan had called by and remarked in passing that her Maeve had gone with Joan MacCormack to visit Joan's nan up in Sligo. This news in itself would have been safe enough – Moira Dwyer not being one to rock the family boat – had Joseph Dwyer not thought to remind his wife that he would be off for a spot of fishing in the morning and she would need to get his dinner in time for an early start. It was to deliver this edict that he was entering the kitchen when Maeve's mother blew Bridget's cover.

'She's in a play by Shakespeare, though, your Maeve?' Joseph was proud of his knowledge of the so-called English 'bard'.

Mrs Whelan was not an ill-meaning woman; the last thing she would have wanted was young Bridget, who sometimes helped out with looking after her youngest, getting into trouble. But she was not quick enough on the uptake to avert a crisis.

'What play's that now, Joseph?'

*   *   *

'Are you sure now it's not a case of better the devil you know, Bridget?'

Sister Mary Eustasia's grey eyes looked tired. Bridget, who had come to return the Shakespeare before leaving, found herself, not for the first time, wondering what in the nun's own life had led her to take the veil.

'Mam says she's scared I'll kill him.'

'And you would, would you . . . ?'

'If he ever hits me like that again I will.'

'In that case maybe you are better gone.'

By this time Bridget was tall enough to look down on her teacher. Addressing the well-governed face, which had seen her through so many family crises, she said, making a joke out of the subject which had brought them close – for she found that some table between the two of them had turned and now the responsibility of making the atmosphere right had fallen on her – 'I'll be best off in England. Didn't Hamlet say they're all mad there anyway?'

'Remember now where you came from,' Sister Mary Eustasia had said, 'the land of St Patrick, who was crazy enough to survive anything.'

By this time Bridget had thought more about St Patrick's Purgatory and the ghost in *Hamlet* who was doomed for a certain time to fast in fires. 'Sure, St Patrick didn't have childer to take it out on, Sister!'

'Write to me, mind,' Sister Mary Eustasia had instructed, as Bridget left, and a month or so later, after she had written with the address of the hostel she was staying in, a packet had arrived which on opening proved to be the red-leather-bound Shakespeare, with a line written in a neat hand in the front:

'. . . the readiness is all' *Hamlet* V. ii.

and under it:

Joyce Mary Eustasia, with warm good wishes

In her sitting room, which looked out on the westering sky, Bridget remembered the nun whom she had seen only once since that first leave-taking.

She had returned to Limerick the year after marrying Peter, and had gone in search of her former teacher. Sister Mary Eustasia, she learned, had retired from the school and was now part of a closed order, further west in Clare. Bridget had driven down to see if she could find the place and, after some negotiation on the phone, an interview had been granted by the Reverend Mother to the Sister's old pupil.

As she drove down steamy, fuschia-lined lanes, Bridget had pictured to herself the nun's eyes, witty as ever. But the eyes of the face which received her were closed fast and Bridget learned, from the nursing Sister, that her former teacher was dying of cancer. The sickness seemed unlikely to detain her long.

During the drive, Bridget had speculated that this was the last time she was likely to see Sister Mary Eustasia, and that she should attempt to voice gratitude for the debt she owed. In her imagination Bridget saw herself fumbling to find the right words, 'I've never really acknowledged . . .' and her imagination also supplied the words with which she would be interrupted.

' "To be acknowledg'd, Madam, is o'er-paid" – Kent!' Sister Mary Eustasia, who liked the minor characters best, would say. 'You had a fine mind, Bridget. It's not often you find that in a country school in the back of beyond and you could not know how much that did for me – so there's no thanks needed, if that's what you were on about!'

The thanks were never given, for Sister Mary Eustasia was beyond speech and lay with a dribble of saliva at the corner of her mouth. Bridget had wiped away the saliva with her handkerchief, and, briefly, the grey eyes had flicked open. But they had glimmered only a second in the dying face; if Sister Mary Eustasia had had any idea of who Bridget was – never mind *King Lear* – it would have been a miracle. So the acknowledgement was never made.

Yet there remained the need for it, Bridget reflected, as the rooks returned to their ink-blot nests in the elms, for it is out of such gossamer threads of chance that we are saved . . .

24

Peter was not conscious that there was a connexion between his drifting into the Brompton Oratory and the meeting with a fellow officer from the Malaya days.

'I say, Pum Hansome!' The word erupted in his ear in the middle of the Brompton Road, and stopping to look back at the man who had uttered it, he saw Atkins.

'Pum', a corruption of 'Peter, Peter, Pumpkin Eater', was Peter's army nickname. He and Atkins exchanged convivialities. They owned to wives and children, a pair each on both fronts, and agreed they must call each other and fix a chance for a longer chat. That neither followed up this threat was hardly surprising: they had had little in common all those years ago in a far country – no reason to suppose that time and home would have caused them to grow close.

But for Peter at least – we know nothing of Atkins's thoughts or history – the meeting was sufficiently unsettling that, moments after, passing the Oratory, he turned and entered the church, near to tears. Churches provide a certain hospitality: for all its domed height, there was a consoling privacy within the quiet blue and gold space where Peter sat and composed himself before going on his way to the lunch he was off to.

It was weeks later when, making his way towards a venue in the same part of town, he again went inside the church and many weeks before he dared to approach a priest. This was long after his marriage to Bridget and the liaison with Frances.

Peter was always grateful that Frances had received the news of his Catholicism with the unassertiveness he found attractive in her. Though you could never call Bridget interfering it was as if you knew that, should she choose, she could stretch out her powerful arm and knock your life into disarray. That she did not choose only added to the slight fear that she induced.

Frances had none of that scary quality. Peter had never enquired into her beliefs but if he had bothered to think about it he might have guessed at a gentle agnosticism.

Frances had toyed with religion after the death of Hugh; that she had not persevered in visiting churches, lighting candles – even, on one or two occasions, going so far as to kneel on hard stone floors – was an aspect of that tentative part of her character Peter found appealing. There was something in Frances which brought out in men either the sadist or the knight-on-white-charger; sometimes – these configurations being merely different sides of the same coin – both. She was without Bridget's invincible strength; but for this reason she listened more.

Frances wondered if the fact that there was no experience equivalent to the terrible migraine with which she had been visited when Hugh died, maybe indicated that her love for Peter was a lesser love than that for her brother. And perhaps it was; impossible to measure degrees of human love, though we are always attempting it: Do you love me? How much? Is it more than him or her? being the kind of subliminal questions with which most relationships are freighted. If Frances was unusual it was because she did not ask such questions of other people but only of herself. Therefore, Did I love my brother more than my lover? became a question she was not afraid to pose.

One consequence of her posing it was that she considered carefully how she should mark Peter's death – not for herself but for him. She had no strong opinion about the afterlife; but even had she been sure ours was the only existence, she would have respected the different view of one who was now existenceless. This is how it happened that Frances travelled to Paris, and made her way along by the Seine, where the swirling autumn mists bore quite a funereal aspect.

25

As anyone who has visited Paris knows, the slow, green river which divides the majestic city is lined on its left bank by covered stalls, where even today the Parisians buy books – for in Paris, at least, reading is still a requirement of a cultivated mind. Among these old paperbacks are also to be found books on art, books on architecture, books of photography, and the altogether tasteful erotica which the French preserve as part of their reputation for culture.

At one such little booth Peter and Frances, wrapped in that exciting, invisible tissue which is an element of the erotic, enjoyed – at first sneakily, then, seeing that the other wasn't shocked, more heartily – the representations of the various configurations which the human mind has invented to extend the pleasures of sexual congress. In one thick-yellow-papered volume there was a drawing of a young woman whose breasts Peter insisted, were the 'dead spit' of Frances's. Closer inspection revealed that the 'young woman' was a hermaphrodite, replete with a vigorous-looking member. 'I suppose it's getting the best

of both worlds,' Peter had said; and Frances riposted, out
of character – as unlike Bridget she wasn't given to frank
curiosity – 'Then would you like me to have had a penis
too?'

After that they had crossed the Seine to the Louvre,
where she showed him the Leonardo of St Anne, the
Virgin's mother, with her daughter in her lap and her
young grandchild, on his mother's knee, playing – in a
small patch of freedom – with a lamb.

St Anne's feet, with their long toes, were planted firmly
on the pebbled ground, while the foot of her daughter
was entwined with the lamb's hoof. But the boy's fat foot
. . . Frances wanted to reach out and pinch it. 'Look at his
grandmother's expression,' she said, repressing another
thought. 'You wonder if she knows what's going to
happen.'

On the day that Peter's mortal remains were shunted
into the powerful modern incinerator to be reduced to a
cupful of ashes, Frances returned to the old gallery to
find the painting of the holy family by the acknowledged
master of the enigmatic. St Anne, her hand on her left
hip, the mysterious azure mountains behind her, gazed
down as before at her daughter. The lidded face, with
the strange, calm smile in which compassion blends with
anguish, had not altered, but its meaning for Frances
had. Looking now, she could see that the Virgin's mother
knows what her daughter cannot yet afford to know, as
all her maternal being is directed at the small boy, who,
pulling at the ears of the struggling lamb, stares back at
his mother in ordinary childish defiance. Yes, Leonardo's
St Anne is aware of what her family is going to have to
bear: that small, mean, brutal tragedy, which was

ordained to ensure a larger comic end – the ultimate salvation of the human race. She must have wondered, St Anne, Frances thought, passing quickly out of the room to avoid the diluting sight of other paintings, if it was worth it. How could you set the loss of your heart's dearest against any objective, however universal? It was too theoretical – a woman would have known that. Sensible Leonardo had ensured that in this trinity at least it was the women who counted.

Outside Frances walked through the florid, self-consciously ornate courtyards back to the river and across the bridge where she and Peter had walked as lovers nearly five years before. Paris had hardly changed – only become a little grubbier; as with everywhere there were more cars, more complacent signs of multinational interests, but better than most races the French knew how to hang on to their own.

By the bridge which leads on to the Île de la Cité, the most ancient quarter of Paris, Frances halted with the air of looking for something over whose existence she might have been in doubt. Then, tucked into a corner of the bridge, she saw it – the flower seller. That, too, hadn't changed: the Parisians still bought flowers before politely visiting their God.

Notre-Dame, with its twin tall towers, stands within a courtyard space of its own, and there Frances stood a while too, looking at the honey-coloured, intricately carved portal before venturing through one of its doors. Inside she wandered purposelessly in the lighted dimness – it was many years since she had been inside a cathedral – but light from a vast rose window made her stop again and look upwards. The sapphire and amethyst window

Peter had talked of. She sat down opposite it and rested her head on the chair before her.

Peter was gone; there was nothing to be done about it – nothing that could be done. Having no prayers to say she didn't pray – there was nothing she could ask, nothing that could be granted. He was gone and she was here and all she had to be glad about was that, unlike St Anne, she had been spared the foreknowledge. That and the sapphire ring Peter had left her.

Lifting her forehead from the hard wooden rail of the chair, Frances looked at the ring again, tilting the plane of her hand until the superior light of noon, playing through the window behind her, caught the jewel, making a tiny echo of that high, other extraordinary blue within its square heart. Those anonymous men who had fashioned the stained glass and set it for the glory of their God, they were dead and gone too. But the glass remained. Then did death matter? She didn't know. All she knew now was that this was where Peter had come after they had made love and it was the closest she would ever again be to him.

The bunch of anemones lay beside her on the seat, like some humble paid companion, too polite to interrupt, yet anxious to be about her own particular duty. Figures were moving about the cathedral, coming and going in its indistinct roominess – tourists, local worshippers come to light a candle or say a rosary, parties of pilgrims – nobody seemed to be bothering about anyone else's business: there was a kind of splendid anonymity there still.

Frances rose and walked deliberately towards the high altar. Ducking under the corded rope she placed the anemones by the statue of God's mother, then turned and walked quickly down the aisle and back outside.

Afterwards, she wondered if she should have thrown the ring into the Seine; but on balance decided that this would have been excessive.

It was this act of Frances's which first summoned Peter from the place of windy dark. He travelled back to Waterloo on the Eurostar with Frances, and, recalling the earlier journey, regretted the whisky, and the brandy and dry ginger, he was no longer at liberty to purchase.

26

It was the Easter bank holiday and Bridget had stayed up in London to serve in the shop on Saturday. Tilly, the girl who helped out, had an eye infection, suspected to be caused by the punch with which she had had her eyebrows pierced. Anyway, the season of the Resurrection was a boom time for garden furniture; it was as well, Bridget thought, that she be at the shop herself.

Trade was brisk; a row had broken out between two women who had laid simultaneous claim to a thirties cane table, and by the end of the day Bridget was tired. She had planned to drive straight to the country but the prospect seemed daunting. Better go home and set off early the next morning instead.

The question of Zahin paying rent for his room had never been discussed. He appeared to have decided that his contribution to the Fulham household should consist of his keeping it straight. And this arrangement – if something so unilateral could be called an 'arrangement' – suited Bridget. Although Bridget would not have called herself house-proud – rather the reverse – it had to be said it was pleasant to come home to the smell of polish and piles of neatly folded ironing. Even the sheets! She was able to dispense with the services of the laundry, which seemed to rip sheets like some serial killer. It was a change to live in a house which had so little to be done in it – almost like staying in a hotel.

'Zahin, however did you get to be so domesticated?' she asked once.

'By watching women, Mrs Hansome. No, really! My aunties as well as my mother. I liked to be there as they scrubbed and cooked. Sometimes when they washed themselves too . . .' A sly smile.

Ignoring this, Bridget had said, 'You should train to be a chef.'

His cooking was remarkable: subtle, delicate.

'I regret my family wish me to be a chemical engineer.'

'Have you thought that might be a waste?'

Bridget, who abhorred proselytisers, was careful not to communicate her views on family life to her guest. Observation had taught her that what people wanted for others was usually based on what they wanted for themselves. This reflexiveness, however, might equally be true of a point of view. She didn't want to seem to undermine 'the family' who figured so largely in Zahin's plans and motives. Maybe – who could tell? – he would make an excellent chemical engineer.

Somehow, though, she doubted it. Zahin appeared punctilious in his studies: he attended his college regularly and retired to his room after supper where he worked diligently, so far as she could judge, until the ten o'clock news. Then he would generally come down to the sitting room, and tea and KitKats were produced. Beyond the domestic he appeared to have no interests or hobbies.

It is usually possible to tell if a house is empty. Standing in the hall Bridget felt this was just the moment she could do with one of Zahin's appearances, like a solicitous genie from a bottle. But tonight it looked as if the genie had other fish to fry.

The evening had turned cold and Bridget, who had been working in an unheated shop, shivered. She had annoyed Peter once by suggesting that the proof of God's existence could be deduced from the bad weather which so frequently attends bank holidays. Occasional 'digs' at topics about which Peter had been stuffy had been one of her ways of keeping her end up. Quite why he had objected to this particular 'dig' she hadn't bothered to consider. But the recollection now of how she had liked to disarm her husband left her feeling forlorn. Well, there it was; she had never pretended to be easy.

The chilly house and the even chillier lack of company prompted a change of plan. Her packed bag was already in the boot of the car. She would do as she had originally planned, leave now, stop on the way, perhaps for fish and chips, or even a hideous motorway meal; then she would have the whole of Easter Sunday to recover at Farings.

The car was parked round the corner and halfway to it Bridget turned back. Was there milk at Farings? She might as well fling together the bits and bobs from the fridge.

As she rounded the corner she saw someone by the front door and her spirits lifted. Zahin home! Perhaps she might delay her departure after all.

But it wasn't Zahin. A much older man was at the door – a man about her own age.

'Can I help?'

'I'm wondering if I have the right address.' A well-dressed, urbane man – he might have been one of Peter's business associates who still appeared from time to time, to condole, or be consoled.

'I'm Bridget Hansome. Was it my husband you wanted?'

The man seemed to hesitate. 'D'you know, I think I've made a stupid mistake. What is this address?'

The number was clearly before them on the door so Bridget gave the name of the road.

'Ah, that's what it is. It's "Gardens" I wanted. My wife says I'm hopeless at directions – she always reads the map. I hope I didn't frighten you?'

'That's all right,' Bridget said. 'You don't look to me like a crook or a rapist.'

The man gave an uneasy laugh. 'I hope not!' He seemed pleasant enough and for a second Bridget entertained a wild idea she might ask him in for a drink. As if sensing this the stranger hurriedly went on, 'I'd better get going . . . Once again, I'm so sorry to have been a nuisance.'

The mistaken encounter produced a further drop in Bridget's spirits. The long day at the shop had frozen the marrow of her bones; what she needed was a scalding bath and a cup of tea – that would set her up. It would be better, later, anyway, when the traffic had thinned, driving to the country.

Bridget took off her coat and boots, filled the kettle and stripped out of her jersey and skirt. She padded upstairs to run a bath. But the door when she turned the handle was locked.

She rattled the handle pushing with her shoulder

against the door. Hell and damnation, what was this?

From inside the bathroom there came a voice.

'Mrs Hansome . . .'

'Zahin?'

A bell-like giggle.

'I thought you had gone to the country, Mrs Hansome.'

Standing in bra and knickers, locked out of her own bathroom, Bridget felt foolish. She had been sure the house was empty; the discovery that Zahin had been in all along disconcerted her. But she was also grateful.

'I was going to have a bath before I left,' she called through the door. An unmistakable scent of meadow flowers drifted out to her with the chiming voice, 'A thousand sorries, Mrs Hansome, I have finished in here – I will run your bath for you now.'

It was past nine when Bridget finally set out for Shropshire. Next door, Mickey had long finished her dinner and was looking for entertainment through the window. She had observed Bridget's encounter with the man on her doorstep, just as earlier that same evening she had watched a young, dark-haired girl, in a leather jacket, saunter up the same garden path. 'I suppose Bridget knows her own mind,' she remarked. Joan Clancey was visiting her sister in Dulwich and Mickey was spending Easter alone; for the time being there was only the unimpressionable air to take her meaning.

27

There was no one either, when she woke the following morning at Farings, for Bridget to observe to that she had been right about bank holidays. Rain was cascading from the gutter on to the flower bed, flattening the daffodils and narcissi. Across the field she could hear the sound of St Anselm's bells, brazenly inviting the parishioners of Merrow to share the Word with Rector Dark.

Count me out! Bridget thought.

The chance meeting with the man on her doorstep had illuminated her own isolation. That and Zahin's clear expectation of her absence. He had charmingly made her tea and toast, had run a bath, filling it with the bath oil he had obviously helped himself to, and had been as full of courtesy as ever; but there was no gainsaying a sense of the cat being away . . .

The rain looked as if it was well set in and Bridget, who had planned to garden, decided to go for a drive. Perhaps the weather might pick up elsewhere.

At the garden gate she met Stanley Godwit walking down the lane. 'Hello there. Lovely weather for ducks!'

'I was going for a drive,' Bridget said.

'Ah, well, drive carefully now – visibility's poor. I've just sent my lot off in the van to Gloria's sister's.'

Sometimes life gives us a chance to practise. Bridget, who had regretted not inviting the stranger in for a drink, was better able to offer an invitation now. 'I've never visited Ludlow – would you like to come?'

'Is it the castle you're off to?'

'I hadn't thought – but if it's there . . .'

Ludlow Castle was built on a corner of the important manor of Stanton, held in 1066 by the de Lacy family. Protected by the rivers Teme and Corve, and the steep slopes to the north and west, it stands in a fine defensive position. The castle, constructed of chunky Silurian limestone quarried from its own site, was one of a line of Norman castles along the Marches, built by the Conqueror to pacify the local countryside and hold back the unconquered Welsh.

Bridget, who was Irish and mistrusted conquerors, was grudgingly impressed. 'It's not as intransigent as most.'

They had walked up to the castle along a lane where the first crinkled young hawthorn leaves were showing. 'Bread and cheese!' the sweep had said, picking a few tender green leaves and tasting them. Now he said, 'You don't like castles?'

There had been violets at the foot of the hawthorn hedge; Bridget would like to have been offered 'bread and cheese' too. 'I don't like what they stand for.'

Or the memories they held . . .

The time she saw *Hamlet*, just before she left Limerick, it was in the grounds of the local castle. Sick with excitement, she had sat on the hard chair with Sister Mary

Eustasia's red-bound book fast under her thighs, safe against any forgetting. Far west as they were, the light was fading from the rose-dredged sky, so that when the first edgy lines of the play were spoken, it was against the eerie sound of the birds, which the Irish call by their generic name of crows (only later did Bridget learn to call them rooks), returning, in the eldritch light, to their nightly roosts in the trees.

Who's there?

Nay, answer me. Stand and unfold yourself.

They walked across the drawbridge and round the walls, stopping to examine the bailey. 'Brass-monkey weather!' said the sweep. 'Shall we find somewhere will give us a snack?'

The town boasted a proper tearoom with a crackling fire, china dogs and copper pans. At the far end was a bookstall, which also offered souvenirs.

They both ordered beans on toast and the sweep toffee ice cream for afters. 'Gloria laughs at me for this,' he said, indicating the ice. 'Calls me a baby.'

'Your wife can drive then?' Bridget asked; she felt the spectre of Mrs Godwit's health should be faced.

'Not since the MS got worse. Corrie drove her and the kids over to her sister's.'

'She doesn't mind your spending Easter Day away?'

'Reckon we see a fair bit of each other most days – anyway, I had to see a man about a dog,' the sweep concluded enigmatically.

That seemed to be enough of that. Bridget lit a cigarette and looked about for conversational inspiration. The bookstall revealed a uniform selection of local guides – nothing to talk about there – also some novels, the kind

Bridget avoided, and, surprisingly, a collection of contemporary poetry. 'Look,' she said, 'H.V. St John.' The poet H.V. St John was enjoying a late revival.

The sweep raised his eyebrows.

'You don't know her?'

Glad of the chance to depart from the topic of the Godwits' family life, Bridget went over to the bookstand and took down a slim volume.

'Listen.' She opened a page.

> *Small children like tragedies,*
> *They do not mind Lear's madness,*
> *They recognise our maladies*
> *In Hamlet's sadness.*
>
> *Large states are compassable,*
> *Childhood nights prepare us for such pains;*
> *It is the matters risible,*
> *The small affairs, which maim.*
>
> *The letter unarriving,*
> *Which brings us to our knees,*
> *Contains a power harrowing –*
> *The stuff of comedies.*

'And that's true too,' said Stanley Godwit. 'Reckon I'll buy a copy of that for Gloria.'

By Monday morning the God of Bridget's childhood had proved Himself; the rain had not abated. There was no chance of any gardening. Better to make the best of a bad job and try to beat the holiday traffic by starting early for London.

Zahin greeted her affectionately; if he was displeased at her early return he showed no sign, but ushered her into the kitchen where he was making pancakes.

A bunch of magazines lay neatly piled on the kitchen table – *Vogue*, *Harpers*, *Marie Claire*. The trip to Ludlow had unsettled Bridget. If Peter had been alive she might have picked a quarrel – though, of course, if Peter had been alive she would have had no occasion to visit Ludlow. 'Have you seen your sister lately, Zahin?'

'Sadly, she has had to return home.'

The boy spoke with finality. Did he mean Iran or merely the family the girl had been lodging with? There was an air to Zahin's manner which an impartial observer might have detected in Bridget's own – polite as it always was, it forbade incursion.

Bridget flicked idly through the magazines.

'Look, Mrs Hansome, this on you would look so fine, see, with your English skin.' Zahin had come over and, crouched beside her, was indicating an expensively simple linen dress. The boy had an eye – maybe he should be a fashion designer rather than a cook.

'And this here, Mrs Hansome – so soft, for you so flattering.' He pointed to a blue pashmina.

The scarf Peter had bought her had been that very colour. 'Thrush egg' she had called it and had quoted Hopkins to him, '"Thrush's eggs look little low heavens".'

Peter had been rather proud of the way his current date broke into lines of poetry. He was suspicious of anything too intellectual; but Bridget was Irish, and for

145

the Celts, poetry is the natural language of the heart. She never used it to make out she was superior; only, as with the scarf, for a mark of approval.

It may be that the scarf – and Bridget's poetic reaction to it – was a determinant in Peter's decision to ask her to marry him. They had gone away for a weekend in the Cotswolds, which might have turned out badly, as Bridget was against anything which invoked picture postcards; so it was fortunate that the weather had been poor and she caught cold, which did away with that danger.

Passing a haberdasher's in Chipping Camden, Peter had spotted the scarf in the window and suggested buying it to protect her throat. It was a shade of blue which showed off her fairness and both had been surprised by the success of the transaction: Bridget for the concern she was unused to, Peter for her patent pleasure in the gift.

Peter expected not to have an effect on people. It was his impact on Veronica – audible and visible – which had so enchanted him; that the handsome, composed Bridget, who had the air of always knowing her own mind, should be capable of being moved by a simple gesture of his, proved a powerful aphrodisiac . . .

Seeing the blue stole on the magazine model, Bridget could not for the life of her remember where her own little scarf was. Was it in the hall drawer? or in her bedroom?

'Zahin, excuse me.'

Upstairs, she rifled through drawers; then, finding nothing, pulled them all out in turn and tipped out all Zahin's careful arrangements: belts, buckles, handkerchiefs, lavender bags, even a solitary suspender adrift from its partner – but no sight of the thrush-egg blue. She clattered downstairs.

'Mrs Hansome, can I help you? You have mislaid something?'

'A scarf.' She was too agitated to keep the impatience from her voice.

'It is a valuable?'

'To me, yes!' Too bad if she sounded curt; she couldn't always be minding the boy's feelings.

It was not in the hall drawer either.

'Hell!' said Bridget, close to tears.

'Mrs Hansome, Mrs Hansome, is it this that you are seeking?'

At the top of the stairs Zahin stood with the blue scarf round his neck.

'Where did you get that?'

Overwhelmed by the feeling which was swelling up in her, she wanted to fly up the stairs and snatch the precious relic from him.

'It was in the chest of drawers in my room.'

Of course. She had put away things she hardly used there in the bottom drawer. Coming down the stairs he unwound the scarf and held it out to her and she smelled the scent of meadow flowers.

'Zahin, has someone been wearing my scarf?'

'Maybe when my sister came over she borrowed it . . .'

Bridget was not, openly, violent but she knew she had left home for fear she might kill her father. Since that time, knowing that for her it was potentially lethal, she had tried to steer clear of hatred.

'When did your sister come over, Zahin?'

'O Mrs Hansome . . .'

'I want to know.'

'Maybe over the weekend.'

'When "over the weekend"?'

'Maybe Saturday . . .'

So it was his sister he had been expecting when she had returned from the shop.

'And you let your sister use my things?'

'Maybe just some bath oil, a scarf maybe . . .'

The memory of that chilly weekend, in Chipping Camden, smote something deep and unexamined in Bridget. She had not given so much to Peter that she could afford to have forgotten his scarf.

'You and your sister can fuck off!'

'Mrs Hansome . . .'

'Fuck off! Fuck right off out of here and find some other fucking fool to fucking well take you in!'

Trembling, exhilarated, Bridget was conscious of having crossed some shadowy boundary. She rarely swore. The odd 'damn' or 'hell', hardly ever sexual obscenities.

The boy turned and ran like a kicked dog up the stairs, and Bridget turned too, from a fantasy of hurling him down them – and went into the kitchen. After some time she heard the front door close but she sat a while before getting up to see if he had really gone. She felt dizzy, and there was a buzzing in her ear. At last she moved out into the hall and listened. Dead quiet. She went upstairs to the spare room, reproachfully clean and empty of any possessions – save one.

The Chinese bowl. Bridget took the bowl and bashed it hard against the corner of the chest of drawers, bought at knock-down price in a Normandy sale. But defiantly, the blue bowl, more solid than its appearance suggested, remained intact.

28

Frances was sorting tights when the phone rang. Because her clothes were in neutral colours – grey, black or navy in the colder months, taupe and cream in the summer, her tights were these colours too. The different shades were supposed to be kept in different bags but in the period after Peter's death chaos had seized its opportunity and made confusion.

Opening her drawer that morning, after her shower, Frances, naked on the bed, began to sort things out.

Sitting about stark naked was, Peter had been fond of saying, one of the things Frances might have been 'made for'. As a matter of fact, she had once been an artists' model and had achieved minor fame when her nude form had been rendered even flatter in a pink perspex sculpture entitled *Frances Seated* (or was it *Frances Standing*? – she never could remember). The sculpture had been bought by the Tate and the sculptor, a tiny, intensely bearded Dane had, more as a mark of gratitude for their combined achievement than for any real erotic interest, made a pass at her which she had judiciously ignored. Possibly it was his sense of relief at this – shortly after, he left his solid Danish wife and took up with a vulpine young racing driver – which had prompted the sculptor to introduce her to Painter.

Painter, who had just started his abstract period, had not needed a model, but it was through him she had met Roy, and this was how she had come to manage the Gambit Galleries.

There were times when Frances missed her former occupation – as we miss what we have talent for. She had been a good model, having a capacity for stillness and the kind of body which reflects planes of light. And she had liked, too, the mysterious conjunction between her body and the artist and the way a third entity, the painting, would emerge. When Peter had made it plain that he liked her to do so, Frances began to spend more time in his company without her clothes.

Sitting on the bed Frances, for the first time since her lover's death, inspected the body reflected variously back to her in the angles of the dressing-table glass. Deprived of Peter's attentions her once familiar shape had grown into something she didn't quite recognise. Her breasts, in defiance of the lack of recent interest in them, seemed to have grown fuller; a sign of impending menopause, Frances concluded gloomily.

When the phone rang she considered ignoring it: the bit was between her teeth and almost all the grey and cream tights had been returned in neat balls to the designated bags. But there was a part of Frances which was always half expecting tragedy, it wasn't safe to leave a phone to ring – and indeed the voice which spoke to her did have a tragic tone.

'Miss Slater?' For a minute she didn't grasp who it was. 'It is I – Zahin.'

'Zahin? Where are you?'

'At a phone box, Miss Slater.'

'Frances, please. Is Bridget all right?'

She had a fleeting vision of Bridget running into Peter's arms.

'She is angry with me, Miss Slater. She has chucked me out.'

So Bridget wasn't dead – at least she hadn't cheated her with Peter.

'Where are you?' Frances asked again.

'At the station, at Turnham Green. Forgive me but I could only think of you . . .'

Climbing into her clothes, Frances lamented the tights abandoned again to anarchy. The child would be here in five minutes. She rushed a brush through her hair and put on lipstick and the kettle.

'Come in, Zahin. Would you like some coffee? No, you prefer milk, don't you?'

Twenty minutes later she said, 'I suppose you can stay here for a night or two but my spare room's not large.'

'Anywhere with you would be paradise, Miss Slater.'

'Frances!' said Frances, vexed. Zahin's extraordinary way of talking got on her nerves. He was a self-indulgence of Bridget's, part of her deliberate, refractory quirkiness for which she, Frances, was now carrying the can. 'It can't be for long,' she said trying to sound businesslike, 'I'm sorry, I'm not like Mrs Hansome – Bridget,' she corrected herself. Really, there was something almost hypnotically compelling in the boy's habits of speech.

He smiled now, radiant, all traces of tragedy dispelled. 'I will be the best guest you ever had!'

That is not the point, Frances thought. I never wanted a guest at all. More socially adjusted than Bridget, Frances was in some ways more particular; it was not entirely an accident that she had never married.

Zahin unpacked his bag and Frances resumed the sorting out of the tights. But with her clothes on, and her privacy gone, the occupation was no longer fun. She began to hoover the bedroom and was astounded when Zahin burst in.

'Miss Slater, let me, I am a "dab hand" with the vacuum cleaner.'

'Dab hand' is Bridget talk, Frances thought.

'Zahin, I like to do my own hoovering. And please, if you are to stay with me, we must have some rules. I can't have you coming into my bedroom.'

To her alarm the blue eyes welled and tears began to course down the golden cheeks.

'Zahin, please. I didn't mean to speak sharply . . .'

'I know how Mr Hansome loved you, I am so sorry.'

'Zahin!' Impotently, Frances sat on the bed while the boy wept.

'He was my friend too. He told me how he loved you, Miss Slater.'

'Zahin, can you try to call me Frances? I shan't feel comfortable with "Miss".'

'O Miss Slater, Frances, I meant no disrespect . . .'

'Righteous indignation is great for filling a vacuum,' Sister Mary Eustasia had said. 'Poor Hamlet doesn't know what he feels, then the ghost arrives and look, suddenly he's a great reason to be angry!'

Bridget was shocked at the force of the hatred which had surged up in her – like a wild, swollen river bursting its banks. But rivers at least leave fertile deposits. Shame made her want to hang on to her outrage, to justify its voluble, satisfying violence. But in the aftertaste of vehemence she knew there was more in this than a petty wrong done to her by some silly, heedless girl.

The outburst was more complicated: it had something to do with the expedition she had made with Stanley Godwit to Ludlow Castle. She felt guilty – but not just because she had behaved badly to Zahin; obscurely, she felt guilty about Peter too.

There had been violets growing in the hedgerow near the castle – violets, which 'withered all' when Ophelia's father died. Was it really her father they had withered for? Violets were for faithfulness . . .

'For heaven's sake, stand and unfold yourself! Or are you just going to skulk in the corner there?' Bridget asked.

The truth was she was rather scared. The piece of dark which had detached itself from the shadows had plainly become Peter; yet, just as plainly, she had been present as Peter's body was reduced to ashes. She glanced at the night light where the seahorses climbed and ducked, obedient to the scientific law which held them in thrall. The 'remains' of Peter, or whatever it was that had emerged out of the dark place, seemed to be staring at them too. Presumably 'whatever it was' was now outside the aegis of 'scientific' laws?

'It's a night light,' she explained. 'I bought it when

you died to keep me company.' The comparison voiced sounded rather uncomplimentary. 'To give me something to look at anyway when I couldn't sleep.'

There was certainly going to be no sleep with the apparition in the room. Bridget wondered whether she should pretend she couldn't see him and go on reading *Hamlet*. She had got to the bit where the ghost started like a guilty thing upon the crowing of the cock. Maybe this one would go away if she ignored it. But she didn't want it to go away: she wanted it to make some sign but it – or Peter, and really it looked just like him – merely stood, fixing his eyes first on her and then on the night light.

'OK,' she said, 'if you are my husband Peter there are things only you will know. Forgive me if this sounds like a test but if you can't speak I presume you can move. Show me where you kept your father's cufflinks.'

Silently, the apparition moved towards the chest of drawers and gestured to the looking glass which stood upon it. It was a glass with a small drawer at the base, where the cufflinks had lived since the day they had gone missing from Peter's own drawer. The drama had been such that Bridget had taken charge of them thereafter.

'Forgive me,' she said, 'but anyone could guess that. Here's another. Where's the key to the clock?'

Again the phantom moved across the room. In ghost stories they glide, Bridget thought. This was more like a private showing in her bedroom of a three-dimensional film.

The figure which looked like Peter stopped and indicated a pot on the other chest of drawers.

'Very good,' said Bridget. This exercise was at least having the effect of making her lose her fear. 'Now one more. How do we keep the window open when it's hot?'

But at this the phantom seemed to hover and a sudden sense that it was distressed reached Bridget. She looked towards the window. 'Sorry, sorry, it wasn't meant as a trick.' The old broom with the toothless head which they used to prop the window wide was still under the bed. She didn't quite like to get out and look but there had been enough questions.

'So you *are* Peter,' she said. 'Or should I say *were*?' And she knew then, from her tone, that it must be him after all.

29

By the end of a fortnight Zahin had thoroughly spring-cleaned Frances's flat. The carpets had been sprinkled with evil-smelling powder and vacuumed, the parquet floors had been stripped down and repolished, the windows sprayed with a brand new product containing vinegar, the grout round the bathroom tiles cleansed with a toothbrush and denture polish, and the stainless-steel sink scoured. Zahin explained, 'You use salt – it is a natural . . .'

'Abrasive?' interrupted Frances. Luckily the flat was small and soon there would be nothing left to clean. But then what?

It was the May bank holiday and she was dismayed to learn that Zahin's college was closed. She thought of ringing Bridget, decided to let sleeping dogs lie a little longer, and instead rang Painter.

'Patrick, I'm sorry to be a nuisance –'

'Which you always are . . .'

'– but Zahin's here.'

'What happened? That Limerick woman turf him out?'

Painter, who had the Corkman's antipathy to all other natives of his island, sounded almost jolly.

'I haven't got to the bottom of it yet,' Frances spoke cautiously, knowing Painter's predilection for spiteful gossip. 'How would you feel if I brought him over? Would it be an imposition?' She knew that Painter was irrepressibly curious: if he had conceived a dislike for Bridget he would relish the idea of getting to know her lodger.

'Bring him over, surely. I've got Mother in the garden – we can have tea.'

The weather had turned warm; the thought of tea in a garden was pleasing after the prospect of hot streets and a drive during which Frances became, inexplicably – for she knew perfectly well the way to Painter's – lost. While reversing out of the garage, she scraped the side of the car. Unfairly, she wanted to blame Zahin.

And yet, of course, nothing is wholly self-originated: how we feel at any one time has also to do with who we are with. Negotiating the roundabout where Peter had been killed, it occurred to Frances to wonder whether, if there had not been an actual person in the car with Peter, there might have been instead some distracting presence on his mind.

Zahin sat beside her passing compliments. Without having yet discovered the basis of the row with Bridget it wasn't hard to see how the child might get on one's nerves. She was grateful when they reached the cul-de-sac where Painter lived and she could stop searching for polite replies.

'This is Mother.'

Frances had never actually met Painter's mother.

Unavoidably aware of her presence from the artist's frequent references to her, Frances had somehow imagined an invalid, tucked away in bed. Now she saw a small, energetic-looking, red-haired woman, with a face like a pug, sitting upright, apparently in full health, in a deckchair.

Painter's mother smiled graciously and said, 'Don't mind him, dear. You can call me Rita – everyone does.'

'Lovely Rita, meter maid,' said Painter and grinned.

Frances thought: He really *is* in love with his mother! 'This is Zahin,' she said aloud.

The boy sprang forward and kneeled beside the deckchair. 'O Mrs Painter, it is a privilege to be in your garden. The English are the best gardeners in the world and I think this one must be best of bests!' he turned about embracing the air with wide-flung arms.

Frances, who expected Painter to say something scathing, was astonished to see him beam at this extravagance.

'Not English, Irish. Mother's garden is a treasure. We have parties come and inspect it.'

This, too, proved not to be a joke: Painter went inside and returned with a booklet titled *London's Hidden Gardens*. 'Page 45 is ours,' he announced proudly and read out, '"Specialities," it says, "snowdrops and polyanthus".'

'The snowdrops have long left us,' remarked Rita. 'But the polyanthus would bring a song of joy to your heart. What I like best is gardenias, but they won't grow in this soil.'

They ate ginger nuts and drank Typhoo tea. Zahin gave Painter tips on various cut-price shops. Painter seemed genuinely taken by him, but then, I suppose he *is* gay, Frances reflected, wandering off to inspect the further reaches of the garden. She had never quite placed Painter's sexuality but supposed from his devotion to his mother that other women were taboo.

Mrs Painter had apparently also taken a shine to Zahin. He was talking to her animatedly when Frances returned from her stroll among the tulips; and the forget-me-nots, which covered every available patch of ground like a blue scintillating Milky Way . . .

Frances passed through the garden but never saw the appearance of a man who stood before her, vainly offering the bunch of misty-blue flowers.

30

Peter had been driving back to Fulham when he first saw the girl. It was only her back he saw, with the long black hair cascading down it. But it was the slight poke of the shoulder blades which stopped his heart. A split-second after this had registered on his memory, the girl turned off into a side street; he had already passed the entrance to it and had to make a U-turn, causing tremendous uproar among the traffic.

He drove slowly down the road, ignoring hoots from a car behind, but no sight of the girl.

That night in bed Bridget said, 'Whatever's got into you?' which was unlike her: usually she accepted his approaches without comment.

The following day he made an excuse to himself to pass by the road again – and again crawled the car up and down it. No joy. He tried to forget the vision he had seen. But it wouldn't leave his mind. The girl had not only looked like Veronica – all his responses cried out that it *was* her – and yet cold reason told him that Veronica, by now, must be fifty-five, and, most likely, fat; maybe even

– though he could hardly bear to force such an image upon his imagination – a moustache?

Weeks passed; he had almost persuaded himself the incident was unimportant, when, passing through Shepherd's Bush from a different direction, he spotted the girl again. It was that distinctive walk – and the shoulder blades. The blood surging in his heart he drew alongside her.

The girl turned her head and smiled at him and he braked too sharply, nearly causing an accident – the face and the demeanour were almost Veronica's, only just not quite . . .

The girl smiled again and, mesmerised, he followed her as she turned into another road where she stopped and waited.

'Please?'

'I'm so sorry, I thought you were someone I knew.'

'I am sorry that I am not she.'

There was a pause during which Peter thought: I can't possibly.

'Well, nice meeting you!' Such banal words. He wanted to lay his head down on the steering wheel and howl – for himself, for the girl he had treated so callously all those years ago in Malaya, before he knew better; most of all, he wanted to cry for the desperate, hopeless *uselessness* that lurked inside him, waiting to mess everything up.

'Would you like me to come in the car with you?'

Peter heard the words but was not sure how he was to take them. Was she offering to come on a date? Or was she a prostitute? He had visited prostitutes but none lately.

'For a drive?'

'If that is what sir wants.'

So she was a prostitute. The idea was not erotic – indeed it tarnished the tenderness which had welled up for Veronica.

But there was no denying it – this girl was quite incredibly like Veronica. And if he took her for a spin in the car that wasn't as if he was 'going' with her – even if she expected, which she certainly would, to be paid.

They drove over Hammersmith Bridge and along to Putney and across into Richmond Park. Peter said nothing and the girl seemed content to stare out of the window. It was on the brink of evening and the sun was vividly dropping in the sky. Peter finally stopped the car and in need of something to say suggested, 'Shall we go for a walk? It looks as if it will be a jolly sunset.'

'If that is what sir would like.'

He came round and opened the door for her and offered his arm, which she took, tucking a small hand inside his elbow. They promenaded, rather stiffly, he praying that neither Bridget nor Frances, nor anyone who knew him would pass (he was worldly-wise enough to be aware that it is on such occasions that people generally do pass by). Arm in arm – like some elderly couple welded together by years of sedate living, he couldn't help thinking – together they watched the round disc of sun drop down to another side of the world.

On that occasion, he drove the girl back to where he had picked her up and was astonished, as he fumbled to pay her, when she leaned across and stopped him from opening his wallet. 'Oh no, please, it was such a pleasant ride. I do not want to be paid.'

Driving away, he thought she had said it not as if she was angry but as if she were giving them both a holiday.

Peter, quite deliberately, had not looked to see which house the girl had entered when she left the car, but, a few days later – impossible to keep her out of his thoughts! – he went back to the street and waited. And this time there was no talk of not accepting money.

31

Frances, who was fussy about her make-up, was almost late for the meeting at the gallery because she couldn't find her eyeliner. A quarrel had broken out between Roy and the young sculptor, Ed Bittle, and she needed to have her best face on to deal with Roy, who put you down if you were not presentable.

Searching in her dressing-table drawer, she found it, among the lipsticks, and was puzzled. Generally she was careful to keep the eye make-up separately, in the bathroom cabinet.

Zahin had been staying with her for three weeks now and the initial strain had worn off a little – but not enough to suggest she would ever want him permanently about the house. Yet Peter had liked the boy, enough to confide in him about her. She couldn't quite envisage it – but the boy's words were the proof!

Frances hadn't liked to probe exactly what Peter had said. She felt embarrassed to raise the topic, and Zahin had that manner – it wasn't aloof, not aloof enough in some ways, but it shared the deterrent effect of aloofness.

The argument between Roy and Ed Bittle was over the commission Roy charged for the sale of the sculptures. The gallery was a showcase for new talent, and Roy, conscious that many purchases made for investment purposes were based on his noted eye for talent, exacted a high percentage from his new exhibitors for the privilege. Often they didn't read the small print of the contract – and that was when Frances would find herself becoming involved.

Entering the gallery, Frances could hear raised voices coming from the room behind.

'You should have fucking well told me . . .'

'I'm afraid it states quite clearly . . .'

'It's a fucking disgrace, that's what it fucking is!'

'Roy,' said Frances, 'I'm so sorry to be late. Lady Kathleen rang. She needs to talk to you about her Matthew Smith.' Lady Kathleen, a multimillionairess, held an unimpeachable position in Roy's affections.

'Will you excuse me . . . ?' Roy left the room with an exaggerated deference to manners.

'He can drown in the frigging Antarctic for all I frigging care,' said Bittle, looking angry and sheepish at once.

'Tell you what, let's go over the road to Marie Rose's and have a bagel and some coffee,' said Frances diplomatically. 'I need some breakfast.'

Outside she took the sculptor's leather-clad arm and steered him across the road. Marie Rose was the name of the tall Malayan woman who owned the eponymous bar conveniently situated just across from the gallery. Apparently she was redecorating – Frances and Ed had to step over several pots of paint.

'He wants to take seventy per cent of everything I sell,' Ed said gloomily when coffee and bagels had been ordered. 'That's not just what you lot sell – it's all the stuff I sell from me own workshop. It's not right.'

'It's his policy, I'm afraid,' Frances said. She was used to this. Roy charmed and flattered, so it was a double shock to discover it was only part of a plan to systematically fleece you. 'He'll drop you unless you guarantee to sell through him alone.' She had been in this position numerous times with other young artists.

'Yeah, but seventy per cent! It's frigging daylight robbery.'

Frances looked at the young man beside her. His nails were bitten to the quick, his face, pale as marble, was drawn back into his ponytail and he had mauve rings under his eyes. It took guts to be a sculptor: to work long physically taxing hours with few chances of sales.

'Almost the only way for someone like you to become known is through a gallery like ours,' she tried to sound soothing. 'And Roy will get you known. That's his upside.'

'Jesus Christ! He needs a frigging upside with a frigging downside like that!'

Frances was touched by the 'frigging' which she understood as some kind of deference to her sex. She looked at the taut young face again; it looked as if it could be trusted to keep its mouth shut. 'Listen,' she said, 'this is how you do it. You work away and don't show Roy all your pieces. Other than the ones he's already seen. Just show him one or two more. If you're good – and you are – he'll sell you for a price and you'll get a reputation. Then, if you want to, when you've established a name,

you can go somewhere else with the work you've accumulated in the meantime.'

'Yeah, and in the "meantime" how do I frigging well
live?'

'Well, I agree that's a problem. But if you can hang on
for a year or two he will make you a success. It's happening already – Patrick Painter thinks you're talented.'

Bittle turned an anguished face to hers. Painter had
told her once that the human face could be defined as
one of two categories: cabbage or horse. 'He was just
trying to cheer me up.'

Definitely horse, she thought. 'I know Patrick quite
well – he wouldn't say anything he didn't mean.'

'Yeah?' The face became ecstatic. 'His work's fantastic.
I really rate him.'

'Under all that showing off he's rather a nice man, too,'
Frances said, feeling confidential.

As she left to go back to the gallery Bittle said, 'Hey,
thanks. You don't fancy going to the pictures, do you,
only there's a movie . . . ?'

Well, why not? Frances thought; at least it would spare
her from an evening with Zahin.

32

Peter had told himself, decidedly, when he had left the heavy-curtained house in Shepherd's Bush, that that would be that. He had a mistress and a wife, both of whom he loved, each of whom was sexually attractive to him. It was crazy to place in jeopardy a life already blessedly full of satisfactions. That evening he visited Frances, unexpectedly, and returned home to Bridget where he made love to her too; and the next morning followed her into her bathroom and repeated the performance as she bent to put the plug in for her bath.

For a sixty-year-old man, in reasonable health, to ejaculate seven times in seventeen hours is not impossible; but neither is it all that common. Though Peter did not consciously connect his unusual potency with the girl, he was aware that a more-than-ordinary excitement had surrounded his experiences at her hand. And a 'more-than-ordinary' excitement is an experience that will nag away until it is replicated.

Even so, Peter was cautious; he had come to know caution early – caution might be said to be his oldest friend. The occasional wary trip to a prostitute, here and there, was one thing; a regular visit, especially in a locality so close to home, was a recipe for discovery. And there was also the matter of his religion . . .

A connexion is recognised between sexual and spiritual energies. Bridget had once read Peter a poem by John Donne, in which the reformed Dean had likened his God to his past mistresses. Peter had been impressed by the brilliant, piquant, dovetailing mind of the poet, whose ardent longing for his God seemed honestly to have gained from his former ardour for his women.

Maybe Peter had the Holy Sonnet in mind; maybe it was that common human tendency to rationalise our baser instincts into something elevated. Whatever the cause, when, inevitably, he returned to Shepherd's Bush to repeat the excitement, the effect was not to lessen but mysteriously to deepen Peter's religious feeling. He felt, quite literally, after seeing Zelda, that his heart was available to his God in a new way.

Long ago Sister Mary Eustasia had pronounced, 'If there is a God – and I, at least, Bridget, must assume there is one – then I suppose He is likely to be a stranger to human ways of reckoning.' Peter hadn't had the benefit of Sister Mary Eustasia's wisdoms; but he had lived many years with Bridget, and we pick up ways of looking at the world from those we live with. In any event, Peter wasn't as puzzled as he might have been by the quickened response to his religion prompted by his new acquaintance: in fact, it could be said that he took it rather in his stride.

33

Ed was waiting for Frances in Marie Rose's. The early-evening showing of the film didn't start for forty minutes, so they ordered coffee before setting off to the cinema. Outside her business persona as manager of the gallery, Frances felt exposed and slightly stupid. Feeling a need for female solidarity, she tried to engage Marie Rose in conversation.

'How's the redecorating going?' The paint pots seemed in much the same place as the day before.

Marie Rose had the figure of a model. It was rumoured that Antonioni, who had made a habit of using the café during a stay in London, had once offered her a part in one of his films. But Marie Rose had laughed the famous director to scorn. It has to be hoped that she was sincere in her rejection since her hair was now an unexpected snow white and it seemed unlikely she would be offered the chance again. Nevertheless, the well-boned face and cat's eyes remained striking.

'Ach! You know, men!'

Early on Frances had discerned that Marie Rose's aggression was born of anxiety. 'It'll be nice when it's finished.'

'If it ever is!' exclaimed Marie Rose, flouncing off, her gold sandals clacking.

'So . . .' Frances said, missing Marie Rose. She couldn't think of anything to say to Bittle. She didn't even know on what basis she was going to the cinema with him – or what he imagined the basis was.

They drank their coffee in silence. It was seven years since Frances had been alone with a man she didn't know, other than for mild socialising or business reasons.

In further silence they walked to the cinema a few streets away. The weather had turned freezing – the green, baleful chill of a May which has perversely decided to turn its back on summer. A passing car threw up dust which got into Frances's eye. Dabbing at it with the remnants of a tissue, pretending it was 'nothing', she wished she was back home where it was warm – even with Zahin who talked too much, but at least one never felt awkward.

The film seemed to be about a motorcyclist who commits a casual murder and subsequently falls in love with the victim's girlfriend. The plot was hard to follow and the actors' voices so 'real' they were incomprehensible. Frances felt herself sink into boredom, then into grief, missing first Peter, then allowing that to slip, in turn, into missing Hugh. She remembered being taken with Hugh to see *The Railway Children*. Hugh had fallen in love with Jenny Agutter, and had forced his sister to write to the star on his behalf. And, of course, being Hugh, Miss Agutter had replied. How did it work, that effect? Even through an amanuensis the young film star had known Hugh 'counted'.

The film's hero (if that was what you could call him) had

confessed to the girlfriend who, though shocked, was clearly not going to allow the fact that her current lover had apparently stabbed her former one in a men's lavatory to make any difference. Peter and Frances had seen *Jules et Jim* together – twice. Perhaps the amoral Catherine who had gone with both Jules and Jim, and finally driven one of them (was it Jules? she always got the two men mixed up, anyway, the one with a moustache) into the river, was no different from the murdering biker? Bridget would probably say not. She must ring Bridget, from whom nothing had been heard since the upset with Zahin . . .

Bridget also thought of going to the pictures that evening – but decided against, there was nothing she really wanted to see alone. She was restless; it was too chilly to walk – instead she got into the car. Nearing the Hogarth roundabout she thought of Peter and drove, on spec, over to Turnham Green.

Frances lived in a mansion block. Walking up the stairs, to the second floor, Bridget was in time to see a girl come out of the door of Frances's flat and get into the lift.

'Excuse me,' she called, 'is Frances in?'

But the girl had already pulled the lift gate across and now stared blankly out from behind its grille. She was unusually pretty, with long black hair and tight white jeans. But she must already have pushed the button as the lift began to descend and, still smiling, the girl shook her head at Bridget as if in non-comprehension, leaving Bridget to ring the bell of the flat – unanswered.

The film had ended – not at all satisfactorily, in Peter's view. He was tagging Frances through the cold London streets, as she hurried behind the striding form of Ed Bittle. The murderer had been permitted to get away with his murder, to live happily ever after. But not for all time, Peter reflected grimly, keeping an eye on Frances. Just let him wait! No one got away in the end. And why was Frances dressed so skimpily in this freezing weather? Didn't she know to look after herself? Bittle, he was glad to see, was saying goodbye to her. So much to worry about, he thought, sliding into the tube as the doors closed, and finding his way to where Frances stood, warm and lonely in the crowded carriage.

34

Bridget was just about to ring Frances when the phone rang and it was her on the other end.

'Sorry to have been out of touch.' Frances was not looking forward to having to speak of Zahin.

'Oh, Frances . . .' Bridget said, pretending not to know for a moment who it was. She didn't want to give an idea that she might have been missing anyone. Also, she had an instinct about the girl she had seen coming out of Frances's flat.

'Only I've been meaning to tell you—' Frances ploughed on.

'That Zahin is staying?'

'How did you know?' Frances, detecting hostility, became cautious.

'I saw his sister coming out of your flat.'

'What! When?'

'The other night.' Now that Frances was thrown off balance Bridget allowed herself to become amused. 'Didn't you know she was there?'

'Certainly not. Look, I don't want him staying – only

he sort of imposed himself. I shall certainly enquire about the sister.'

'He led me to believe she was in Iran, or some-where . . .' Bridget threw in, wanting to make mischief.

'When did you come by?'

'Yesterday,' said Bridget shortly, anxious not to give any impression of being at a loose end, 'I thought you might fancy going to the pictures.'

'That's where I was – at the cinema, with a client.' Though Ed Bittle, with his turnip-white face and bitten nails hardly seemed to fit the notion of 'client'. He had been nervous when he said good night; observing this, Frances had forgiven him the frightful film.

'Well, anyway . . .' Bridget trailed off.

'Bridget, are you going to be around this weekend? Can I call you back?'

It was Bridget's weekend for staying in London. The weeks without Zahin had passed and the house was already showing signs of his absence. Conscious that she was acting out of a sense of obligation – always a deter-rent to pleasure except with the self-righteous – Bridget called round to see Mickey.

Mickey, while not telepathic in the Celtic manner, nevertheless was possessed by some inner genius which kept her instructed in the comings and goings of her neighbours. She knew without sensible evidence, even before Bridget's call, that things had changed next door.

'Not in the country?' she enquired, bluntly. 'I suppose you've nothing better to do then than call on an old woman.'

Mickey's age and health were, in fact, both matters of

pride to her. At seventy-five she possessed a haleness which would have done justice to a life spent in regular visits to expensive health clubs. In fact, other than trips to the pub, or to the corner shop to buy Embassy cigarettes, she never took any exercise. A box of groceries was delivered fortnightly, originally from Cullens, now Waitrose.

Mickey's ruling passion was watching the films of Clint Eastwood. One was showing now and she turned down the sound as Bridget came through from the hall into the over-heated front room.

'I'm interrupting,' said Bridget, looking for an excuse to leave.

'It's *Misty*,' Mickey explained, 'the moment when she picks him up – only he thinks it's him doing the picking up. She flatters him, you see. That's men for you, always so sure of their own charms!'

Bridget had never quite liked the film in which Clint Eastwood falls for a psychopathic girl and has his life, and that of his girlfriend, turned upside down.

'I just called to say hello.'

Until now she had not really been aware how much she had worried that this might have been Peter's fate.

'That boy's gone, hasn't he?' Mickey's satisfaction was evident. 'Thought he was trouble. Like a cup of tea?'

They sat in the garden. Bridget, looking at Mickey's regimented beds, thought: I'll need to find someone to weed. Zahin, without her ever noticing him doing it, had kept the garden almost as impeccable as the house.

'Who was that young girl, then, that was round all the time while you were away?' Mickey asked. 'Didn't like the look of her. Not that it's any of my business, of course!'

Frances was supposed to be going to an old school reunion that day. The school she had attended was expensive and exclusive. It was a day school and because her family lived in the country she had been made to board with Mrs Maddox, who had hairy legs. The legs would not have mattered so much if Mrs Maddox had not also worn white ankle socks. Even as a child it had filled Frances with shame to see the long black hairs on Mrs Maddox's white calves.

The other school experiences had not, by and large, been comfortable either. Fearful of the effect of Mrs Maddox's legs, Frances had never felt able to return any hospitality when she was invited to friends' houses for tea after school. At the weekends she usually went home, which was all right if Hugh was there but dull if it was just her parents. The school prided itself on its intellectual attainments and had a marble-covered wall where the names of girls who won scholarships to Oxbridge were inscribed in gold. There had never been any chance of Frances's name being on the *Honor Deo* list – she had done Art for A level, a subject which was not admired. Also biology, which for some reason the school considered a subject for the weaker students.

So when the Old Girls League secretary had sent a circular announcing a 'get-together' of the girls who left in '78, Frances's first impulse had been to screw up the letter and throw it in the bin.

Frances had seen no one from her school days since she left miserably sure that she was the possessor of only one A level with which to approach the hazards of adult life. The fact that it turned out she was awarded an A in Art and a B in Biology (doing better than she had dreamed) had not redeemed for her the school's associations. But curiosity is a powerful corrective – even to fear. Frances fished the letter out of the bin, uncrumpled it and e-mailed the League secretary.

Before setting off for the school, offsetting one fear against a greater one, she had phoned Bridget intending to tell her about Zahin. What a nuisance – now she would have to ask him about the girl Bridget had seen coming out of the flat – doubly annoying, since she wanted to remain composed before the reunion.

'Zahin, can I have a word?'

'It would be the greatest pleasure.' Zahin's responses were all too much the same to be quite real.

'Zahin, has anyone been here? I mean, while I was out?'

The boy frowned, apparently untangling some tremendous puzzle. Then, brightly, he said, as if reaching an answer he knew would find favour, 'Only my sister . . .'

'But, Zahin, you should have asked me. Anyway, I thought she was in Iran.'

'I am so sorry, Miss Slater.'

Oh no, my boy, Frances thought, You are not getting away with that! 'It is "Frances", Zahin and you are not going to distract me by bursting into tears. When did your sister call? You should have introduced her to me first.'

'You did not come home from work. I did not know . . .'

So the girl had been round while she was out at the

cinema with Ed Bittle. It was true she hadn't told Zahin she would be late. 'OK, but you should have let me know when I got in that you had had a visitor.'

'After my sister left I went to sleep. Then this morning you were getting ready for your school. And now you look so pretty . . .'

'Oh, Zahin,' said Frances, exasperated, 'please stop paying me all these compliments!'

In the film Play Misty For Me *there is a song written by Ewan McColl. The song describes the songwriter's feelings for Peggy Seeger, the woman who later became his wife. Peter, watching the video in Mickey's front room, heard these words:*

> *The first time ever I saw your face,*
> *I thought the sun rose in your eyes,*
> *And the moon and stars, were the gifts you gave*
> *To the dark and the endless skies, my love . . .*

and remembered three women and the different gifts they had given him.

35

Frances's car was still in the garage having the scratches – the legacy of the trip to Painter's – repainted. Her old school was a short distance away and she had planned either to walk or take the bus. But the confrontation with Zahin had made her late. She didn't want to arrive hot and bothered. In the end, she rang for a taxi.

But the taxi driver, flouting the time-honoured ruling which decrees that all taxi drivers shall be bastards, stopped first for a bag lady to meander across the road and then, worse, to let into the congested line of traffic a coach carrying a party of Down's syndrome children. The coach's incursion made way for other drivers, swift to take advantage of this piece of professional imbecility. While Frances fumed, the children pressed their noses to the coach windows, making their happy, pink, moon faces flatter than ever. By the time the taxi reached Brook Green she was late, a thing she disliked being at the best of times.

'More haste less speed,' observed the driver as she almost tripped over the hem of her dress getting out of the cab.

'Thank you for that,' said Frances. And then stung to unusual asperity, 'Since you seem to be so free with tips you won't need any from me.'

Apart from Zahin, another reason for Frances's bad humour was that she had been unable to fasten the skirt of her favourite wheat-coloured linen suit. Troubled by the likely worldly successes of her peers, she was concerned to make at least a good appearance. The long dress over which she had nearly come to grief getting out of the taxi, was in place of the suit, to hide any signs of unwelcome girth.

A wave of familiarity hit her as she ascended the stone steps and entered the hall. Almost at once a voice called, 'Frances!'

'Christina!' Christina Stack had also 'done' art – the pair of them had been 'dim' together.

Christina's label on her cherry-red jacket announced that she was now called 'Stein'; she had photographs of a large house in Dorset, with a pony and three children. Frances had forgotten this would be one of the ordeals she would have to face: the sight of children, which she herself had never had. And husbands, of course.

Christina's husband turned out to be a barrister, well able to supply both the house in Dorset and the pony. Other people also had husbands but quite a few were divorced. Some had never married and what a relief that in spite of the discarded suit, Frances was still one of the better dressed!

A tall woman with big earrings detached herself from a group and came over. 'Hi, I'm Susannah. I'm looking at everyone's skin.'

Frances, who was startled to recognise in this groomed,

confident woman plump, tearful Susannah – who had excelled at netball and lacrosse, but suffered mysteriously from something connected to her periods – instinctively put her hands to her face. 'I should think mine's deteriorating by the day.'

'Looks pretty good to me. Are you on HRT?'

'I hadn't thought about it.'

'You should. You don't look as if you're at the "change" yet. Are you?'

'No,' said Frances offended and bounced into a candour she immediately regretted – actually, she had been meaning to see a gynaecologist. She had forgotten the reputation for directness which made girls from her school occasions for fear. Hardly 'girls' any more, she reflected, eyeing her peers who, in varying conditions of confident early-middle age, were queuing up for quiche and two types of salad, plus orange juice or one glass of dry white wine.

Lunch was rather more fun. One of the old girls gave a speech about the need for 'women like us' to influence public opinion. 'Why ever would we want to do that?' enquired Frances's neighbour, who, as a schoolgirl, had had a head of flaming red hair and a personality to match. The hair had tempered to auburn, and Lottie now ran a bookshop – 'not very successful', Frances was glad to learn. Nor did Lottie have a husband, or children. The speaker, a square woman in a powder-blue, box-jacketed suit with gilded buttons, whose face was better known to Frances from the newspapers than recollection, most assuredly had a husband, as well as quantities of children and a powerful parliamentary position. The very thought of 'public opinion' made her feel tired, Lottie said. She and Frances agreed to meet one day and re-explore Hogarth House.

Hogarth House was in fact one of the places Peter had taken Zelda. Zelda had seemed to enjoy the experience, although she had been bothered about her eye make-up running.

'It doesn't matter,' Peter had assured her, 'you look lovely however you are. I don't know why you bother with make-up.'

Zelda had intimated that not to 'put on' her 'face' was an impossibility only to be suggested by the laughable ignorance of an English gentlemen. She was wearing her white jeans and was worried also that these might be stained by the grass. Peter, who wanted to lie next to her, had taken off his shirt and offered it as a makeshift rug.

It was the thought of Zelda's young bottom encased in the tight white jeans, which, on that fatal day when the lorry driver lost concentration, had caused Peter to change his mind about the route he was taking and had led him into the one-way system which is death.

36

Zahin was out when Frances got home, which could only be a relief. She kicked off her shoes – bought specially from Hobbs and not yet properly worn in – and lay down on the sofa inspecting her hands. Bridget's hands, she had noticed, were mannish, the fingernails ragged and not always quite clean. Looking at her own – long and pale with scarlet-lacquered tips – she missed the sapphire ring. Hadn't she put it on?

Maybe because of the fuss with Zahin she had forgotten it before hurrying out, though she was almost sure she hadn't, since she had had it half in mind – should the matter of her single status threaten to become humiliating – to give an impression of its being an engagement ring, the gift of a fiancé, dead of cancer, for example, or some other socially acceptable disease. In the event, the meeting with Lottie had removed the need for any such deception. But where was the ring?

Perhaps it was still on her bedroom table in her mother's glass powder bowl where it lived when not on her finger. But the cut-glass bowl yielded nothing more than a dried-up rosebud from some distant dinner with Peter, she couldn't even remember which.

Frantic now, Frances riffled through her bag for the number of the League secretary.

A voice on the answerphone commanded her to 'speak slowly and clearly' – just as well, as panic does not encourage clarity.

'Lindsey, it's Frances Slater. Stupidly, I seem to have lost a ring – a sapphire ring – quite valuable. Could you find out if anyone found it today when clearing up?'

'It was lovely to meet you again,' she added – untruthfully, for she didn't think they had even exchanged so much as a glance.

Anxiety about the ring precluded further rest so that when the phone rang she was glad to answer it. But it was Ed Bittle, and not the League secretary.

'Hi,' said Ed. 'I was wondering how you were.'

'Not too bad,' said Frances, cautiously. She hoped this was not more Roy business.

'Only . . .' said Ed.

Frances waited. She felt drained – the reunion, then the loss of her ring. She really didn't want to have to do anything for anyone. But she had helped Ed – and those we help we feel tender towards, which is one reason why helping others is not always the wisest policy.

'D'you fancy a curry or something?'

'Do you know, not really,' said Frances, trying not to sound rejecting. 'Only I had to go to my old school today and it's tired me out.'

'Oh,' said Ed's voice, crestfallen.

'Tell you what,' said a part of Frances relenting, 'if

you'd like to come over we could get a takeaway, if that doesn't sound too unglamorous.'

Apparently it was sufficiently glamorous for Ed to arrive thirty minutes later, wearing his leathers and with his hair standing up, like some urban elf, in small waxed spikes. It appeared that he had driven over on his motorbike at top speed from Stepney.

He fancies you, warned the knowing part of Frances. Don't be absurd, said the other, rational, part. I'm fifteen years older than him.

Ed's motorbike drove off to the Bengal Tiger and Frances took the opportunity to smooth the bedcover and reapply lipstick and mascara.

So why are you doing that, then? asked the knowing part. If you imagine anything could take place with Zahin here . . . ! said the rational part, primly putting the other in its place.

Frances warmed the foil containers in the oven, then took them out again colder than before. 'I've forgotten to light it,' she apologised.

There was an unwholesome smell of gas in the kitchen so they ate in the living room, under the coquettish glance of the Kavanagh nude. Although she would normally have felt mortified by the error with the gas, Frances found with Ed she didn't care. The poppadoms had fragmented in his bike bag and most of the mango chutney had leaked out of its container and deposited itself among the shards.

Most human emotion is reactive. Perhaps because he was so anxious himself Ed inspired a kind of soothing calm. Difficulties were made light of and Frances found herself becoming expansive, almost witty, describing the gallery's various upheavals over the years.

But at midnight, conscious that Zahin might arrive any minute, she tried not to look at her watch.

'I'll be off then,' Ed said, with the superior discernment of the slightly paranoid. He made no move to go.

'It's been lovely,' said Frances enthusiastically. And nothing's happened, she pointed out to the knowing part, which was lying low.

'Shall I see you again then?'

'Yeah . . . ?' said knowing, biding its time.

'Well, I –'

She didn't know how he had managed to get his arms round her but she didn't resist when he steered her backwards to the bedroom, and only whispered, 'Be careful, I have a lodger . . .'

But there was no sign of the lodger when an hour later she said, 'I'm sorry,' as Ed offered to go.

'It's not you,' she said, apologetic at the door. 'It's me – I'm not quite right yet from someone else.'

See! said knowing, thoroughly irked. That's what happens when you don't listen!

Peter, vigilant as Frances anxiously watched Ed's departing shoulders in their leather jacket, in turn watched her, and understood how, unexpectedly, she was reminded of Zahin.

37

Frances called Bridget the following morning. 'It *was* his sister, you were right.'

Zahin had not returned. Frances couldn't say she much cared what had happened to him. Although she knew that it was quite unfair of her, she felt angry with the boy for what had happened with Ed.

Ed had removed the long dress with chisel-scarred hands, surprisingly small and deft. What had happened after that had been a mystery, because just at the moment when she should have melted, she had frozen and they had had to call it a day – or a night, she supposed, recovering a sense of humour. It was Peter, of course, or the ghost of him – his memory – which had got in the way.

Bridget said something incomprehensible which Frances had to get her to repeat.

'You don't mean the child is back with you?'

'It seems so. He was in the kitchen when I came downstairs this morning.'

'For heaven's sake!' said Frances, thunderstruck. 'The

little monster!' Some part of her wished she had known the evening before that there would be no one to interrupt her with Ed Bittle. Maybe then . . . but probably it was for the best. At least she was rid of Zahin's taxing politeness.

Bridget had been enormously relieved to see Zahin when she descended, in Peter's dressing gown, to the kitchen. In fact, it was the smell that had summoned her: an unmistakable smell, of roast coffee and warm toast.

Neither of them said anything about the reasons for Zahin's departure but when he granted Bridget one of his dazzling smiles she knew she had missed him. Frances would never understand, she thought protectively.

During Zahin's absence there had been time for a satisfying amount of dust to settle, debris to accumulate. Zahin set to, tackling the housework as if the house had been taken over by a band of noisome squatters. Sitting in her old oak chair – a bargain in an Auvergne sale – Bridget watched the zealous operation with affection. It took a kind of genius to clean so thoroughly. He wore, she noticed for the first time, the make of rubber gloves generally used by surgeons.

'Zahin, are you wearing nail polish?' There were unmistakable hints of red showing through the thin rubber. Her mind flickered up to her dressing table and back again. She hardly ever wore nail polish; only occasionally, to weddings for example, and then only Cutex Clear.

Zahin, who was bending down, sweeping under the sink, where none but a fanatic would ever look, did not immediately answer. When he spoke his voice was muffled.

'It is my sister. She likes to try it out on me before she puts it on herself.'

Bridget thought she might as well let the matter of the sister drop. So long as the little minx didn't wear any more of her things it was no concern of hers.

'We must have a feast,' Zahin announced later, house filled with the satisfying scent of lavender Pledge. 'To celebrate. We should ask Mrs Michael.'

This was a stroke of genius: to consolidate his return by seeking to win round the enemy. Bridget congratulated him inwardly and outwardly offered fifty pounds for supplies.

'No, no, it is my treat. To make up for my sister's bad behaviour . . .'

This was the only reference to their quarrel other than the superhuman cleanliness which met Mickey when she arrived with Mrs Thatcher hair, freshly tinted and blow-dried, and wearing, on the lapel of her blue suit, the Mickey Mouse badge which the clientele of the Top and Bottle had given her for her seventieth.

'O Mrs Michael, such a darling brooch.'

'Get away with you!' exclaimed Mickey, resentment melting with fickle ease into enchantment. 'I must say, Bridget, the place looks a lot better since when I was here last.'

The last time Mickey was a dinner guest was in fact the evening that Peter had first taken instruction from Father Gerard. Father Gerard was a large, slightly lumbering man with bags beneath his eyes, which gave a faintly decadent air. Perhaps it was this, or the coincidence of name, but at first sight, Peter thought, he looked improbably like Gerard Depardieu.

'So, you have come to be instructed,' Father Gerard had said. 'And my first question to you is this: Do you have faith?'

'My God,' Peter had answered spontaneously, 'I have no idea!'

This turned out to be the right answer. Father Gerard beamed as if Peter had presented him with a fat donation to the mission in South America, whose work was illustrated on a multicoloured chart behind his head. He embarked on an introduction to the Catholic cosmology: this earth and the three levels of the next – heaven, hell and purgatory.

Rather in the way that the name of a clandestine love cries out to be spoken, Peter had introduced the topic at supper that night. Mickey was dining with them because she was 'all electric' and there had been a power cut in the street.

'D'you believe in the afterlife, Mickey?'

Bridget was making gravy, and Peter hoped to avoid attracting notice.

'There's two kinds of people, Peter: those who believe and those who don't – I'm one of those who don't, but my mum was a believer and I've always hoped for her sake she was right – bless her.'

'Do you think it makes any difference,' Bridget had asked, abruptly arriving with a leg of lamb, 'whether you believe? Either a thing's true or it isn't – facts don't alter, do they, whether they are believed in or not?'

'There's two kinds of people . . .' Mickey was saying, again.

The phrase came from her favourite Clint film: *The*

Good, the Bad and the Ugly. Clint, 'the Good', says it to Eli Wallach, 'the Ugly', in a graveyard where the loot is buried, next to the grave of the money's originator. 'There are two kinds of people, my friend,' Clint declaims in his inimitable voice, 'those with guns and those who dig. You dig!' Even without seeing the film you can tell, from the way it is phrased, who is in possession of the gun.

On this occasion Mickey was referring to the food Zahin had prepared, explaining that there were those who were foolhardy enough to sample unfamiliar food and those, like herself, who preferred to stick to what was tried and tested – a pity, for Zahin had excelled himself and the length of Bridget's French farmhouse table was garnered with plates of exquisitely arranged food. An old heel of Cheddar was found, which was grated on to Mickey's plate with such salad as she was willing to sample – tomato with not too much onion; definitely not the bean, or the stuff which looked like rice, but wasn't. It was a shame, Mickey felt, after all this time coming to supper again at Bridget's, that they should be having cold.

Mickey's – or Clint's – phrase had been a watchword with Peter and Bridget, one of those shorthands which first establish, then maintain intimacy. And the saying has validity: in any situation often there *will* be two kinds of person – those who will be brave and those cowardly, those rash and those cautious, those well- and those ill-mannered, and so on.

But there is a third kind of person, who is both brave and cowardly, rash and cautious, well- and ill-mannered, and on the whole this kind is the most common. Father

Gerard's question to Peter, and Peter's response to it, revealed this about him: that he both had faith and, equally, didn't have it. Over this Father Gerard expressed frank satisfaction.

'At least I don't have to be spending all that time undoing the faith to find the doubt beneath, Peter. This way we know where to start!'

Father Gerard sprang on an expression of doubt as if it were a potsherd from a rare and ancient pot and he a keen-eyed archaeologist whose task was reconstruction. Like all fanatics he exuded an energy which, when it wasn't tiresome, could be attractive. For Peter, who had lived most of his life in a miasma of uncertainty, the fervour of Father Gerard was reassuring: it suggested to Peter that what he had embarked on, entering the Catholic Church, was the right thing to do.

There exists also a fourth kind of person. For this kind, ambiguity of response is not only true but the truth of it is known to him or herself. Such a person will be aware that, in certain circumstances, they might collude with the Nazis, or rob a friend, or murder their mother – or, perhaps they might not: time, and the particular situation, alone could tell. This insight rarely brings the possessor fortune or happiness, but it means they can be trusted not to put too much faith in their own opinions. Among those who survived Peter, neither Bridget, nor Mickey, nor Zahin, nor indeed Father Gerard was such a person. Frances might have been, and Peter, himself, was; but it took Father Gerard – or, more accurately, the procedure Father Gerard was entrusted with – to reveal this truth about Peter.

38

Frances had not confided her suspicions to Bridget that Zahin's sister might have taken the sapphire ring. The ring was hardly a subject she could safely broach – and since Zahin's return Frances thought she detected in Bridget a renewed prejudice in Zahin's favour. Very likely that would extend to the sister. Anyway, Frances was not the sort to make easy accusations. She had been intending to wear the ring to the reunion – better explore that avenue first.

The botched encounter with Ed Bittle had left her jangled. A brisk walk would do no harm – and really she must get back in shape, so she might as well kill two birds ... She set out in her track suit for her old school.

Not expecting anyone to be there on a Sunday, Frances was rewarded by the sight of the imposing front doors standing open. Going up the steps she saw a woman mopping the marble floor – and for the first time realised that this floor was often in her dreams.

'Hi,' said Frances. 'I'm sorry to barge in.'

The woman stopped mopping to inspect the source of interruption.

'That's all right, darling,' she said. 'I shouldn't be here myself but my daughter's sick and I couldn't come in last night. There was a party they had here.'

'I know,' said Frances. 'I was at it. That's why I called by – I may have lost something here.'

'What's that you lost then?'

'My ring.' Frances tapped the ring finger of her left hand. 'A square-cut sapphire you haven't found it?'

'I haven't, darling, but I only got here myself ten minutes. That your engagement ring you lost?'

Frances looked at the woman's hand which grasped the handle of the mop. A multitude of hooped brilliants glittered and sparkled on the fingers. 'Yes,' she agreed. 'My fiancé gave it to me before he died.' It seemed a shame to waste the tragedy.

'That's too bad. Listen, if Claris finds it for you she keep it safe. What's your name, then, darling?'

'Frances – Frances Slater.'

'You go look round where you like, then, Frances. Claris'll look out for it too.'

Frances made her way back down the stairs her eyes peeled for a fragment of bright blue, but with no success. The room where Susannah had enquired about her skin proved equally barren. Nothing in the dining room either, though you could hardly look everywhere. She made her way to the cloakroom where she had gone to wash her hands. The same site as the old loos but now transformed into washrooms resembling some smartish hotel. She was conscious of a disapproving thought: Can all this luxury be good for young girls? How mean she was getting! She herself had used these very washrooms, in their unfurbished state, to put on, with a trembling hand, eyeliner to meet Paul Madden, from the boys' school. Paul Madden had gone on to manage a successful rock band – she'd have been grateful for one of these mirrors then!

No ring in the washrooms either.

Claris had finished mopping the black-and-white marble when Frances reappeared. She agreed to keep 'an eye out' and accepted Frances's telephone number 'in case'.

Not finding something you value is worse than losing it in the first place. Frances tried to jog away her despondence on the way home, but, getting tired, stopped at a café and ordered a caffè latte. An acute longing for Peter came over her. He would have minded about the ring and anxiously joined in the search. It seemed some ill omen that she should lose her most treasured memento of him – maybe it was a punishment for the moment of weakness with Ed . . . ?

'You see, Peter, we have become feeble as a species – the idea of punishment makes us feel queasy, wouldn't you say? And yet let us look at the question: what is "punishment", when we think about it?'

Despite Father Gerard's words, Peter, as it happened, was no stranger to punishment. His stepfather was an advocate of it – a subtle one, but subtlety is no great deterrent when it comes to inflicting misery, often the reverse. When it was noted how Peter and his mother shared certain jokes, the language of understanding, a treat for the other children would be proposed, at a time when Peter could not reasonably join the party. Several pantomimes, circuses and boating trips mysteriously materialised when Peter was staying with a friend, or playing in a school rugger match. Marcus – who later became a prison governor, and used this regular lesson in injustice to good effect – was too short-sighted to be good at sport; Clare, the baby, was always available for off-the-cuff outings.

The effects of this partiality were apparent later in life – though both Marcus and Clare sent flowers and condolences neither attended Peter's funeral but at the time Peter took it all with no outward fuss. He became reconciled to others' pleasure as a source of pain for himself. It was not, anyway, the fact of missing the clowns, or the dame in drag, or the picnic at the regatta – it was the fact of being deliberately excluded which hurt, and the frightening sense of power that this gave to the excluder.

'But purgatory is not exclusive, Peter,' suggested Father Gerard, his slightly droning voice as usual at odds with the levels of his enthusiasm. 'Not at all. Except for a few blessed souls whose state of sanctity renders them immediately ready for heaven, most of us – and I count myself very much among this bunch – will need time to find forgiveness for our venial sins – and that is what venial means, you see – it comes from the Latin *venia* and means forgiveness.'

Forgiveness was not a concept which, until now, had had much reality for Peter. He might be said to have 'forgiven' his mother for seeming to turn her face from him, but he himself would not have called that 'forgiveness'. In the quite straightforward way which modern psychologists will always wrongly question, he loved his mother, and knew that she – for her own reasons – in turn loved his stepfather. He perfectly understood her difficulty. As to being himself 'forgiven', he had not the least sense of what that might feel like. And if you have no experience of being forgiven, you can hardly forgive yourself.

If Peter remained reticent about his reasons for approaching the Roman Catholics it was because he himself did not really understand it. He never made an explicit connexion between what he had embarked on, his meeting with Atkins in the Brompton Road, his misty sense of his own betrayal and the place of the nuns in Veronica's life – which according to her they had saved. (Veronica had been found in a basket, 'like Moses', she had later been told – but not in anything like so salubrious an environment as bulrushes.) But a sense of shame had surrounded the memory of Veronica – obscurely he knew, or sensed, he had acted shabbily.

'Look, it's a caring concept,' Father Gerard had said, his eyes alight with the zeal of hope, 'an opportunity for ordinary, fallible people to be cleansed – and that's what Purgatory means, Peter – a place of purging. It's a refining process really – a kind of spiritual health farm on a vast scale, if you like. Free as well. No credit cards in the afterlife!'

If Peter found anything to object to in Father Gerard's lively contemporary comparisons, he never said so. He was too busy finding relief in the thought that what you had done could, after a fashion, be undone again. And he was reassured by his instructor's pronouncement that purgatory, whatever it was, was not likely to be the sort of place where you knew other people were off enjoying themselves at circuses. It seemed quite democratic, a point that Father Gerard was keen to emphasise.

'They made a mistake, the so-called reformers, abandoning the notion simply because there's no mention of it in the scriptures. The Church existed long before the scriptures were written. People forget that! Look at it this way, we're all, every man jack of us guilty of some misbehaviour we haven't come to terms with. Tell me, Peter, how could we ever rest in eternal bliss with no chance to set the record straight! Answer me, Peter, that!'

Sometimes when we give way to depression and let ourselves sink down, other, lighter, moods may bubble up. Frances, drinking her coffee, was cheered by a passing elderly man, wearing a top hat and a red rose in his buttonhole – off to some wedding, perhaps? – who, sighting her seated at the table, raised the tall hat and gave a distinctive bow. And Peter, who had disliked caffè latte and never would drink it, was grateful for this act of old-fashioned courtesy towards his mistress.

39

Bridget might not ordinarily have remembered the hastily flung-off suggestion that the people of Merrow come round for a drink. But maybe she had motives for reviving it. One bank holiday had passed; with another looming it seemed the moment to reintroduce the idea. Perhaps she didn't quite like the prospect of hosting a social event alone, or perhaps she wanted company? Anyway, she rang Frances.

'Do you fancy a trip to the country this weekend at all?'

'Not if Zahin's coming too!'

The association with Bridget was teaching Frances to speak her mind. Neither she nor Peter had been very good at that. That morning, lying in bed, she had thought how little, really, Peter had asked for himself.

Bridget gave one of her barking laughs. 'Don't worry! He'll be here: he's on a campaign to twist Mickey round his little finger.'

Frances couldn't understand this attitude of Bridget's towards what looked like naked manipulation. She gave an impression she almost enjoyed it – certainly she seemed to indulge it.

What Frances didn't understand was that for Bridget watching Zahin's posturings was almost as good as being at a play.

'Will you notice, Bridget,' Sister Mary Eustasia had said, 'the difference between the Players, whom Hamlet welcomes with open arms, and his so-called friends who try to manipulate him.'

Why, look you now, how unworthy a thing you make of me! You would play upon me; you would seem to know my stops . . . Hamlet says to Rosencrantz and Guildenstern, who are only playing the parts of friends, in reality colluding with the murdering king. And Hamlet was right to mind, the young Bridget had thought. *It is as easy as lying*, he says, seeming to challenge the puzzled pair to play on the recorders, but really meaning to show them that he has seen through their act and that he's on to how they are attempting to 'play' him. But they're no match for their fleet fellow student, poor, slow-witted Rosencrantz and Guildenstern. They go to their deaths in the end because they don't understand the difference between honestly acting a part and impersonating a truth. And yet it is a fine line . . .

She was reflecting on this as she watched Frances busily looking in the cupboards at Farings for bowls to put crisps and nuts in. 'Really, Bridget, you haven't brought very much for them to eat!'

'It'll make sure they don't stay long!'

Bridget, like many people when facing the realities of their social planning, was regretting the party. It had seemed fine enough when she had tossed it into the awkwardness of the meeting with the Godwit family. But there had been the awkwardness since of the trip to Ludlow. She had called the sweep and learned that Corrie and her husband would be up for the late May bank holiday weekend. She had also called the Rector, Bill Dark, her neighbour, Mrs Nettles, and the local doctor and his wife, whom she considered it prudent to be on friendly terms with.

And of course there was Frances. For half a second, she caught herself wondering what Stanley Godwit would make of Frances. He might like her nose which resembled a bird's beak.

It was clear to Frances that if the party were to work she was going to have to run it. Bridget, whose scheme it was, after all, was plainly going to do nothing. She had suddenly gone off to fetch a book and was now lying on the sofa, with her shoes off, reading.

'Shall I cut some cheese into cubes?' Frances asked, more as a way to recall Bridget's attention.

'Eugh! How bourgeois! They can cut their own cheese if they want any.'

'Very well,' said Frances offended. 'I'm going up to have a bath.'

But Bridget didn't hear her because she was rereading the play scene.

'Of course,' she said aloud, but only to herself. 'I see now, it was a choice. It was up to Hamlet. He could choose what kind of ghost it would turn out to be . . .'

Frances said afterwards that the party was one of Bridget's worst ideas. The Godwit father and daughter and a more than usually pink husband arrived in a disconnected group in which they more or less hung together all evening. Frances made efforts to engage Corrie, but it was uphill work of the question-and-answer kind which tends to defeat sympathy. It is true that Corrie's husband tried to talk to the Rector, but the latter so hugged the drink that any filling of glasses had to be done in negotiation with him, which meant constant interruptions. Bridget, who was resistant to Frances's expectation that all human encounters should be made easy, made no attempt to be sociable. The doctor's wife rang to say that her husband was 'coming down with flu', which Bridget opined to no one in particular was 'not, in a doctor, very promising'. Stanley Godwit looked awkward and out of place while Mrs Nettles, in spite of her name, proved to be a mild-natured old woman with no conversation.

By the end of the evening Frances, who had worked the room twice, was exhausted, so that when, having said goodbye to the guests, Bridget remarked that she believed Mrs Nettles was suffering from unrequited love for Bill Dark, Frances retorted that she believed this was just a fantasy of Bridget's of the kind which Bridget clearly took malicious pleasure in concocting. Bridget, boosted by this response, had replied that it was as well one of them had some imagination or poor Peter would have been bored out of his wits.

This was the last straw – as perhaps Bridget intended it should be. Frances retired to the recently installed sweetheart bed, where she spent the night in wakeful fury.

Bridget was also awake but more calmly. She had spent the evening longing to resume her reading of *Hamlet*. Living with Peter had eroded her habit of night-time reading. And it was still a thing she had some resistance to back in the Fulham house. But here, where there was no difficulty in sleeping, quite often she read till the green light had made its way through the thin curtains. She read now with a lover's excitement . . .

In the Offertory of the old Requiem Mass there is a petition that the soul of the departed might be freed from the pains of perpetual punishment. 'Sweet', suggests one eminent authority, 'is the consolation of the dying man, who, conscious of imperfection, believes that there are others to make intercession for him, when his own time for merit has expired; soothing to the afflicted survivors the thought that they possess powerful means of relieving their friend.'

'This is a moot point,' Father Gerard had said, his forehead furrowed, 'and is very much a matter of current debate, you understand, Peter – but since the early Fathers it has been the teaching of the Church that the attitude of the living can swing the afterlife of those who have gone before us.'

'Like the way parents can affect their kids' futures?' Impossible not to be affected by Father Gerard's habits of speech.

'Exactly!' Father Gerard's expansive potato face radiated approval. 'A loving mum or dad smooths a child's path through the troubles of this world. In our supplications for the dead we alleviate them from the burden of their sins and steer them towards the everlasting light – a trouble shared is a trouble halved – lighten the load, Peter, that's what we are enjoined to do. Lighten the load!'

*　　*　　*

'A trouble shared is a trouble doubled,' Bridget had sometimes said when Peter had occasionally dared to ask what she was thinking. The fact is that such moments of thoughtfulness were often the result of her minding Peter's 'house calls'. This was one of the things about her life with Peter she now regretted. She wanted very much to see him to tell him what was on her mind. If she had any recollection of the Catholic teaching about the afterlife it was hazy – but what she did remember were Sister Mary Eustasia's words about the ghost.

'Whatever kind of creature comes back from the grave with tales of his own torment? Is that a loving father, now, weighing down his son with frightful news like that? Hamlet should have listened to the Player King instead. There's the real tragedy, Bridget!'

Bridget had gone to see her second production of *Hamlet* when she was working at a hotel in Bath. This time there was no need to put on concealing make-up. She could have gone with Terence, the second sauce chef in the kitchens. Terence was sweet on Bridget and had presented her, when he had heard the blonde Irish girl with the laugh was keen on poetry, with a mauve-bound copy of Tennyson's poems which had belonged to his Grandad.

Bridget didn't much care for Tennyson but she did have a soft spot for Terence who reminded her of a giraffe, so tall and thin he was, with that nervous blotchy skin and Adam's apple bobbing up and down in his spindly neck like a ping-pong ball. For all that she was fond of Terence, she was deliberately obtuse over his hints about the two of them maybe going along together – her having let slip that she was taking her night off at the Theatre Royal –

and sharing a Chinese afterwards . . . ? She wanted to have a chance to concentrate on the play unencumbered by fear, or the social obligation of worrying how anyone else was enjoying it.

The six months before taking the job in Bath had been spent by Bridget in Rouen, where she had learned to like things French. Among the things she learned to like was the philosophy of Jean-Paul Sartre, which she picked up from another Jean-Paul who worked in a bar, where Bridget also picked up less abstract matters.

Jean-Paul had introduced her to the philosopher's notion of the human tendency to play a part. 'The waiter, you see, plays '*imself*, Brigitte. In this way 'e is and – this is the brilliance of Sartre! – is *not* merely a waiter . . .'

Bridget, who was herself 'merely' a waitress at this time, was taken by this concept. For all their other differences the Jean-Pauls' and Sister Mary Eustasia's philosophies had something in common. She remembered this as she sat in the Theatre Royal, watching, for only the second time, the play within her favourite play.

'The Mouse Trap' Hamlet calls it. Poor Terence had blushed horribly when it emerged – much later, when she had repented and was chatting to him about her evening's entertainment – that this wasn't the play by Agatha Christie which had been running in London, even all that time ago, seemingly for ever . . .

And then it started like a guilty thing upon a fearful summons . . . Bridget jerked awake. The cock in the farm by Mrs Nettles was crowing – early again, for, strictly speaking, it was still night. The play had run on in her mind as she slept – or wandered, as it seemed to her, between worlds: between the world of Mrs Nettles's cock and the cock which dispatches the ghost from Denmark's battlements. Was that where Peter also wandered, in the space between this world and the next – or one of the next anyway? In her half-awake state she seemed to see many worlds, receding mistily into the dark. Suddenly, it came to her that there were two ghosts – or rather two illusions of the man who had been Old Hamlet: the armoured apparition, who appears on the battlements of Elsinore commanding his son to seek revenge, and the Player King, who acts the part of Hamlet's father. And for the first time it struck her that these might both be shades of the man Hamlet's father had been, offering very different ways of approaching his death – ways so different that you might almost say there were two kinds of ghost in *Hamlet*.

Bridget sat up in bed pulling her husband's check shirt round her. The battered red book had fallen to the floor and her fingers, cold at first, couldn't find the right place in the rice-paper-thin pages. Here they were, the lines Sister Mary Eustasia had liked to quote: *Most necessary 'tis that we forget/To pay ourselves what to ourselves is debt* the Player King says, when his wife, the queen, insists she will remain faithful to him for eternity. And yet what does the ghost on the battlement want but a repayment of what he believes he is owed? A life for a life – which shows you should be careful what you ask – for in the end his creator lets him have it sixfold – eightfold, if you count those inseparables, Rosencrantz and Guildenstern!

Bridget stared into the shadowy corners of the room where she and Frances had slept together the night she moved into Farings. No Peter – nor the ghostly shape of him. She thought that for the first time she began to see behind the play's many-layered arrases, which played different versions of reality. What was the difference between the illusory ghost and the illusory Player King on the stage? Or between impersonation and acting? Or lying and the truth? What, if it came to that, was the difference between the quick and the dead? Did the living merely 'act' reality? But in life there was no clear, tangible 'reality', only choices, and as you chose you closed your own version of reality round you, like a garment, until it fitted and became your particular fate: vengeful father, faithless wife, betrayed daughter, justifying son . . . And then that also became the fate of those near you. If Hamlet had chosen the Player King as spokesman on his father's behalf, and cancelled the 'debt' his father was owed, Ophelia and her father – who was a pest it was true, but a harmless enough old busybody – Laertes, Gertrude, Claudius, even the slightly absurd Rosencrantz and Guildenstern, not to mention Hamlet himself, might all have lived – prospered even. All flawed people to be sure – but then Hamlet himself remarks that if we were all treated as we deserved which of us would escape whipping?

And the ghost, might he then have made his way through purgatory – wherever that was – to whatever it is that lies beyond? And whose ghost was he, anyway? Was he Old Hamlet's or was he also his son's? It seemed to her that maybe he was neither but the possibilities that lay between the two. Because, she was beginning to see, there was between people an infinitude of possibilities which might be realised. Where did one's responsibility to the dead lie? According to Shakespeare it looked as if it was in the hands of the living – the 'quick' – to decide . . .

40

'I'm sorry,' Bridget said frankly. 'I behaved like a cow last night.' She had removed Peter's shirt and put on her own Provençal dressing gown when she came down to find Frances eating breakfast in the kitchen.

This took the wind out of Frances's sails. Not a naturally combative person, nevertheless she had been rehearsing a speech most of the night and was reluctant to jettison its well-made points.

'I just want to point out that *one*, you invited me up here and *two*, it was your idea to give a party!'

'Quite right,' Bridget said. 'It was entirely my idea. I behaved abominably.'

It is always disagreeable to receive an apology before one's temper has cooled. Frances had packed the bag with the embroidered apples on it, which she had bought to take on the trip to Paris with Peter. To go upstairs and unpack it now would feel like a defeat.

'And by the way,' watching Frances, Bridget tried not to smile, 'I don't expect to be forgiven just because I apologise.'

Anger has its own momentum. Frances ate her toast

in silence looking out of the window where the rooks were training their offspring in the art of sky-diving. It must be easy to be a bird: you grew according to the law of your species and never had to worry about how you lived, or what was right or wrong – you just got on with it, or ended up in the belly of a hawk, or as rook pie.

Bridget watching Frances found herself wondering when Frances and Peter had last had sex. The old, curious part of her would have liked to disconcert Frances and ask. But she must try to behave: Peter had suggested that if anything happened to him he would like her to look out for Frances . . .

Peter and Frances had last met at a restaurant on Kew Green. And the fact is that they had quarrelled. This was a piece of bad luck since, on the whole, quarrelling was something they avoided.

Peter was late, and Frances, who generally made no reference to Peter's unpredictable timekeeping, made a slightly barbed comment.

As she said afterwards, compared to the kind of remark that many women make in such circumstances – hers having arisen out of a plethora of lame excuses on similar occasions – it was insignificant. But an appeal to how others might behave is useless in an argument. Peter, like most of us, was blind to his own blind spots: he believed his timekeeping was rather superior – it was just the world, in the form of traffic jams, late trains, dilatory buses etc., which got in the way. Frances, who was rarely late – ten minutes at most, and fretted when she was – had accepted this fiction about her lover with good grace. But even Homer nods.

Most of us have a sore point on which our character gets tested. In Frances's case it was the perception that she was being dealt with unjustly. She had curtailed a conversation with an important art critic – one on whom the reputation of a show could hang – to get to Kew in time for the dinner appointment. And she had negotiated the same traffic, pretty much, as Peter had that evening. To be told that it was the traffic's fault, and then that she was no better at timekeeping than Peter, smarted. As a consequence they had eaten the meal in virtual silence.

And, if truth be told, Peter's lateness was only tangentially to do with the traffic. He had called to see Zelda on his way to Kew, meaning to stay a bare five minutes, but, in the way of such things, the minutes had extended into the worst of the rush hour around Shepherd's Bush.

We are always most touchy about our virtue when most out of touch with it. Peter had a way of humming or whistling to himself when his equilibrium was disturbed. Bridget, familiar with this idiosyncrasy, would have found a means of making him laugh – a person passing by with a ridiculous haircut, or a dog which resembled its owner – but Frances, thinner-skinned, was more easily hurt. Hearing Peter, apparently nonchalantly, humming 'Loch Lomond' seemed like the final straw.

'I think I'd better get home,' she said when offered brandy. 'I had to cut something short to get here in time and it means I'll need to make an early call tomorrow.'

This was a lie – the critic was a notoriously late riser – an early call would have put paid to any goodwill towards the gallery.

Peter, rightly feeling the response was intended as a snub, said, 'Sure. D'you want to make another date . . . ?'

'We're a bit busy just at present at the gallery,' said Frances, stabbing herself in the heart as she spoke.

'I'll give you a ring sometime then . . . ?'

'Sometime, yes. You know where to find me . . .'

Peter left a larger than usual tip to the waiter to ensure that at least one person in the world should think well of him. He escorted Frances to her car and they kissed stiffly, holding their bodies so that not too much contact could occur.

Frances waited a respectable amount of time, to be quite sure Peter had driven off, before putting her head in her hands. It was a shock, a few minutes later, to look up and see Peter's face pressed against the glass beside her. She wound the window down.

'What?'

'I love you, France.'

'I love you, Peter.'

'Don't be an idiot then . . .' and they had driven, urgently, to the cemetery where Frances had hiked up her skirt – happily a full one – to climb the railings (not too taxing, perhaps because if the dead are to wander they are not likely to be deterred by spikes or height).

Peter had caught Frances in his arms, a prelude to repairing the breach between them before the lenient, sightless gaze of the marble angels.

Bridget was hardly less shockable than a marble angel. As Frances rose to clear her breakfast things in the kitchen at Farings, she stood for a moment against the window

in profile. Bridget, looking at her, put the cigarette she was about to light back in the packet. 'Go up and unpack your things,' she said, quite gently. And Peter, from his vantage point amid the tumbling rooks, looked down at his wife with fond approval.

41

'I'm afraid there is no mistake. And I would say, small as you still are, you are well into the third trimester.'

Ms Ellen Nathan had iron-grey hair, cut very well, and excellent taste in earrings. Frances fixed her gaze on one now – amber, with the relics of tiny, costly, ancient flies visible in its golden-syrup interior. What she thought first was: Thank God I didn't sleep with Ed Bittle.

Our spontaneous thoughts – not necessarily the ones we act on – often prove the most emotionally accurate. The thought which followed was not really a thought at all but an ecstatic: It must be Peter's baby!

Frances had got into the way of assuming that she was infertile. Her cycle had always been erratic and it had seemed only fitting that, since Peter's death, it appeared to have wound down altogether – she'd never monitored it anyway. She had vaguely been considering consulting a gynaecologist; it was, in fact, the remarks of Susannah – about HRT – at the reunion which had prompted her to make the appointment.

'You have the body of a much younger woman,' said

Ms Nathan. 'There's no need for there to be any problems. Of course we shall get you scanned but we should do an amniocentesis –'

'No,' said Frances firmly. 'I prefer not. I shall want the baby whatever.' Once she had uttered the word 'baby' that was that – there wasn't to be even a breath about 'complications'.

'Very good,' said Ms Nathan. Her amber earrings gleamed approvingly. 'Healthy women in their forties are the physiological equivalent of prehistoric women in their twenties.' Frances wondered how she knew this. 'There's no need for all this modern panic. I can book you in, if you like, at the private hospital where I have beds – or you will be just as well cared for in the NHS hospital where I am a consultant.'

'Let me think about it,' said Frances, who felt some pressure from the tone to choose the NHS hospital. That sort of caving-in might be all very well when it was just herself to think of; it was a different matter now she had Peter's baby to consider.

'Don't think too long!' said Ms Nathan. 'We'll do an ultrasound but I would guess you've only two months, three at the most, to go . . .'

It was in fact seven months, two weeks and three days since the evening in the cemetery when Peter last held Frances in his arms, before reluctantly disengaging his body from hers. They had parted – for good, as it turned out – by her car, where he had dropped her, and although they had parted many times before, afterwards she felt it was not hindsight alone which made her recall this parting as especially significant. Wanting to keep him with her, she had not bathed that night before bed, and it was this which had ultimately led to the unexpected conception.

The appointment with Ellen Nathan was in the morning. Fortunately, there was a whole day's work to get through before she need start thinking about the future and making plans.

Back at the gallery Roy had left a note: *Lunching with Lady Kathleen at the Gay Hussar. Painter called – can you ring him? – R.*

Roy liked to inscribe the features of a smiling face in the upper portion of the R in his name, which, generally, Frances found tiresome. But when dramatic events take place we are reassured by continuity – this morning, Frances was almost grateful for the R's irritating smile.

Ed Bittle was hanging about at the back of the gallery, apparently attending to some minor mishap to one of his boulders. (The boulders, it had turned out, had come from an area near Farings, this kind of coincidence, as Bridget had explained to Frances when the latter had remarked on it, being far more common than people suppose.) Ed had found some excuse to come into the gallery most days. His work was selling well, partly thanks to the fact that Painter had decided to lend his support to the young sculptor, and had given an unprecedented interview, where he had gone on record saying that this was a major new talent. This article was why Roy wanted Frances to ring Painter.

Frances decided it was better not to pretend that Ed wasn't really there, so she went across and asked if he would like coffee? – she herself was having herb tea. He came and hovered in the office where she did the paper work, and where the kettle and battery of different drinks were kept. Roy only drank maté, a form of health beverage – particularly disgusting – alleged to promote longevity. Frances usually drank coffee, Colombian or Blue Mountain; then there were the teas, Lapsang for Lady Kathleen, in case she should call (she never did), Darjeeling for Roy's boyfriend, Typhoo for Painter. Luckily there was, in addition, the range of health-promoting herbal teas left by the receptionist before last, whose boyfriend had been – very likely still was – a drug pedlar.

Frances made herself a cup of 'Tranquillity Tea for Inner Peace and Harmony'. Perhaps it was the effect of the tea but she felt perfectly tranquil facing Ed.

'Listen,' said Ed, his tense, white face gleaming under the pitiless electric light, 'I have to talk to you!'

Frances thought: It might be a boy, and one day he might fall in love unsuitably and I would want her to be kind.

'Of course,' she said. 'I've some things to do but why don't we go across to Marie Rose's for lunch?'

There were invoices due, a fax from a gallery in New York with whom there were reciprocal arrangements for exhibitions; and Painter to ring. It was not yet quite twelve so Frances dealt with the two other matters first, and then, at 12.15, rang Painter.

He answered at once. 'Yes?'

'Patrick,' said Frances, 'Roy said you wanted to speak to me.'

'Why the bloody hell haven't I heard from you?'

'Is that why you rang?'

'Is there a better reason?'

218

'Patrick,' said Frances, defensively, 'I saw you only a week or so ago.'

'When you came round with that child – how is he, by the way? Extraordinary beauty.'

'He's gone back to Bridget's,' Frances said, 'and a great relief it was, I must say.'

'Didn't like him?'

'There's something creepy about him. My brother Hugh used to have what he called a "creepometer" – Zahin would have scored ten.'

'Any road,' said Painter, 'with him there it gave me no chance to talk to you. There's something I want to ask you – come round as quick as you like.'

'How's the *Sunday Sport*?' Frances asked.

But Painter only repeated that he expected her round soon.

Then it was time to go to Marie Rose's.

Ed walked with Frances to the other side of the road, while keeping his body as far from hers as was possible crossing a small busy road in central London where the traffic cedes only the narrowest gaps to pedestrians. The redecorations at Marie Rose's were proceeding fitfully. To get to the table which was most private required stepping over planks, which Frances did with caution, conscious of the small piece of Peter inside her which any accident might threaten. She and Ed Bittle sat down to face each other across the narrow table.

'What will you have?' asked Frances: she felt she should take charge.

'I'll have a Coke.' Ed spoke as a condemned man might ordering his last meal.

'Anything to eat?' Frances enquired brightly.

'Yeah.' Ed scanned the menu grimly. The food at Marie Rose's was not inspiring – there was really only sandwiches and salads; these, once somewhat exotic, were now to be found, or their equivalent, in even the least enterprising bars and cafés which pepper London. 'A beef sandwich.'

'With mustard?'

'Yeah, OK.'

'English or French?' Frances persisted. She was experiencing a kind of dread at the thought of leaving the mundane.

'English, no French. I don't care.'

'Ed,' said Frances after Marie Rose had taken the order. 'Please stop being so tragic – you hardly know me!'

'What the fuck's that got to do with it – sorry.'

'It's everything to do with it,' said Frances, more sure of her ground now the subject had been broached. 'For a start I'm pregnant.'

She had not intended telling Ed, but, like so many things not intended, it had slipped out. Now she saw that without meaning to she had given a false impression.

Dramatically, Ed's face brightened. 'You should have said.'

'It's not the sort of thing one says easily.'

Sometimes the truth seems hardly charitable. Frances saw that the false impression was going to be useful: Ed's distress stemmed from having been rejected rather than any serious feeling for her. 'But I wanted to tell you now so you would understand it wasn't anything about you . . .'

Ed had gone a surprising shade of magenta. His thin skin moved so rapidly between white and red it resembled

220

the skin of the love object of some minor Elizabethan sonneteer.

'Fuck! Motherhood is the most fantastic thing on earth. Can I draw you when the baby comes?' He spoke with the ardour of an artist and for a moment Frances regretted that the small, delicately formed life inside her closed other avenues. He was a nice boy and one day would make the right girl happy.

'So you see,' Frances went on, 'if we could be just friends . . . ?'

Though why I say 'just', she thought, crossing back over the road, this time with Ed solicitously steering her elbow – for a real friend is worth anything.

On the matter of 'friends' the next problem was going to be telling Bridget. She should do this at once. Frances dialled the Fulham number and found herself answered by Patrick.

'Patrick! I meant to dial someone else!'

'How can you, when you knew I wanted to see you?' Painter sounded genuincly peevish.

'Well, I was going to do that when I'd got the difficult calls over first.'

'There's no one's more difficult than me,' said Painter, who was rarely far from the truth.

Although by the time she reached Isleworth it was by most people's reckoning dinner time, Painter offered Frances tea and biscuits. 'No thanks. I'm not drinking any caffeine.'

'Not on one of those piss-awful diets, are you?' Painter asked mildly. 'I was reading about one of those in the *Sunday Sport*. Sounded to me as if you give up everything you like and then you feel so bloody miserable you shoot yourself. Not that I need any excuse to do that . . .'

'Picture trouble?' Frances asked. She was grateful not to have had to explain the reason for her giving up caffeine.

'In a way,' said Painter, mysteriously. 'Come and have a look.'

One of the tortoises, which, since it took the best light, liked the room where Painter habitually worked, was noisily crunching a lettuce leaf. Ginger, Frances supposed – the female was slightly bigger than her mate.

'She's picking up her energy after laying,' Painter nodded towards the mottled, chomping shell. 'Seven eggs, so we might have little ones soon.'

'Where does she lay them?' asked Frances, with a new interest in the reproductive habits of all species.

'In the garden. They bury them – I dig 'em up and put them in sand in one of Mother's flowerpots and keep 'em in the linen cupboard.'

'And how long is the gestation period?'

'Eight weeks. When's yours due?'

Frances, who was looking at a large canvas on which a series of lilac and cream squares made receding three-dimensional curves of the two-dimensional space, felt a shock like electricity run through the crown of her head to the soles of her feet. 'How did you know?'

Painter was looking at her full on. His green eyes, slightly out of true, were gleeful. 'I was painting women's bodies since before you knew what they were meant for. Time before last when you came round I spotted it.'

'I didn't know myself then!'

'Ah well, now, I did wonder . . .'

It appeared that not much was wrong with the picture

after all. Frances had supper with Painter and his mother on a card table in the conservatory. They had slices of tinned ham from Denmark, tomatoes and radishes from Mrs Painter's garden, cucumber and salad cream from the corner shop. Afterwards there was jelly with tangerines in it, which Frances refused. She also rejected the tinned Ambrosia rice, which Mrs Painter suggested was good for the baby's bones, but accepted a triangle of processed cheese in silver paper, something she had last eaten at kindergarten. Painter forbade her alcohol even though she assured him that Ms Nathan of Upper Wimpole Street had agreed a glass of white wine was perfectly in order.

'Don't trust doctors,' said Painter. 'Where are you having it, anyway?'

Frances said she had decided on the local NHS hospital which had a good reputation and where Ellen Nathan was a consultant. 'She's keen for me to go there and on the whole I think the nursing's better. I'll be happier with ordinary people.'

Painter said he believed that wise; 'the rich', he said, wanted to dodge pain and were therefore offered too many drugs. He himself was worth several million, but it was doubtful he considered himself among their number.

42

Although Bridget had been distracted at her drinks party she had not been unobservant of her guests. She had considered it best to leave Stanley Godwit alone, but she had tackled his uncommunicative daughter.

'I never asked what you did?'

Cordelia volunteered that she had once been an accountant, but was now a tax inspector.

'Heavens,' Bridget exclaimed, 'I thought it was supposed to be the other way round.'

'What?'

'Being a tax inspector – I thought that generally came first and then you used your know-how learned as an inspector to help people dodge tax.'

This turned out to be a mistake.

'Dodge tax? No one who has worked for the Revenue would do any such thing.'

In *King Lear* the last we hear of Cordelia concerns her frown. It looked as if this characteristic had been bestowed on her namesake.

'I hope mine does!' said Bridget undaunted. 'She's a

224

very nice young woman called Saskia, about your age.' Cordelia looked as if at any moment she might demand to know the address of this perfidious representative of her previous profession so Bridget steered the conversation on to other lines. 'And your husband the psychoanalyst. That's a fascinating job, now, unravelling the minds of the tormented.'

'He's not a psychoanalyst,' said Cordelia. 'He's a psychiatrist.'

'And that's different?'

'Completely,' said Cordelia and asked where the bathroom was to be found.

Frances had already left for London when Stanley Godwit called the following morning.

'Nice party.'

'It wasn't really,' Bridget said. 'I'm a poor hostess.'

'Corrie said she had a nice talk with you.'

Bridget, who doubted this, felt that a cup of tea was in order. Sister Mary Eustasia's Shakespeare was open at *Hamlet* on the table by the sofa and when she returned from the kitchen with two mugs of tea, the sweep was reading it. He put it down and remarked that there was a divinity which shaped our ends, rough-hew them how we will.

'Do you believe that?'

She had noticed before that he blinked when asked a direct question.

'It makes sense.'

'I wouldn't like to think it's all been decided for us.'

'Shakespeare says "shapes", doesn't he – not "makes"? That's not deciding for us.'

Bridget wished she had some cake. There were some

225

Cheese Thins left over from the party, rather stale by now, everything else had been scoffed by Bill Dark. It seemed unlikely she would ever have a conversation with *him* about predestination. 'Was it really your wife who called your daughter Cordelia?'

Stanley Godwit picked up the Shakespeare and flicked through the pages as if seeking the answer to her question. 'Guess it was my idea.'

'I don't have children,' Bridget said. 'But if I had I'm not sure I would have dared call a child after someone who dies so appallingly.' She seemed unable not to say things which might sound rude.

'I know what you mean,' said Stanley Godwit, drinking his tea unperturbed. 'But it's a question of attitude – you get the feeling that she doesn't mind death herself, Cordelia. Fearless! Corrie, now, is brave. You could count that as an asset to a person.'

Peter had always half expected death, which is not the same as welcoming it. Yet there was something attractive in the prospect too – he couldn't have said quite what, maybe the absence of responsibility that it would bring. Father Gerard changed all that.

'Life doesn't end with death, oh dear me no,' he exclaimed, lunging forward in his chair as if to demonstrate in his own person the position necessary to adopt for the life to come. 'We might even say that death is only the beginning!'

Peter accepted this new ordering of things with the compliance which was part of his character. If he lamented the loss of a place where all obligations were to be dissolved, he never admitted as much to his instructor. It sometimes crossed his mind, though, that Father Gerard would be well employed by England's rugby team, his exhortations were so muscular and rousing.

'You see, Peter, if we die with all our misdemeanours full about us, through the process of purging – and the helpful prayers and actions of those we leave behind, of course – gradually our souls are cleansed of sin. It's rather like –' Father Gerard struggled just a second – 'yes, it's rather like a tablecloth stained with the marks of too many good dinners, being washed and rewashed in an eternal washing machine!'

Father Gerard explained there were other sins than the venial kind. There was mortal sin, for which more was apparently needed than the eternally recycling washing machine. And then there was the sin which seemed to come merely from being born. About this sin Father Gerard was no less enthusiastic.

'Original sin, or the sin of our origins, our first mum and dad. As I like to say,' the potato face prepared itself for mirth, 'it's not "original" at all, of course! No one escapes it so you might say it's as common as dirt!'

Peter might have been troubled in his mind as to whether Zelda constituted a mortal sin. However, much of the time he pushed such considerations to the back of his mind. Zelda herself was untroubled by moral questions of any kind, although Peter did once confide in her about Frances.

'You have a sweetheart, apart from me?'

The good thing about a whore is that there is no need to lie. Yet, in a sense, Peter's answer was a lie, for, by omission, it left Bridget out of the picture. 'I have a mistress – her name is Frances.'

'And she is beautiful? And you love her?'

'Not as beautiful as you – but, yes, I love her.'

Possibly it was some sense of self-protection which made Peter say nothing about Bridget. Perhaps it was some feeling that, deep down, a mistress and a whore had things in common and could therefore, without disloyalty, be disclosed. Or perhaps it was a literalness in his character which made him merely answer the question asked, for it is true that 'sweetheart' does not, as a rule, imply 'wife'.

'The sins of omission are every bit as serious as those of commission,' Father Gerard had advised. 'If you do not declare your income to the Inland Revenue then that is theft, according to the law of the land, as surely as if you were to steal from Woolworths.'

Peter had never had any desire to steal from Woolworths, and his income tax forms, filled out by a pretty girl found by Bridget, so far as he was aware were innocent of any lack which properly ought to be disclosed. The fact that he had failed to disclose to Zelda that he had a wife, however, made him feel guilty.

The guilt was not so much about Bridget, but about Zelda – or perhaps not Zelda herself so much as the role she had come to play within him.

Philosophers have debated whether the source of wonder lies in the observed or the observer. Peter was not a philosopher and did not try to make this artificial distinction. Zelda had recovered for him a sense of wonder he had only experienced once before – with Veronica. Therefore whatever Zelda was, to him she was wonderful.

A consequence of this was that the sense of the precious became transferred to life itself. For the first time Peter found he actively wanted to be alive, and this was a novel sensation. The triangle formed by his imagination whenever he made love to his wife or his mistress had shifted: now in place of Veronica it was Zelda he always saw in his mind's eye.

By the time he met Zelda he had already been taken into the Catholic Church but the words of Father Gerard often came back to him.

'The Trinity is a great mystery – perhaps the greatest,' Father Gerard had asserted. 'God in three persons, like the different flavours of a Neapolitan ice, Peter – strawberry, pistachio and chocolate, each distinct in its own way and yet each an essential part of the whole ice cream . . .'

Peter wanted to be obliging but even he could not quite accommodate this image from the helpful imagination of his instructor; the association of ice-cream wafers was too close to the other kind of wafer he tasted at the Mass, in which, it was said, lay dormant the very substance of the body of his Saviour. It was as well for his indefatigable mentor that he never came to know Peter's own model for the tripart nature of his God: the associated persons of his three mortal beloveds – Bridget, Frances and Zelda.

'I like Donne for the same reason,' Bridget was saying. She and Stanley Godwit had continued their discussion of Shakespeare. 'He understood human foible too. Even when he was Dean of St Paul's he never allowed himself to forget that he had charmed the drawers off countless mistresses.'

She had made a second pot of tea. All the awkwardness of the previous encounters had evaporated.

'Did they wear drawers by then?' Stanley Godwit's eyes were the grey-blue of the Irish sea. Thinking of the day he had helped her down the cliff path, she glanced down at his hands.

'How do you know so much about poetry?' she asked quickly; though it was true she also wanted to know.

'I was an "English" HMI – a schools inspector, but I quit when they introduced the National Curriculum. My dad was a sweep – he taught me the trade when I was still a kid. It's a clean occupation compared to most.' The hard palm wrapped itself round her softer one.

'Like Matthew Arnold? Sweetness and light?'

'I doubt if Arnold'd have made a sweep. He was a fair enough schools inspector though.'

Later Bridget said, 'You can see the hills from here, through the elm trees. Housman's hills. He was right they are blue.' The guilt seemed to have gone.

'Poor sod,' said Stanley Godwit, putting on his socks. 'Living with all that under wraps.'

'You mean his sexuality?'

'I mean loving young whatsit and not being able to say so.'

'I wonder if it really matters *who* you love,' Bridget wondered. 'It's *that* you love that counts, isn't it?'

43

It turned out to be easier than expected to tell Bridget about the baby.

'Yes, I noticed at Farings.'

Had everyone seen she was pregnant but herself? 'Why didn't you say anything?' asked Frances, irked.

'Not my business. I presume it's Peter's?'

'Unless it is an Immaculate Conception it could hardly be anyone else's.'

Bridget snorted disconcertingly at this and offered Frances coffee.

'No thanks, I've given up caffeine.'

'I hope you're not going to become a health bore?'

'Probably, until I have the baby,' said Frances a trifle stiffly.

They were in Bridget's kitchen. Frances had called, steeling herself with a sense of duty. Bridget seemed remarkably relaxed. But you could never tell with Bridget; she might turn savage at any moment and bite your head off.

'Where's Zahin?' Frances asked after a minute. She was hoping not to have to see him.

'Gone to see his sister, I think.'

'Have you met her?'

'Not yet,' said Bridget. She was having trouble bringing her attention back from thoughts of Stanley Godwit; so that she could enjoy these properly – 'improperly' was closer – she wanted Frances to leave.

'I'd better go, then,' said Frances feeling slightly defeated but not sure why.

But at that moment the bell rang and it turned out to be Marianne with a delivery of painted chests. Bridget, conscious that her desire for her guest to leave may have made itself felt, became unusually solicitous.

'Marianne, my friend Frances – Frances is having a baby. Tell you what – we'll get Marianne to do a special chest for the baby's toys – she paints things trailing with leaves and daisies.'

Marianne insisted the crystal she wore round her neck be suspended over Frances's stomach.

'That's a little boy,' she announced. 'Clockwise is a boy, anti's a girl – I've never known it fail. What are you going to call him?'

'I hadn't thought,' said Frances. She had particularly requested that she not be told the baby's sex when the results of the scan came through.

'What's his daddy want to call him?'

Bridget, aware that Frances might think this was said deliberately, said, 'Marianne, could you get me the next delivery in time for the end of July?' This had the desired effect: a flood of excuses meant that the paternity of Frances's baby was forgotten.

'Listen,' Bridget said when Marianne had finally departed promising the painted furniture no later than

August – which meant September – 'If I were you I'd get this all over with in one boiling. Tell Mickey while you're here, why don't you . . . ?'

The tea leaves in Mickey's cup indisputably indicated a girl child. 'Now you listen,' Mickey said, 'my mum swore by the tea leaves. She knitted an entire outfit in pink for me when I was born. Same for my brother, Sean – a whole set in blue: the tea leaves don't lie.'

'Which means either Marianne's cosmology or Mickey's is going to suffer a blow,' Bridget remarked when told. 'Unless you've got twins in pod?' But Frances knew that wasn't so.

'I'm too small and anyway they would have mentioned it when they did the scan.' She felt that Marianne was right and that the child she was carrying was Peter's son; but when you thought about it anyone had a fifty per cent chance of guessing a baby's sex!

Zahin, when he returned on Sunday morning, was enthusiastic at the news. 'O Mrs Hansome, a baby, a miracle!'

'Well, not quite, Zahin, I dare say it was produced under the usual conditions.'

Bridget had not bothered to form any view of Zahin's life beyond the domestic role he pursued with her. He had never made any mention of girlfriends, nor, except for the elusive Zelda, were there any signs of him having female companions. It seemed quite possible he was ignorant of the usual preoccupations of men and women. Or perhaps he just liked the company of older women better? Certainly he and Mickey had become very close.

Zahin, in fact, was engaged on a project: he hoped to persuade Mickey to start up a sandwich business with him and had already made enquiries about a franchise at a local set of offices. If this came off he might be spared having to train as a chemical engineer. Although he was fond, in his way, of Bridget, he preferred it when she went off to her country home and he could get the house just as he pleased. With Zelda there was nothing to do but experiment with her hair or make-up, there was only so much you could do there; he was careful these days, since the fright over the scarf, not to let Zelda put on any of Mrs Hansome's clothes.

Frances had been grateful that Zahin was out when she had called round at Bridget's. Her attitude to the boy had mushroomed into definite distaste. She remained suspicious about his sister's role in the disappearance of the sapphire ring – and suspicion adds greatly to our dislike of anyone.

Lindsey, the League secretary, had called back leaving a message that a marcasite brooch in the shape of a poodle – was that perhaps what Frances was looking for? – had been found. Otherwise nothing. No word from Claris either, but then Frances hadn't really expected to hear.

She felt at a loose end on her return from Bridget's, so was glad when Lottie rang and suggested they made the promised outing to Hogarth House.

Lottie was properly interested in the baby. 'Who's the father? Don't say if you don't want to – I was in pup once by a bassoon player but I had it put down.'

Perhaps because Lottie was a person who deliberately presented herself in a poor light – and the opposite is so often the case – this unsentimental approach to the termination of life didn't disturb Frances. The two women walked under the horse-chestnut trees where Peter had lain with Zelda's arm on his chest and felt that he was as happy as a king – happier probably, as kings, at least these days, are not famous for happiness.

'Promise me that if you are ever in need you will come to me,' Peter implored; and when Zelda turned her eyes of astonishing blue upon him, and asked how she could possibly do that if she didn't even know where to find him, Peter's answer was to take from his wallet one of his business cards and present it grandly – dismissing the inner voice which questioned the prudence of such a gesture.

'But this is your office – you want me to come to your office?' Zelda had enquired. Peter had then considered and concluded that Bridget would be less likely to ask questions than either his secretary or the office manager, Mark; he had reached across to recover the card, scrubbed out the address in Holborn and in place added that of his home in Fulham.

Frances described to Lottie a talk she had attended where the lecturer had been of the opinion that Hogarth had a thing about women's underwear.

'But don't most men?' asked Lottie.

Frances said she didn't know; Peter, she thought, hadn't – well, not particularly: he seemed as pleased to see her without as with.

Lottie told her about a groom she had a fling with in Hampshire who would only let her wear stockings – silk, as well – no tights.

'It cost me a fortune at Harvey Nicks – I couldn't afford it, I had to sack him,' Lottie said.

44

Bridget was glad, on the whole, that she had stuck to her routine of visiting Farings fortnightly; she needed the weekend in London to reflect on what had taken place between her and Stanley Godwit. Not being a person who based her own morality on how others behaved, she had not for a second contemplated being unfaithful while Peter was alive.

This view of things amused her when she realised she had been bothering about whether she was being 'unfaithful' now. By all ordinary accounts, Peter was dead. She hardly took notice of 'ordinary' accounts – was 'dead' strictly what you could call it, anyway? The figure who had appeared at her bedside – was that Peter, or some version of him? The live Peter would certainly have minded her sleeping with another man – this Peter, she sensed, she couldn't say how, had quite a different approach.

Then there was the question of Mrs Godwit. Stanley hardly mentioned his wife; but this, Bridget felt, came more from something more complicated than a dearth of emotion. Having been in the position herself she wasn't sure if she minded more or less about sleeping with another woman's husband.

The following weekend Stanley Godwit arrived at Farings with something wrapped in a brown bag.

'You probably have this . . .'

The Sermons of John Donne, bound in leather.

'No,' said Bridget, 'I don't, as it happens.' Taken off guard she sounded brusquer than usual.

'I have two – this one's spare.'

Bridget looked at the distinguished, ancient binding. 'The other copy must be pretty exceptional!' Seeing she was going to get nowhere that way, she went on, 'Tea first or . . . ?'

They had the tea second, looking out over the hills. Bridget thought: I can't have been so lucky – this won't last, nothing does – and said aloud, because if there was anything disagreeable she liked to get it over with, 'Does your wife know you are here?'

'I couldn't say.'

'Sorry to be nosy – but in case there's anything I should watch out for . . .'

Stanley got out of bed and she looked admiringly at the muscles of his back, which showed the signs of hard physical work. The back was as different from Peter's as – well, comparisons are odious, wasn't that what Sister Mary Eustasia had used to say? 'Odorous' they had turned it in the playground. Stanley smelled good too – the surest test of physical compatibility.

He came back to the bedroom with the volume of Donne. 'Look.'

She read, screwing up her eyes to make out the tiny, elderly print.

I doubt not of my own salvation; and in whom can I have such occasion of doubt as in my Self? When I come to heaven, shall I be able to say to any there, Lord! how got you hither? Was any man less likely to come hither than I?

'I like that,' said Stanley Godwit. 'If Dean Donne could say that of himself maybe there's hope for me.'

'I have been thinking marriage is a decision,' said Bridget, carefully. She was aware that there was something larger she was being told, and that, quite possibly, she was putting herself in the way of heartbreak – some unhappiness certainly. 'I'm sure you're never unkind to your wife.'

'It's not safe to be too sure about anything,' said Stanley Godwit, 'least of all our own behaviour.'

Bridget, who agreed with this, was visited by a perverse need to restore some of her usual defences. 'I'm afraid I'm not much interested in self-help philosophy.'

There was a pause, then Stanley Godwit got out of bed and began to dress.

'Time I got going,' he remarked, with perfect good humour.

Bridget sat and watched him, deliberately not covering her naked body with the sheet. When he was at the door she said, 'Don't go. Please. I'm sorry.'

'The thing is I can't give you much.'

His back was to her, which was a mercy in the circumstances. 'I know that.' She'd got hold of her voice now. 'But stay anyway, while you can.'

'All right,' said Stanley Godwit, turning back. 'Does "staying" mean me getting undressed again?'

*   *   *

'Confession does not always have to be verbal,' Father Gerard had said, but Peter had not found a way of 'confessing' Zelda, because, at heart, he did not regard her as a 'sin' at all – something with which the Catholic – or any – Church would hardly agree.

Yet who can know the mind of God? Peter, for one, would never have claimed to; and it seems likely that the unsure, the unopinionated, the disowned, the puzzled, even the downright errant, come closest to what we are told of that particular mystery. Before inviting those who were without sin to stone the adulterous woman to death, the man from Nazareth bent down and wordlessly wrote in the sand 'as though he heard them not'.

It was Frances who told Peter the preface to the famous words. They were at the National Gallery where, a little archly, she pointed out the painting by Rembrandt of the woman taken in adultery.

'Look, that's what would have happened to me!'

'"Let him first cast a stone . . ."'

'It's the bit before I like,' Frances said, 'when Christ draws in the dust.'

Painter had referred to this event when she had first seen the Rembrandt with him. 'The best bloody draughtsman of all time!' Painter had exclaimed. 'No one to match him. He knew what the boy meant by drawing in the sand.'

'What did he mean?'

'In those parts a drawing in sand wouldn't last five minutes. It was the boy's way of showing what he thought their opinions were worth. Look how Rembrandt's got their eager little faces, all agog with self-righteousness!'

Self-righteousness was not one of Bridget's stumbling

blocks, which was maybe why, she decided, she didn't feel too badly about Stanley Godwit's wife. Nevertheless, she tried to steer clear of Cordelia when, the following day, she saw the Godwits' daughter coming towards her. But in the way of such occasions Cordelia spotted Bridget and made a beeline.

'Hi there, Cordelia, I'm here to buy sausages.'

'You won't get any.'

It was true that Bridget had never successfully made a single sausage purchase at the pork butcher's.

'Why is that? I never seem to be able to get any when I ask?'

'They sell out.'

'Why don't they order more if they're so popular?'

There seemed to be nothing more to be said on the subject of sausages. Cordelia walked along beside Bridget in moody silence and Bridget, feeling that recent events dictated a special politeness to Stanley Godwit's daughter, was stuck for a more fertile topic of conversation.

'My mother asked if you'd like to visit.'

This was a blow. Bridget played for time. 'I wouldn't want to put her out – an invalid.'

'It's no trouble – she's in remission at present.'

Hell and damnation, Bridget thought. 'Are you up here every weekend?' she enquired. She couldn't help feeling there was a touch of the policewoman about Cordelia.

'I try to come when I can.'

Bridget promised to telephone the Godwits – Yes, she had the number – and call by for a drink. Roland was coming up to fetch his wife and the children that evening.

'Isn't it rather a long journey to do there and back all

in one day?' Bridget found herself asking. It appeared impossible not to say somewhat the wrong thing to Stanley Godwit's daughter.

45

Zahin was pleased with the way his sandwich business was shaping. He had compiled a business plan with expected Profit and Loss, which he had run past one of his cousins – the accountant – in St John's Wood, the one he had kept dark from Bridget. It wasn't wise to mix different portions of your life. The cousin had suggested some market research – with the local offices, where Zahin was hoping to get the sandwich business off the ground. A questionnaire had been devised, requesting people tick their preferences: white bread or brown, rye, granary, mixed grain, baguette, rolls, pitta, bagels, etc., as well as a choice of fillings. Cheeses of various kinds, with pickle or tomato, predictably, came out on top. But there were surprises too: salmon – also salt beef, which he would not, himself, have thought of; mayo with almost everything seemed popular.

With Bridget away in the country he had been able really to get on with things – so much so that these days he hardly had time for Zelda.

More and more, Zelda was getting to be someone he

saw when he was bored. It was true Mr Hansome had liked her – but with Mr Hansome dead there didn't seem so much point in dressing Zelda up in her sexy clothes, painting her face and her nails and so on. Not that Zahin believed girls shouldn't take care of their appearance at all times. He disapproved of so many of the modern, scruffy girls he saw around in London – hardly wearing make-up – if at all – not bothering to make themselves look pretty, or sexy.

Though he sometimes missed Mr Hansome he preferred the company of Mrs Hansome and Mrs Michael. Mrs Michael had a big collection of videos; it was soothing to lie on her sofa and watch Clint Eastwood, while Mrs Michael made cups of tea and chatted to him. She knew a lot about the latest cleaning products, which she saw on the telly – one good one, she'd told him, for washing wood which didn't take off all the shine – guaranteed 'natural', with orange peel, Mrs Michael said, among its ingredients. Neither Mrs Hansome nor Mrs Michael made demands – he was tired of having to try to be how other people wanted. Miss Slater he didn't like so much – she didn't like him either, he could tell. Mr Hansome had told Zelda that Miss Slater was his sweetheart; Miss Slater dressed nicely and he supposed that was what Mr Hansome had seen in her, though she wasn't a patch on Zelda when he'd got her properly dressed up. Personally, he, Zahin, preferred Mrs Hansome's big, blonde looks to Miss Slater's. If only Mrs Hansome would let him, he could dress her and make her up too – some definition in her lipstick and eyeshadow, and some nice lowlights in her hair, and you wouldn't know her . . .

*   *   *

243

' "When you are old and grey and full of sleep . . ." ' Stanley Godwit had quoted before the discreet audience of distant hills, running his fingers through Bridget's fine, silver-riddled hair. 'I'm glad you don't dye it.'

Bridget remembering this as she stood waiting for the bell to be answered in the porch of the Godwits' house, adjusted her skirt and wished she had chosen another one. She had hovered between vanity and prudence and prudence had won out – the skirt she was wearing was eminently sensible.

It was Cordelia who came to the door. 'Oh, hi!'

'Hi there!' said Bridget. For some reason – no, she knew the reason – she found herself adopting a hearty, guide-mistress tone with Cordelia.

Cordelia showed Bridget into a room with French windows looking out onto a neatly kept garden. French marigolds and salvia, quite unlike the rambling garden at Farings. She looked to see if there were bean poles – yes, a wigwam of them, twined about with the little scarlet flowers haunted by bees.

Mrs Godwit, in trousers and trainers, was sitting on the sofa. Thankfully, no wheelchair was in sight. 'I'm Gloria. I'm so sorry I missed your party.'

'Bridget Hansome.' Her own voice sounded gruff. Stanley's wife was more socially adept than Bridget had imagined. She felt accountably shy.

'Do sit down, no, not that one, that one's Stanley's, but the chair beside it is quite comfortable. I couldn't get a word out of Stanley about you, so I thought I'd better ask you over to see for myself.'

They drank sherry out of tulip-shaped glasses, which looked like the remnants of wedding presents from long ago. Cordelia's children, a boy and a girl, rather dull, drank Pepsi. Bridget refused nuts and crisps but asked if she might smoke.

'Certainly, I'm sure we have an ashtray somewhere, Corrie . . . ?'

But Bridget said not to bother and accepted an olive instead from Corrie's boy.

Stanley drifted in and out of the room. 'Do sit down, Stanley, or go and clear out your garage and leave us in peace,' said his wife. 'Really, he's driving me mad at the moment!' At any moment she might utter the word 'Men!' and look heavenwards, where Bridget felt her own husband might more likely be found.

Cordelia, coming back from a fruitless ashtray search said, 'Perhaps it's the male menopause?'

'Is there such a thing? My husband was always restless.' Bridget felt it the moment to introduce one.

'Oh, how tactless of me! I had forgotten about your husband. Stanley told me. Of course, I'm very lucky to have Stanley.'

Yes, you are lucky, Bridget thought later, walking, with the sunset before her, back down the lane, over the stile and along the footpath to Farings. She wondered if Stan had really intended to give his wife the book of poetry he had bought in Ludlow. She hardly seemed the sort to enjoy poetry. There was something too knowing about the eyes. The kind, grey-blue eyes of Stanley Godwit opened in her mind; she did hope that at her age she wasn't going to fall in love . . .

And yet which of us can resist falling in love? Of all the manifold temptations open to humankind it must be the

245

most captivating. Peter had not even tried to resist it when, as he frankly told Zelda, he found himself falling in love with her.

Zelda had not thought to discuss Mr Hansome's declarations with her brother; she and Zahin liked such different things. Zelda had her work with her clients, where financially she was well-rewarded for her efforts. She understood that her duties were to make them happy – and if it made them happy to believe they were in love with her, it was not her job to contradict them. In fact, quite the contrary: contradiction, she was aware, being bad for business. And it was useful too, that Mr Hansome should be a bit soppy about her because it meant he didn't enquire too much about why she wouldn't do certain things with him. Not that this troubled her with other clients who liked it – wasn't it why they came to her in the first place! But Mr Hansome came to see her for a different reason – because she reminded him of someone he had been in love with long ago. She didn't mind that – though she herself didn't have much time for love. This was not something she needed to discuss with Zahin, who only wanted the money she was able to get for them. Zahin was hardly the kind to fall in love either . . .

Peter, reflecting, in the place of windy darkness, on the mysteries now revealed to him, remembered how Frances had told him of the inscription drawn in sand, and suddenly understood the meaning of that gesture.

46

Because Bridget's shop was closed on Mondays she was always able to take time after the weekend getting back to London in a leisurely way. She had packed the car and was taking a last look at the rooks, when Stanley Godwit appeared at Farings' garden gate.

'I was just off. You'd have missed me if you'd come five minutes later.'

'I miss you already.'

They looked into each other's eyes.

'Come back next weekend, Bridget.'

It is odd how often when we greatly want a thing we say the opposite. 'I can't – I have to be in London for a trade fair.'

'Skip it.'

'Is this wise, Stanley?'

'I don't care, Bridget, do you?'

'Stan, will you write to me?'

Bridget drove along the M50 so fast she was booked for speeding.

'Damn, I suppose you aren't up for bribes?'

'I'm sorry, madam?'

'I'm afraid I'm in love, officer, I wasn't thinking about what I was doing.'

'It's for your own good, madam. If you don't watch yourself next thing you'll fetch up dead and might take someone else with you into the bargain.'

'Would you say that death's a "bargain", then, officer?'

'I'm sorry, madam . . . ?'

What is a 'bargain', anyway? Bridget reflected, having parted with her driving licence in return for an ominous-looking green form. Something of value, got cheap? Maybe it was life, then, that was the 'bargain'? Could you call all that she had been through 'cheap': her father, running away, working in the hotels for peanuts? But there had been compensations: Sister Mary Eustasia, Shakespeare, Peter – and now, though she hardly dared to voice it, even to herself, there was Stan.

With the green form in her bag, she drove with studied correctness so that it was late when she finally reached Fulham where she was glad to find that Zahin was not at home. Fond as she had grown of him she needed to be alone. Or, perhaps not quite alone . . .

'Peter?' she asked – for she was almost sure that was his particular piece of darkness, in the corner of the bedroom by the big French *armoire*. 'Come out, it's quite safe.'

Zahin was definitely off somewhere, she had checked – there was only her in the house, in the bed that she had once shared with the man whose apparition stood wordlessly across the room from her.

Silence, except for the drone of traffic, ploughing its way up and down the Fulham Road. The seahorses rose and fell in their colourful, hypnotic rhythm.

'OK,' Bridget said, 'be like that! I just thought you might like a chat.'

She was dropping off to sleep, and beginning to dream of Stanley Godwit, walking with him down the lane at Farings, when a familiar voice spoke.

'It's not as easy as all that.'

'Peter?'

She had sat bolt upright, hitting the back of her head on the metal-work art nouveau lily, whose sepals unfurled – dangerously proud, Peter had always said – from the bedhead.

'Peter?'

'Who else did you think it might be?'

'O Pete! Is it *really* you?'

It was many years since she had called him 'Pete'; not since the first day she had suspected his infidelities.

'I suppose it depends what you mean by "really".'

'You haven't lost your sense of humour, at least!'

He had emerged now from the shadows and she saw that he was dressed in his old tweed jacket and cords. His face was clean-shaven, with none of the dark stubble which had grown so fast on his jaw in life, giving him, she had used to say, the look of a Mafia boss turned respectable. He was, in fact, exactly, but without the disfiguring cuts and bruises of the accident, as she had seen him last – in his coffin.

'I suppose you don't have to shave any more?'

'It's one of the compensations.'

He had moved closer to the bed and she patted the place beside her. 'Do you want to sit down?' It was where he used to sit when he sometimes brought her tea, after her trips away – when, most often, he had been trying

249

to make something up to her. 'Can you, in fact, sit?'

'Yes, but there's not the same need – to take the weight off one's feet, I mean.'

'I suppose not.'

A slight awkwardness fell. What did you say to a dead husband you had known for over thirty years? 'How is it being dead?' That sounded too brutal, but she wanted to know.

'Much like life – hard work.'

'Pete – did you just read my mind?'

'Another of the compensations – if that's what it is.'

'I suppose that can have drawbacks.' She might have added, that she, being a fair mind-reader herself, knew this from having lived with him, but that would have been impolite.

'I do know, now, what it must have been like for you.'

'You really *can* read minds, then – I was just a good guesser.'

'Pretty good, I'd say!' He smiled fondly.

'So, if it's not a rude question, what are you doing here? Not that I'm not delighted to see you, mind.'

And she was – truly delighted. She wondered if it had anything to do with her having fallen in love with Stanley Godwit and then quickly tried to expunge the thought.

'You can't unthink a thought – and yes, partly, it is that you are feeling more chipper.'

Here was a turnabout; now she was the one with the reason to feel embarrassed.

As if sensing this the thing-that-had-been-Peter went on. 'We don't appear to those who aren't up to it. We need the right reception, shall we say.'

'But I saw you before . . .'

'I couldn't have spoken to you before. Are you going to run away with that man?'

'Oh, Pete, I don't know. I shouldn't think so. He's married.'

'The wife's rather a pain. I checked her out.'

'But you know that's got nothing to do with it.'

'Oh, I know that now!'

'Can you tell me . . . ?'

'Some day – not yet.'

They sat and looked at each other in the cautious silence. Bridget tried, unsuccessfully, not to think how different this was to looking at Stanley Godwit. It seemed discourteous to be so transparent – and yet her thoughts about Peter were also those of love. Later she wasn't sure how much time had passed with him there before she fell asleep and woke at dawn to the sound of the door closing not quite quietly enough in the hall. Zahin coming home after some night-time activity. What a blessing she had no children and hadn't to lie awake at night, worrying about their safety. She wondered if Peter missed not having had children with her, now he was . . . wherever it was that he was . . .

Or again *wasn't*, she supposed, drifting back again down the green Shropshire lane, her hand in the hard palm of Stanley Godwit, on their way to an unknown destination.

47

Zahin was not at all put out when Bridget informed him that she would be away this weekend as well.

'Not to worry, Mrs Hansome, I will look after the house.'

'You sure you don't mind?'

'There is my studying to do, Mrs Hansome, and Mrs Michael has asked me over to watch *The Crying Game*.'

This was a departure – Mickey watching a film with no Clint in it. 'Was that your idea, Zahin?'

'It is good to change our habits, Mrs Hansome.'

Well, I'm certainly changing mine, Bridget said to herself, motoring down the M4 towards the M5. In the past, she would never have missed a trade fair – since Peter died, she had hardly even been to France. The recognition produced a pang of guilt: she knew Peter had missed her, yet she had never tried to accommodate his dislike of being left alone. But now, when Stanley Godwit wanted her, she was running up to see him at his first request. He had sent a picture postcard of an Arctic tern with a single line written on the back: *Hope this isn't the stuff of tragedies* – so he had been reading the St John. Did she love Stanley more than she had loved Peter? Or was it that now she knew what loss felt like she was more afraid to lose him? How could you calculate? Anyway, what had Sister Mary Eustasia said about comparisons . . . ?

Zahin was delighted at Bridget's change of plan. Too guarded ever to let feelings show, he gave no outward sign of what he felt at being able to get on with experimenting with his sandwich fillings. He was not a person of intense pleasures but his pleasures, when he felt them, were satisfying. He had put into play some further market research, visiting a huge variety of sandwich joints about town. Now he was ready to develop his own menus.

He had decided to adopt a 'This Week's Star Filling' policy, to spice up the more conventional items which, following the results of his questionnaire, would be staples of the sandwich menu. With Bridget out of the way – and wearing, he detected, a new perfume: Mitsouko by Guerlain – Zahin was able to roll up his sleeves and spread out all the ingredients on her kitchen table. Today he would be trying out crayfish with apricot, beetroot and spicy sausage, and his own personal favourite: smoked duck with red onion and salsa. Later, when he was satisfied with the results, he might ask Mrs Michael over to sample them. Although she didn't always like what he had produced he knew she liked to come across to Bridget's kitchen and poke about. Then they would go back to her house together, and watch the video and discuss plans for 'Zandwiches Zpecial – The Last Word in Sandwiches', which was what the business was going to be called.

Stan had arranged to meet Bridget early on the

Saturday morning. The plan was that they would drive to the coast where they had been before to go birdwatching. This meant Bridget had the whole of Friday evening to get through before she saw him, so she wasn't as put out as she might have been to see Bill Dark making his way up the path – at least it would fill in time.

'Hello, Bill.'

'Bridget, I saw your car and thus took a liberty . . . How splendid to see you up here again so soon.'

Seeing the direction of his glance Bridget put him out of his misery. 'Sherry, Bill?'

'Good idea. I must say, you're looking well, quite radiant, if you don't mind my saying?'

A compliment from the wrong person is worse than useless. Bridget stole a look at herself in the lavatory looking glass. He was right, though, she did look well – she had lost weight and her cheekbones had begun to show again.

After several glasses of sherry the Rector snuggled down the sofa towards Bridget and made a pass.

This was too much.

'Oh, come now, just a little cuddle between friends. No harm done!'

'I'm sorry,' said Bridget, springing up and walking across to the other side of the room, as far as it was possible to be from the sofa, 'but time for you to leave, Bill, I think.'

'Nothing venture, nothing win, I always say.'

'And I say, "Nothing doing",' said Bridget, firmly, bolting the front door behind him.

After that it was bath and bed; but she couldn't sleep. She began to read *King Lear* – but the sight of the name,

Cordelia, felt like a reproach and in the end she just lay in the dark trying – since she knew how dangerous it was to anticipate – not to feel excited.

The morning crept flirtatiously through the curtains with intimations of impending heat. Bridget, who had put on, then taken off again, three different outfits – all chosen for their seeming indifference to appearances – finally settled for a faded cotton dress she had bought in a Montelimar market years ago. At least it would be easy to remove. After looking at her face in the bathroom mirror she also put on some blusher – which she had been surprised to find when, back in Fulham, she had ransacked her dressing-table drawer looking for make-up.

Then there was nothing for it but to wait and not drink too many cups of tea, to be sure she didn't have to stop on the way to the sea.

At 7 a.m. she heard the noise of a diesel engine and was at the top of the lane so there was no need for Stan to turn the van round.

'You're punctual.'

'I should be – I've been up since five.'

'Me too!'

They grinned at each other, shy and conspiratorial.

The white van drove through flower-crowded, steep-banked lanes. The air was steamy with damp clay and bracken, and the musty almond smell of meadowsweet, whose delicate cream-froth bracts were pierced by the long phallic heads of loosestrife. Gertrude's flower: the *long purples,/That liberal shepherds give a grosser name . . .*

'What name do you suppose that was, now, Bridget?'

Sister Mary Eustasia had asked. 'Do you see how delicately Shakespeare suggests the queen's veniality? She's sex mad, that's what it is – can't keep off the subject, even when reporting poor Ophelia's drowning.'

Bridget had sometimes wondered what Sister Mary Eustasia would have made of Peter. She herself doubted that 'sex mad' was the right diagnosis of Gertrude. Hamlet's mother needed to belong, that's what it was, to anyone, even if he were – maybe even because he *was* (for aren't sex and death incalculably linked?) – the murderer of her dead husband. Maybe, like for Peter, sex for Gertrude was a play of intimacy? Sister Mary Eustasia, eager to demonstrate her readiness with the taboo topic of sex, for once had missed the point. If there was a point, which Bridget also now doubted. The 'point' about Shakespeare was probably that he saw the dangers of having any 'point' at all . . .

Her mind, free and expansive, flowed into another June day, more than thirty years ago, when she had found purple loosestrife growing along a riverbank in Oxfordshire. She had been with a man who had sold watches in the Portobello Road, on the stall next to her own. Keith, he was called. Later he had been angry with her when she told him about Peter. 'But I never gave you grounds to think this would be permanent!' she had protested. As if anything was permanent anyway. But she had been unfair to Keith: she herself had thought Peter 'permanent'.

It was easy being with Stan. His silences merged with hers. And he knew when to break them.

'There's a thermos of coffee if you'd like to wet your whistle.'

'Does your wife mind you coming out like this?'

'Gets me out of her way.'

Bridget told him about Bill Dark. 'Bloody cheek of it – I've a good mind to go round and punch him on the nose!'

'That's rather sexy,' said Bridget, pleased.

The sea was mint green. They descended, Bridget more ably this time, the steep path to the tiny deserted beach. Stan jumped her down the last plunge into his arms. 'I wanted to do this when we were here before.'

'You should've – I wouldn't have stopped you.'

The sea was cold despite the sun, but Bridget took off her French frock and ran through the waves. 'Come on in!' she bellowed.

'Looks as if it'd freeze the balls off.'

'You know that's a naval term, don't you, not filthy at all?'

Of course he did.

Bridget showed off, humping her bottom out of the water.

'You look like a pink dolphin!' Stan was impressed. '"His delights/Were dolphin-like, they showed his back above/The element they lived in" – which play?'

'*Antony and Cleopatra*!' she yelled back.

The sun spangled the assenting sea as their arms thrashed, making diamond-bright fragments of the water. Across the bay a vista of light and shadow receded hazily towards the steep cliff where they had descended. Above the clifftop soared the seabirds, pearly, dream-like, their wings carving scimitar arcs into the vaulting sky.

Bridget's eyes, dizzy with water drops, saw Stan's head

rear up from beneath a great wave; around him, as if he were some ancient god, her salty lashes created a penumbra of light. Thank heavens! For a heartbeat she had thought him gone to Davy Jones.

'Here's one for you!' she yelled in relief. '"Though the seas threaten, they are merciful!"'

'Dunno. *The Tempest*?'

'Right!'

Afterwards they rubbed each other dry on a single, stiff towel, because Bridget had brought none and Stan had dared risk only the one being found missing from his linen cupboard at home. But they had each brought sandwiches and they fed each other – ham and mustard, cheese and pickle, 'The stuff of life,' Stan said. Then they lay down on the yielding pebbles and the overseeing sun warmed their bones and their bodies, and soon one thing led to another . . .

'I've never been happier,' Stan said, as they began the drive home, their faces and shoulders burning.

'Shh! A bad fairy might hear.'

'I believe in fairies.'

'Of course you do, a sensible man like yourself!'

Perhaps, then, it was a bad fairy that had the Reverend Dark pass by the top of Bridget's lane when Stan dropped her there that evening.

'Evening, Mrs Hansome. Evening, Stanley. Lovely evening.'

'Hello, Bill,' said Stan, trying not to look sheepish. 'You're a bit out of your way, aren't you?'

Bridget said, 'Were you going to call on me, Bill?' and looked at him hard.

'Just taking a constitutional – doctor's orders, you know!'

'You shan't want a lift back to the village, then?'

'Thank you, Stanley, no. I'll accompany Mrs Hansome down the lane, if I may?'

Stan shot a look at Bridget – who turned away so that she wasn't looking when the van drove off.

Halfway down the lane Bridget said, 'If you say anything to anyone about this I'll suggest you sexually assaulted me.'

'Now what would I say to anyone . . . ?'

'You heard,' said Bridget emphatically, turning into her gate, 'and I am not inviting you in!'

Sunday was agony: Bridget tried to read, then she made a stab at weeding the garden. After that she lay on the grass and did nothing. Every fibre of her body ached for Stan – for the pressure of his body on hers.

She thought of herself and Peter, back in the days when he had bought her the thrush-egg scarf. What a meal she had made of that with Zahin and his sister. Why was that? You made 'a meal' of things when the thing wasn't quite true – no, that wasn't it, it was true she had loved the scarf. But the emotion she had recalled it with, was that 'true'? There was some unpleasant taint – to do with jealousy, or guilt? – about Peter. Perhaps this emotion she felt now wasn't 'true' either, this feeling of being stooped double with desire . . . ?

Far up, the rooks wheeled and swirled, their wings drawing ellipses, hooping in interconnected arcs the mercilessly cheerful, forget-me-not sky. Bridget's eyes, dazed by staring into the sun, made mirages of the clouds.

Sometimes we see a cloud that's dragonish... That's what poor Antony had said, contemplating his own vicissitudes before he committed suicide – or tried to. A 'bungler' he called himself, when he botched the job. Antony, Cleopatra's lover, was not unlike Peter – though she herself was hardly Cleopatra!

'Peter?' she called to the roofless sky, but not even the rooks returned an answer.

One of the birds' long, sooty feathers on the ground caught her eye. She picked it up for a bookmark. But there was no concentrating on a book – not even one given to her by Stanley Godwit.

Boredom mingled uneasily with excitement; she rang the Fulham house and Zahin answered. He was studying hard, he said, revising his chemistry. Bridget expressed leave to doubt this. 'What are you *really* doing, Zahin? Is Zelda with you?' Remorse over the fuss she had made about the scarf gave her a conscience about the girl. It seemed ages since there had been signs of her having been in the house. But Zahin said he hadn't heard from Zelda – he was going over to Mickey's later . . .

That evening there was a knock at the door and Bridget flew to find Mrs Nettles – was all the neighbourhood of Merrow going to visit her except the one man she wanted to see?

'Oh, hello, Mrs Nettles.'

'I just called to see if you were all right. Only, Rector Bill mentioned that you were poorly.'

'I'm as right as rain, Mrs Nettles. What can the rector have meant?'

'He said he'd met you and you'd come over all funny.'

'He's pulling your leg, Mrs Nettles. You know what he's like!'

Mrs Nettles, who, more than once, had asked to be called Mandy – it was just that Bridget couldn't cope with the juxtaposition of the two names – looked puzzled. 'Is the rector humorous? I hadn't noticed.'

'He's a scream,' said Bridget, feeling that any minute she might scream herself.

'I'm slow, I never latch on to how people are.'

'You're just fine the way you are, Mandy,' said Bridget conceding defeat.

She was packing the car to leave on Monday when Stan arrived. The gap between the bottom of his trouser legs and his socks looked very vulnerable.

'Sorry, I couldn't get away before. Gloria's had another relapse.' His kind sea eyes were dumb with what could not be said.

'Oh, when?'

'While we were off at the beach . . .'

Embarrassment is catching. 'I see.'

'I told you I couldn't give you much.'

'It's OK,' said Bridget, 'you told me.'

This time she drove as slowly as she could bear back to London. One ought never to ask for too much, she told herself.

48

Mrs Painter had warned Frances that births are commonly heralded by unusual displays of cleaning. Frances had looked polite, but inwardly, when this piece of information had been presented to her along with a collection of brightly coloured knitted baby clothes, she had dismissed it as an old wives' tale.

'Don't like pastels,' said Painter (who rarely used anything else in his palette), 'so I had her do them in decent colours.'

'These were your idea, Patrick?' Frances was turning in her hand a small violet hand-knitted cardigan and matching hat with a scarlet pom-pom.

'She'll look better in colour.'

'Why do you say "she"?'

'It's a girl – I can tell by the way she's lying.'

Two nights later, Frances, unusually wakeful, remembered that she hadn't rinsed down the draining board before going to bed. Halfway through cleaning the bath, the rubber gloves she was wearing developed a hole, and she had to search in the cupboard beneath the sink for another pair. Nothing there but a pair of the surgical gloves Zahin used – unfortunately far too small. The lack of gloves forced Frances to abandon her cleaning but by morning it was apparent she had better call the hospital. Lottie too – who had promised to be on hand if needed . . .

'Take some ice packs,' Lottie advised. 'I'm told the pain is horrendous.'

In the end all Frances brought was herself because there was no time for more before the ambulance arrived.

Patrick and the tea leaves were right: it was a girl child, born in an hour, with tiny fists and a small, red, boxer's face.

'She's adorable,' said Frances, transfixed.

'Each to his own,' said Lottie. 'I knew I was right not to have any! How are you feeling?'

'Wonderful!' said Frances.

'It sounded hellish. Were you in ghastly pain?'

'I didn't feel a thing,' said Frances, blissfully.

'You were screeching like a fishwife,' Lottie said. 'I've never heard such effing and blinding.'

The first response to the birth was from Ed Bittle who sent a glade of white lilies.

'What are those for – the annunciation?' asked Painter, who arrived himself that evening with a bunch of sweet-peas from the garden wrapped in a copy of the *Sunday Sport*. 'He's got you confused, thinks you're a virgin.'

'I think they're lovely,' said Frances, loyally.

'Here you are!' said Painter, taking a frail, candyfloss bloom from where it nestled in the bosom of a *Sunday Sport* girl and laying it against the baby's cheek. 'Pink for a girl – not white for a bleeding angel. You could

263

always call her Sweetpea, after Popeye's baby. You have a look of Olive Oyl about you.'

Frances, correctly, took this for a compliment. 'I'd thought of calling her Petra,' and once she had said it she knew that this had always been her daughter's name.

Ms Nathan called by and was crisply congratulatory. 'Well done! She's a credit to you, and I hear came nice and quick too. If only my young mothers were as obliging.'

Frances had become used to the train of foreign women who traipsed through the ward vaguely mopping disinfectant under the beds. One day it was Teresa from Portugal; the next, Elsa from Sierra Leone. So when a trim, dark woman began to mop vigorously under the bed Frances thought nothing of it but went on reading the book Painter had brought her about Henry Moore.

'You ever find that ring, then?'

Frances looked up. 'Claris!'

'That's right. You remembered.'

'Why are you here? Of course I remember you! No, I never found the ring.'

'Ah, that's a shame. It's one of my cleaning contracts – the school, then the hospital. God returned you something for the loss, though, didn't he? You never said you was expecting.'

'I didn't know myself!'

'That kind's best. My Pearl was one of them. I loved that child more than all the others. A gift from God she was too. I never knew her dad.'

Frances said, 'Petra's father died. She'll never know him either.' It was comforting to feel that Petra and Claris's daughter had something in common.

'Is that right? Then that child's sure going to make up

for that loss too. Her daddie'll be watching over her right now, that right, sweetheart?'

Claris bent and swept up Petra, who had just wakened and was gazing upward with soft unfocused eyes, at a presence neither woman could see. Impossible, Frances thought, to look at those eyes and not be reminded of Hugh. It's like a great web, she reflected, Hugh and me and Peter and Petra, and then Bridget and Patrick and Zahin, and now Claris and Pearl – we're all linked somehow – even the dead.

'There's not another love like it.' Claris laid Petra back in her bassinet. 'You look after yourself, now, darling. Take plenty rest.'

Another surprise was that Painter came to the hospital every day. Because Petra had been born premature and underweight, and Frances had no one at home to look after her, Ms Nathan decreed they should stay in longer than forty-eight hours. In the end they stayed a week; Painter came in a taxi to collect them.

'Mind the baby, mind, mind!' he shouted as they made their way through the hospital with Petra a tight bundle in Frances's arms.

'Patrick, everyone's got babies here.'

'None like ours! The others look half-baked.'

Halfway home Frances said, 'I forgot to say goodbye to Claris.'

'Good God, woman, who's Claris? Turn round, turn round! We have to go back!' Painter roared at the taxi driver, but when the cab began to swing across the road Frances said, 'No, no, it's all right. I just want to get home.' Claris could be found another time.

Painter ensconced Frances and Petra in the flat and

went off, returning with carrier bags stuffed with food.

'Patrick, there's only me – Petra doesn't eat. What's in those bags will feed an army.'

'You need feeding up!'

But with Painter gone, the flat, once such a haven, felt alien. Perhaps it was the presence of Petra but some sea change – Frances could not put her finger on what it was – seemed to have occurred.

'Maybe you need a garden,' Lottie suggested. 'I don't know anything about it but I'm told kids like to look at leaves.'

It was more than a week before Bridget came, and then it was with Zahin. 'Sorry we haven't been before – I've been up to my eyes . . .'

'O Miss Slater, she is adorable!'

'Thank you, Zahin, I think so too.'

'My sister Zelda would love her – she loves babies.'

Frances, carried away by the novel charms of mother-hood, invited Zelda to see the miraculous child. 'Any-way,' she said to Bridget after Zahin had gone off to make tea, 'I'd like to get a closer look at Zelda – I'm curious, aren't you?'

'Not particularly.' Bridget was fighting a desperate, savage, serpentine jealousy. She had never wanted children, and yet the sight of this small representative of Peter's genes activated something vicious she had thought defeated.

Frances, guessing something of this said, bravely, 'You can hold her, if you like,' which was the last thing she wanted to have happen.

Bridget took the tiny bundle in her arms. Peter's daughter. She tried to see some resemblance to her husband in the small, bunched features.

'She's more like my brother – Hugh,' Frances said, reading Bridget's thoughts.

'I didn't know you had another brother.'

'He died.'

'You don't seem to have much luck with your men,' said Bridget, returning Petra abruptly to her basket.

It was as well that Zahin returned with a teatray. 'I remembered where everything was, Miss Slater '

'Frances,' said Frances, automatically.

'– and that you like it weak, see, I have brought hot water and the full-cream milk for Mrs Hansome.'

'Zahin,' said Frances, seeing a chance to get rid of some of Painter's supplies, 'there's ginger biscuits – masses of them – in the kitchen, Mrs Hansome might like one with her tea. And by the way, there's a pair of your rubber gloves in the cupboard under the sink. Don't forget to take them with you when you go.'

Ed Bittle began to be a problem. He rang constantly to ask after Frances's health – happy to hear it was good because then he could come and draw her! In the end his calls became such a nuisance that Frances accepted an invitation from Mrs Painter to stay in Isleworth.

'Patrick'll feel happier with Petra on the premises,' remarked Painter's mother, prodding the Moses basket with her embroidered-slippered foot.

It looked for a while as if there might also be a problem with Roy. Roy had murmured something about replacing Frances, now she was 'occupied'. This notion was put paid to when Painter, in a call, mentioned a rival gallery who had been courting him for years. 'Of course, I would never leave Gambit, because of Frances' was all that need be said, for a bunch of perfumeless red roses to arrive with a note: *Dearest Girl – take such care of yourself, and our little Petronella, of course. R.*

The smile on the R was unusually gracious.

Frances was grateful for Painter's interventions. And it was pleasant, too – Lottie was right – to lie in the garden, with the perfect Petra beside her in her Moses basket, and read, and watch the peacock butterflies and red admirals scattering delicate painterly wings over Mrs Painter's buddleia.

She wished Peter could see his daughter as she lay, curled, sleeping in her rush basket in the shade of Mrs Painter's lilacs. Would Peter have liked Petra? Would he have even wanted her to have the child?

We cannot know the worst that befalls those who have parted with this life, but numbered chief among them might be the pang that Peter felt as he watched over Petra.

The dead cannot cry; thus, it was dry-eyed that Peter silently observed his newborn daughter.

49

Zahin was not openly impatient when he learned that Bridget would be staying in London for the third weekend in a row, but he came as close as he ever had to expressing displeasure.

'But the weather at your country house, would that not be pleasant, Mrs Hansome . . . ?'

'Zahin, I believe you want to get rid of me . . .'

'Oh no, Mrs Hansome.'

He does though, Bridget thought grimly. Even in her own home she was superfluous; not even when Peter died had she felt so low. Mickey called by and looked almost embarrassed to find Bridget in her own kitchen. Mickey spoke mysteriously of tuna fish and mayonnaise.

'Zahin, is Mickey organising a tea, or something? She seems preoccupied with sandwiches.'

Zahin decided it was the moment to come clean. 'It is my new business I am starting. Mrs Michael and I are going into partnership.' He explained about 'Zandwiches Zpecial' and the logo that he'd had specially designed:

an open sandwich with a smiley face constructed of portions of tomato and hard-boiled egg.

'And the headquarters of operations is my kitchen, I suppose.' Bridget was almost hurt. 'What about your sister? Is she part of the plan to take over my house?'

But Zahin didn't want Zelda associated with his sandwich project. In fact, he didn't like her being mentioned at all. Almost sullenly he said, 'I don't know where my sister is right now.'

'Didn't you promise she would go and visit Frances and Petra? I gather they've gone to stay with that disagreeable artist in Isleworth . . .'

Later that day a distinctive-looking young woman made her way down the Charing Cross Road and stopped at one of many phone booths. If she was perturbed by the scrawled invitations that could be read within she gave no outward sign, unless an unnecessary repair to her eye make-up indicated some unusual need for self-protection. That same afternoon, while Mrs Painter was taking her rest (studying the card for the Sweepstake Hurdle in the *Express*) and Painter was preoccupied, repainting, for the third time, a tiny square of lavender, the girl stepped, almost shyly, through the side door into the Painters' garden. She stopped and looked warily around, like a nervous cat, before sighting the Moses basket on the lawn.

Frances, returning from the house, where she had gone to fetch lemonade, was alarmed to see Petra in the arms of a young woman in tight white jeans and a skimpy red top.

'Hey!' she yelled. 'Put that baby down AT ONCE!'

The girl turned a blank face in Frances's direction.

Then she bent to replace Petra – now screaming – back in the basket, before running from the garden.

'That's the last time!' Zelda said to herself. 'The very last.'

Her hair was a mess, she had a stitch in her side and her jeans had almost split in the effort to get away from that horrible woman. From the top of the bus she had clambered on to, Zelda looked down to see Painter, who, alerted by Frances's shouts, had run with furious speed after the interloper, down three streets to the spot where the bus had swallowed up her fleet form.

Petra was still crying when he got back.

'Bitch got away!' Painter fumed. 'We'll get the police along – I'd know her again.'

Frances had calmed down. 'Need we? I think I've an idea who it was.' As soon as the girl had left the garden, and she had made sure no harm had come to Petra, Frances had known. 'It was Zahin's sister, I'm almost sure. I did invite her to come and visit Petra.'

Bridget, when Frances rang, said Zahin was not at home at present but she would ask the moment he came in if his sister had been to call on Frances. 'The description certainly fits the girl I saw at your flat – white jeans, dark hair.'

'Looked like a tart to me!' Painter said. They were eating, Petra on Painter's lap, in the garden. 'Get some of this down you –' offering Frances Guinness – 'good for breastfeeding.'

'No thank you, Patrick, I loathe stout – the name alone is enough to threaten my waistline.'

'Really, Patrick,' said his mother, indulgently, 'such language!'

'I hope she hasn't infected Petra with anything,' said Frances, who was new to the neuroses of parenthood.

Bridget was puzzled, when Zahin returned, to learn that he wanted to make a bonfire. 'It's roasting hot, Zahin. Can't it wait till the weather's cooler?'

As a rule, there was no one more gracefully persuasive than Zahin, but on this occasion he became simply stubborn. 'It is important' was all he would say.

'OK, but you must inform the neighbours. Mickey, of course, will let you do whatever you want . . .'

Fortunately, the neighbours on the other side were away on holiday. In fact, half the street was, so only Bridget was inconvenienced by the acrid smoke billowing from Zahin's fire. Bridget, who could be tactful and in scrutinising Zahin's face had noticed that it looked as if it might have been streaked with tears, did not ask what it was he was burning; it looked like bundles of clothes – though you'd have thought these could more easily have been disposed of at the charity shop on the corner – for donkeys, she seemed to think it was.

Father Gerard, whose dogma was formed in South America, did not fudge the question of hell.

'Nowadays we don't imagine an eternal fire, or devils with pitchforks, oh dear me no! There are those who have claimed it is a place of eternal silence, coldness, filled with ash – but most of us prefer simply to see it as a place of everlasting separation from God's grace. Like a child shut away from a parent's care – the worst of punishments, wouldn't you say, Peter?'

This, though effective, was not the most fruitful of Father Gerard's comparisons. Peter had spent too much of his youth barred from his mother's attentions by his stepfather to do other than switch off from the prospect a similar, but more long-term, deprivation.

Maybe it was this which led to his preferring the idea he had heard in a poem Bridget had quoted to him once:

> Some say the world will end in fire,
> Some say in ice.
> From what I've tasted of desire,
> I hold with those who favour fire . . .

Even so, Peter made no connexion between his desire for Zelda and eternal damnation. The human mind is endlessly plastic, and the intensity of Peter's desire felt to him like something elevated, purifying even. And yet, without question, what he was engaged in was, in the eyes of his Church – certainly Father Gerard would have said so! – a mortal sin. And mortal sin, he was warned, if unrepented, led straight to that unimaginable place, well-represented by artists, until the twenty-first century, with pictures of horned devils almost cheerily tossing condemned souls into blazing pyres or icy wastes.

'What happens if a man dies without being able to confess his sins?' Peter had once asked, and Father Gerard had explained that in that event allowance was made for an act of perfect contrition. 'If a man truly hates his sin at the moment of death, Peter, then that is sufficient to ensure God's infinite mercy comes into play, in which case all other bets are off!'

Mercy – infinite or otherwise – is probably better comprehended through experience than description. One of its less subjective, more universal, manifestations might be the tendency of danger to promote in human beings some saving answering power. At the moment of his death Peter saw in his mind's eye three persons – and saw them, for the first time, as they really were.

Another aspect of objective mercy might be associated with clearness of sight. To see 'truly' is perhaps what is meant by seeing under the gaze of eternity, which is another way of saying 'with the eye of God'. At the moment of death Peter saw truly and understood – and, understanding, forgave what he saw.

Bridget knew that Peter was not a presence in the bedroom that night. There was only the darkness which reflected back the unmediated darkness within herself. Unable to sleep, she put on Peter's dressing gown and went outside.

Bridget made her way barefoot down the path to the bottom of the garden. The sky was lightening in the summer dawn and the glints of red above echoed the still smouldering remnants of Zahin's fire.

Picking up an unburned stick Bridget poked into the glowing embers a remnant of clothing – something white. Now why was Zahin burning what looked like a perfectly good pair of jeans? What a strange boy he was. She wished she knew what Peter had thought of him.

50

By July Bridget knew all about the letter 'unarriving' and could bear it no more. Despite the green form, she drove like a maniac up to Farings and then spent the Friday evening unable to do anything with herself.

On Saturday she forced herself to garden. The runner beans had come on and she picked a trugful – more than enough for a single person.

She had just finished digging out some potatoes when the gate clicked, and turning round with an answering 'click' of the heart, she saw not Stan but his daughter.

'Oh, hello, Cordelia.'

Cordelia was frowning – but that was nothing new; she came and stood too close to Bridget peering at the garden fork.

'What kind are they?'

'Desirée, I think.'

'Funny name for a potato – "Desired".'

'Did you come about anything special?' asked Bridget, who considered it best to keep things as clear as possible.

Cordelia sat down on the bench which Bridget had

bought on the last French-buying round before Peter died. It hadn't been a successful trip; but the old bench she had liked and had hung on to.

'This needs a coat of paint,' said Cordelia, staring critically at the peeling slats of timber.

'Do you think so? I like it as it is.'

'I like our life here too as it is,' said Cordelia, bluntly.

There was a silence during which Bridget did some rapid assessing.

'Rector Dark spoke to Mum.'

'Ah!'

'He said you were in the van, with Dad.'

'We were birdwatching,' said Bridget, wondering why what was almost the truth sounded so lame.

'He hinted to Mum there was more to it – not that he actually *said* anything – it was more his manner.'

It was never wise to reject people outright. 'Yes,' said Bridget, 'I know that manner.'

'Anyway, Mum's upset so I thought I'd come and speak to you.'

Bridget looked over towards the constant rooks. The feather she had found she had kept as a bookmark in Sister Mary Eustasia's Shakespeare. *This feather stirs; she lives!* King Lear says of the dead Cordelia, before he dies himself. If she is dead – Shakespeare suggests that Lear doesn't think so. Was it just delusion then, or had the imagination – or love, or the mix of the two? – the power to hold back death? But the converse was also true.

'You know what,' Bridget said, 'your father told me you were brave. You are. Like your namesake.'

'Oh, her! I can't stand poetry and all that stuff. Dad was always on about it.'

Oh! the difference of man and man, Bridget thought. 'I'm sorry about your mother.'

'I'm sorry too,' said Cordelia looking at Bridget unflinchingly. 'She smelled your cigarettes on Dad the day we went to Aunt Karen's. And she found that book you gave him. Poetry, wasn't it? Mum's like me – she doesn't like poetry.'

It seemed best to leave at once. Bridget drove back to London the same night. How ironic that Gloria Godwit should believe she had bought Stan the H.V. St John poems. Through her mind ran obsessively a fragment of another poem, one that Peter had liked, about the end of the world. They were right, the poets – desire was a kind of hell, no, not 'a kind' – there was nothing 'kind' about it – it was hell, plain and straightforward!

By some lucky chance – or perhaps she was reckoned to have had her fill of bad luck? – the car was not picked out by a single speed cop or camera. Bridget had left Farings at seven and arrived, in record time, at the Fulham house just before ten. Zahin was sitting at her dressing table when she came into the bedroom. Not expecting Bridget back until the following day, he had failed to take his usual precaution: an old metal dustpan against the front door, an alarm against unexpected intrusions.

Speech is slower than instinct. 'Zelda?' enquired Bridget.

'O Mrs Hansome.'

'Zahin!'

The look of dismay deepened. Zahin sat, pathetically squeezing in his hand the ball of cotton wool with which he was removing his eye make-up. The dressing table was strewn with foundation, lipstick, powder, eyeshadow, all the paraphernalia of a last outing for Zelda before the full responsibilities of 'Zandwiches Zpecial' were to be taken on – Bridget recognised the blusher she had worn for Stan.

'O Mrs Hansome . . .' Zahin repeated. His usually melodious voice, rising to a sharp wail, sounded like a cat's fighting.

'Let's have some tea,' said Bridget, ever pragmatic.

In the end there wasn't much to say. That her lodger was in the habit of dressing as a girl was not in itself very interesting to Bridget. What bothered her was something else – something which at first struck her with almost palpable force, and then neatly and suddenly slotted into place. It explained why Zahin had come to find Peter in the first place; but it was something she most certainly did not wish to discuss with the boy. There was only one person alive with whom she could ever imagine having that conversation.

The sobs had abated as soon as Zahin was satisfied that Mrs Hansome would not tell his family. It appeared there really was a sister – a girl of exceptional modesty; it was imperative that no one get to hear of her brother's activities lest it permanently blight her chance in the marriage market.

'Of course I shan't tell anyone, Zahin. People's sexuality is their own affair.'

But was that still the case if you shared that sexuality with your wife? And also with your mistress?

51

Even to herself Bridget had found it hard to explain why, with Peter dead, she had stopped going to France. On the face of it the only impediment to her going had, so to speak, been removed . . . Her husband had never liked her regular visits abroad.

Bridget had been aware that this, in part, had led to Peter's wanderings. But it is difficult to curtail any activity on another's behalf, the more so when it seems innocent – what she had been engaged in was merely a matter of business, hardly wine and roses. Since escaping home, and her father, she had never compromised her own freedom, at least where she was sure no harm was meant by it. But maybe that had taken too little account of the sensibilities of the man she had lived with.

It had occurred to Bridget that in this matter she had had some hand in Peter's search for alternative company, and this, no doubt, had its place in her acceptance of Frances. Although she would never have admitted it openly, to have Frances to talk to had been a comfort of its own kind. That there were limits to Frances's understanding was, to be honest, an aspect of that comfort: Peter might have felt more salient with Frances, better able to conceal, or at least skirt round, his sense of his own infirmities; but with Frances alone he would never have felt fundamentally secure.

But now, when she, Bridget, was in need of an understanding which, in particular, was capable of transcending limits, those 'limits' of Frances's left Bridget also on her own. If not Frances then France was an older, more sophisticated friend it was safe to confide in.

Bridget decided to make a run to the area north-east of Paris. This took her by Rheims where she planned to stop for the first night. She was out of practice with Continental drives; an early stop would do no harm and give the chance of a good start the next morning.

Having found the reasonable hotel – improbably owned by a smart young Chinese couple – where she had stayed before, Bridget went out to take a stroll.

The town of Rheims, as with many French towns of similar age, is formed around its cathedral, approached by an avenue flanked with lime trees, where long ago the kings of France came to be crowned.

Bridget, in the tracks of the long-dead kings, strolled up towards the western face of the flat-faced edifice, whose porches are carved with grotesque examples of human foible and the forms of smiling angels. It was a close afternoon, and already the midges hung in dizzy clouds, occasionally nipping her bare arms. Irritating creatures. She lit a cigarette.

The high wooden doors were wide open, as if ready to embrace her, and a priest in need of a shave emerged through them blinking into the light.

Even if one is not of a religious turn of mind a great cathedral can offer a rest from the world – but Bridget turned aside from the invitation to enter. It was too long since she had been inside any place of worship. Her flight from religion had been total – well, almost total, there had been Sister Mary Eustasia. But in the face of this crisis even the understanding of her old teacher, whose willingness to vault limits (you could almost see the relish with which she would tuck up her habit the better to get a decent run), God knew, had taken her pupil to unsuspected heights, seemed to falter . . .

Bridget walked round to the south side of the building, where more angels aloft bent their vague beam upon her. She sat down on a bench and lit another cigarette.

Possibly this idea she had conceived about Peter and Zelda was all lurid fantasy – the human imagination, of this she had long been convinced, often most resembles a cesspool. But sitting with the insistent, whining midges, beneath the old angels, who had shared their mild, myopic gaze with centuries of human folly, Bridget knew the sudden insight which had visited her the night she had surprised Zahin was not fancy: Peter had not only known Zahin – he had 'known', in the other sense, Zelda as well.

'I'm sorry,' she said down the phone at the hotel. 'It'll be the once only. There's something I need to talk about.'

No answering spark: Stanley Godwit's voice came back at her, depressingly flat and formal. 'We'll see what we can do.'

'I'm calling from France,' Bridget said, trying to keep her voice on an even keel. 'There'll be no number recorded on your phone. You can say I'm a customer calling from a mobile, with birds in the chimney – or bats in the belfry, if you like!' and hung up before she became too arch.

Stan called at Farings the following Saturday. Bridget, back from France, had driven at once up to Shropshire. It was a lowering, moody, brutal-seeming day.

'Like to come to the sea?'

'Have you time? And should you?'

'I have permission, this once.'

Astonishing how two events, otherwise identical, can be poles apart: even the rooks, combing in droves the stubbled fields, appeared to have taken on a different character – like aged, stooped clergymen stretching their legs on some high-minded ecclesiastical outing. The same drive, through the same high lanes laced with the fecund-smelling flowers, seemed, now, to brood only anger, jealousy, hurt – all the plagues I believed I had escaped for good, Bridget reflected. But then nothing is ever quite for good . . .

At the head of the cliff path she stopped and recited:

> *'The very place puts toys of desperation,*
> *Without more motive, into every brain*
> *That looks so many fathoms to the sea*
> *And hears it roar beneath . . .'*

'*Hamlet*, act one, scene four?'

'The same!'

This time he did not jump her down the cliff path.

They sat on the beach, side by side on his anorak, not quite touching.

282

'I'm sorry,' Bridget said again. As if silence was all that remained to them, they had spoken of nothing in the van. 'Only there's something on my mind, and I need someone sensible to talk to about it.' It struck her that she had never really viewed Peter in that capacity.

'Fine,' said Stan.

A fool could see it wasn't. He picked up a flint washed smooth by the relentless action of the sea, and threw it at a post on which a herring gull was perched. The stone hit the post but the gull, never flinching, continued to sit magisterially.

'It's about the boy who has been staying with me at my house.'

'The Iranian lad?'

'Zahin. Yes.' It was tempting to read contempt into the herring gull's cruel yellow, red-spotted bill.

'You like him.' It was a statement rather than a question.

'I do. I like oddballs – "lame dogs", Peter used to call them.'

'He's a lame dog?'

'I suppose so.'

'I suppose we all are in a way.'

There was a cold breeze coming off the sea and the dark, petrol-coloured water was fringed with spume and lightly choppy. Bridget sat watching the waves, insurgent and actual, beat their way towards where the two of them sat on the shingle, with not even a sandwich to share – she and Stanley Godwit, who had made what felt like true love on the same spot just a month before. *Like as the waves make towards the pebbled shore,/So do our minutes hasten to their end . . .*

'I've been telling myself travesty isn't as odd as all that. I mean, look at Shakespeare.'

'He's a cross-dresser, the boy?' What a godsend there was no need with him to spell things out.

'And, I suspect, a prostitute, yes.'

'I see.'

Stanley Godwit appeared to contemplate the same sea. We're all in the same world, but do we see it the same? Bridget wondered. What had her husband seen in a young boy's play of womanhood?

'And the lad was a friend of your husband's?' The sea-grey eyes looked shyly.

'Yes,' and then going on because it was clear he wasn't going to, 'I think Peter was a client. I sensed there was something, now I look back on it, because I was careful to avoid enquiring too far into their – acquaintance, if you know what I mean?' And there was that caller at the house, the one she had toyed with going to bed with herself! The one who had reminded her of Peter. Even from the eyes of her own curiosity she had turned away.

'Didn't want to know?'

'Well, would you?'

Stanley Godwit threw another pebble; this time it missed the post. 'Depends. I like the truth, myself, it feels safer.'

But 'what is truth?' Bridget asked herself. Do we ever know? Could Peter really not have known that Zahin – Zelda – was a boy? Perhaps he hadn't. That inability – or unwillingness? – to look beyond the way the world presented itself to him had been part of Peter's charm. An innocence. It was not an innocence she had shared, even as a girl, and she saw that this had made up part of her resentment towards her husband. She had presented herself to him, fair and square, as she was, and he had paid her back by preferring a fake – a fictional version of femininity.

'It's the audacity I can't quite take in.'

'I tell you what –' said Stan, after a pause in which Bridget calculated how many pebbles it would take to make a successful drowning – probably about six of the really large ones in each pocket, but then there was the problem of the pocket size – 'there's a scene in *Antony and Cleopatra*, when Cleopatra talks about the humiliation of having "Some squeaking Cleopatra boy my greatness". D'you know the one I mean?'

'When she's worried she might be taken prisoner by Caesar?'

'I reckon only Shakespeare could have done that: had the greatest female sex symbol of all time, played, as we know, by a boy actor, talk indignantly about how if she's led captive in triumph before the mob, the Romans will have some boy actor got up to impersonate her – to insult her femininity. Now there's audacious for you! It's a sleight of hand, but it tells you something!'

'What does it tell?'

'I don't know,' said Stanley Godwit. 'I'm not clever enough to say. All I know is that, in Shakespeare, anyway, disguise has a meaning. But what the meaning is is a mystery . . .'

'My teacher used to say something like that.'

'The Players, you see, Bridget,' Sister Mary Eustasia had said, 'with them, now, Hamlet knows where he is. The young boy who plays the part of the queen – we know he is a boy because Hamlet lets us know this when he begs to hope the young man's voice hasn't broken. Think of the Elizabethan audience, though! They are watching a play, which has inside it another play, with a young boy in it – the young player – playing the part of Hamlet's own mother, who is herself a character *we* are watching on the stage, who is also sitting watching a play. So, we, the audience, are watching a play about an audience watching a play in which a young lad is dressed up to play the part of the woman who is watching him. And her part is also played by a boy, but this time we are supposed to be fooled by it! And what is it all for – this "glass of art"? To reflect back to us our own preening, pretending selves. Can you ever imagine a more amusing introduction to the enigma of "reality"?'

But what are we, and who is watching us? Bridget had silently wondered.

'Stan, the day we went to Ludlow, was it me you were coming to see when I met you at the gate?'

'Who else, Bridget?'

'I wondered.'

'I couldn't wait for them to get out of the house.'

'Now he tells me!'

'I couldn't have told you before.'

No, he would never be disloyal. 'Thank you for telling me now.'

And the book of poems she had innocently been the instrument of his buying. 'You never gave that book, did you, to your wife?'

'I bought them for myself because you liked them.'

The stuff of comedies!

'What are we, Stan? Human beings, I mean, not just

you and me. What's the point of us? Are we someone or some *thing*'s entertainment? Like Hamlet's "Mouse-trap"? What are we *for*?'

'I'm not clever enough for that either. Love, maybe?' Together they watched the same round ruby sun drop towards the wide arms of the same sea. 'The thing is,' Stan said, 'I can't leave my wife – not in her condition.'

The price of a good woman is beyond rubies.

'I understand.' Bridget shifted her gaze from where the sun had finally yielded itself up to the sea's fiery embrace and fixed it instead on the herring gull.

'And with someone like yourself I –'

'I understand,' said Bridget again. 'Don't say any more. Please.' The herring gull left the post and took off loftily into the indifferent sky.

After a while Stanley Godwit said, 'It's funny, isn't it? You meet someone and you know that if you had another life you could have done as well with them, better maybe, but you can't because of the life you've already chosen.'

'I know,' said Bridget. With the herring gull gone there was only the sea to stare at. And not even the all-embracing, everlasting, multitudinous seas could absolve this.

'Makes you wish you had foresight – but then, lack of foresight's what marks us out as human, I guess.'

'Do you know, you are a very annoying man,' Bridget said, finally turning her gaze from the encroaching tide. 'What you keep saying about not being clever – I believe you have spent most of your life concealing the fact that you are really extremely clever!'

They looked at each other and she knew that what she

was doing was trying to etch on her memory the strange
sea colour of his eyes.

'Not clever enough to have found you in time,' Stanley
Godwit said.

52

Stanley dropped Bridget at Farings and she drove back to London the same night. The house was quiet when she returned, too quiet for Zahin to be in residence.

By Zahin's standards the kitchen was unusually untidy. Some of his milk had been spilled on the floor by the fridge. Too tired for sleep Bridget, with the energy of exhaustion, looked beneath the sink for a cloth to wipe up the milk. There was a pair of Zahin's surgical gloves there. Picking them up she saw a bulge in one of the flaccid fingers and when she shook the glove something small and hard and round fell out.

'I didn't know,' Peter said. He had approached the bed but not yet sat down upon it. Perhaps he was waiting to see how she had taken the truth she had discovered? 'Cut my throat and hope to die, I didn't realise that she – *he* – was a boy.'

'I'm not sure that's such an impressive oath in the circumstances. But didn't you when you . . . ?'

'No, that's it, you see. We never did. Mostly we just

fooled about. I thought it was because I was different from her – I'm sorry, he's still a "she" to me – other clients and that she wanted me to treat her with respect.'

Bridget, forgetting Peter's immortal powers, thought: How naive!

'It was, very, but then "naive" is what I am – was. That's part of what I have to make up for here, now.'

'What are you doing here, Peter?'

She had asked the question before; now surely she had a right to know.

'I'm in purgatory – pure and simple – and it is very pure and very simple, when you understand it. It's like Father Gerard used to say – you get punished by your sins, not for them.'

'Father Gerard?'

'A Catholic priest I used to know. He wasn't right about everything – it's not what you're forgiven when you die, it's what you forgive that counts.'

Bridget's mind conjured Old Hamlet, the ghost of Prince Hamlet's father, whose thorough-going unforgivingness had wrought mortal havoc on the human beings he left behind. 'I think I could have told you that.'

'I doubt you'll spend long in purgatory, Bridget.'

'I don't know – I seem to have acquired a taste for adultery lately.'

'Yes, I'm sorry about Stan.'

He looked mournful. Bridget, observing this, wondered if anyone looked after him now – or was that, too, part of what he had to learn.

'Perhaps it doesn't matter,' she suggested. 'Perhaps if you love somebody who or what they are, or whether they stay or go, or you stay or go, isn't important.' The remark was either extremely banal or extremely wise. 'What does purgatory consist of, these days?' she went on hastily. 'It can't be like it is in Dante, can it?'

'Dante!' said Peter, and he gave a ghost of a laugh. 'You were reading him when I met you. I fell in love with you just like that!'

'It strikes me there's been rather too much of the "just like that" sort of thing in your life.' Bridget, who wanted to put her arms round him, played at being crisp.

'That's another of the consequences I have to bear now – watching the results of that "sort of thing" as you call it, looking on at the two of you.'

Bridget studied his face: it looked – what did it look? Honestly, just plain tired. 'Not for too long, I hope,' she said. 'Anyway, why just the two of us? What about Zahin – Zelda?'

'That's different. Zelda wasn't real, you see, so she died when I did. Only the real survives here.'

Bridget was overcome by her need to comfort him. 'Well, Frances has her – I should say, your – baby and you know I'm always all right. So if it just depends on us you should be free, soon, to go off to wherever it is you go to after this. What is it, by the way?'

'Unspeakable.'

'Oh dear!'

'No, really, I mean it. It can't be spoken of. Just as well considering the nonsense human beings have spoken over such matters.'

So already he saw himself as other. 'Will you be OK?'

'I've no idea.'

He was just the same as when he was alive, Bridget

thought, and yet there was a difference. 'You mustn't worry,' she said.

'I do though.'

That's what was different. Not that he worried but that he knew he did. 'We'll be OK – all of us. People are. They say they won't get over things, but they do. It's human nature.'

'Oh, human nature!'

'Don't be so snooty – just because you're not one of us any more.'

He smiled at her, misty and congenial, and she knew he would soon be leaving.

'Goodbye, then,' she said, wanting to have said it first.

'Goodbye,' he said. 'Did you know "Goodbye" means "God be with you"?'

She wanted to cry out: You know, don't you, that I always loved you, and love you every inch as much, even though you aren't alive. But he knew that now; that was the other difference.

'Know-all!' She looked at the seahorses. 'It's funny – there seems always to have been three of us until now. First you, me and Frances, then me, Frances and Zahin. Now Frances has Petra and Zahin has his sandwich business it's finally just you and me.' And finalities, good or bad, bestow a certain relief. 'I suppose soon even you will peter out . . .'

'That's a terrible joke, Bid! I was really on my own all the time until I came here, you know.'

This made her sad. 'I didn't know.'

'Don't be sad for me. I'm here to learn.'

'Well, I've been learning too since you've been gone.' Though he hadn't gone – that was the oddest thing; for all his seeming invisibility he was here with her now more truly than he had ever been. It struck her that maybe for the first time there was a complicity between the two of them, like herself and the rooks ... She remembered something. 'I wondered, I half thought I saw you with the rooks once ... ?'

'Oh yes, the rooks! It was fun flying.'

There didn't seem much more to be said.

'Will you give me some sign then, I mean when, you know, you go for –?'

'I'll give you a sign.'

'– good – or bad?'

He nodded. 'Good or bad. By the way, I'm sorry about the ring.'

'What?'

'The sapphire ring – the one I gave Frances.'

'I got over that a long time ago.'

The death-pale face looked at her.

'Oh, all right then, I did mind, still do a little ... Remember, I'm only human!'

But this time he didn't smile and when he spoke it was with the voice of the real. 'I am sorry – it wasn't that I loved you less.'

Bridget thought: *Most necessary 'tis that we forget/To pay ourselves what to ourselves is debt.*

'That's the first time you've ever told me you were sorry.'

'I'm sorry about that too. I wish you'd taught me about Shakespeare.'

'You know, Pete, I've learned more about Shakespeare from you than anyone – you and Sister Mary Eustasia. Though she was wrong about Gertrude – Gertrude didn't marry again because she was venal, it was because she was lonely.'

'I'm sorry you're lonely, Bid.'

'Well, that's what being human is, isn't it? Being lonely. I suppose it's different with you . . . ?'

'It's different, yes . . .'

Wordless, they exchanged looks, until even in the tactful darkness she had to look away. And when she next looked up there were only the seahorses, rising and falling, giving the illusion they would go on for ever.

53

In the end the only way for Frances to stave off Ed Bittle, Painter insisted, was for her to pose for him. 'You never did sit for me anyway.'

'You didn't want me! You were into abstracts.'

'I never remember not wanting you!'

He worked steadily, sizing her up with his dispassionate, lop-sided gaze. 'A life drawing is like making a baby,' he said once. 'There's you, there's me and there's the picture. You only get the picture right if there's a fit with the other two.'

Ed called and went away offended. He confided to Lottie, whom he had met at the hospital when they were both visiting Frances, 'She promised she would sit for me!'

'I'll sit for you,' said Lottie, who was taken with Ed's motorbike leathers.

Frances had planned to leave the Painters after a week – but somehow the 'week' drifted into September. The late summer was unnaturally hot; Petra lay on the rug on the lawn without nappies, and the Ginger Nuts – the seven tiny tortoises – took the sun alongside her. It seemed a pity to break up the nursery, Painter said.

He also insisted in paying Frances when she modelled for him. 'But Patrick, I can't take this – if anything I owe you for board and lodging!'

'I suppose you think I can't afford it,' said Painter, choosing to take offence. 'Sit up straight, woman, your left dug's drooping!'

'That means it's time for Petra's feed.'

Bridget visited once with an altered Zahin. He called Frances by her first name, and gave Petra a velveteen rabbit with which he tried, quite ordinarily, to make her smile.

'She's not old enough to smile yet, Zahin.'

Zahin told them all about his sandwich business and Mrs Painter found a recipe for soda bread. His voice had lost the bell-like tone and had become quite gruff – suitable for a young man about to make a fortune.

Before Zahin and Bridget left, Frances politely asked after Zelda. But Zelda, Bridget explained, had gone back to Iran, wasn't it sad? – though another sister of Zahin's might be coming over soon – and his mother had also promised to pay a visit . . .

'That boy behaved unusually normally,' said Frances, after the two had left. 'I suppose everything's all right there?'

'That Bridget'd sort anyone out – she's a tough nut!'

'You take too much notice of appearances.'

'What else would an artist take notice of? Sit up – you've collapsed into a coil.'

But with September drawing towards its end Frances

felt it was time to leave. 'I must go, Patrick, or I'll never get my independence back.'

'So?' The green eyes looked enquiringly.

'I can't – we can't – live here with you for ever.'

'Why not?' Painter had an exhibition coming up; meticulously, he was repainting imagined defects in the tiny coloured squares.

'You've got your painting . . .'

'What's that got to do with the price of eggs? What's wrong with living with me, anyway?'

'It would be an unusual arrangement.'

Painter turned round. 'I'm told I'm considered "unusual", but what's so funny about asking a pretty woman to live with you?'

Frances felt herself colour. 'But Patrick . . .'

'You think I'm queer, don't you?' Painter said. He was looking at her sideways from one out-of-true eye.

Frances flushed deeper. 'Well –'

'Just because a man loves his mother doesn't make him queer! I never took you for conventional.'

'There's nothing wrong with being homosexual.'

'Speak for yourself!' said Painter, rudely.

'It wasn't just that!' protested Frances.

'What then?'

'You never had any girlfriends.'

'There's hardly any women I find attractive – Celia Johnson's dead and Anne Bancroft's spoken for. You're one of the very few available women I fancy.'

'Thank you,' said Frances; she felt chastened.

'So how about it? You can come and live here.'

Frances thought about it. 'I don't think I'm cut out for marriage,' she said.

'Why not? There's no need to marry, if you don't want to.'

'Living with just one person – it's too much for me. I think that's why I've been a mistress. I seem to work best in a three.'

'In that case,' said Painter, 'I'm ideal. There won't just be me – there's Mother!'

'But she might die,' Frances blurted out.

'She'll die, but there's Petra – and I'll die, and then you'll die – we'll all die one day. Even Petra. What does it matter?'

Perhaps it doesn't, Frances thought. Perhaps I've taken everything too seriously.

Something sharp attacked her toe. Frances looked down to see a tortoise nibbling at her feet. 'Hey!'

'It's your red nail varnish – thinks you're a tomato!'

'I'll think about what you say,' said Frances, 'but I must go home first.' She was flattered by the tortoise's nip.

'Promise you'll think? By the way, I'm glad you've stopped wearing all those dreary colours. That varnish's a good colour on you, goes with the silver sandals – what's it called?'

'It's called "Persian Nights".'

'You thought I fancied that pretty Persian boy, didn't you?' said Painter, and laughed raucously.

He helped to pack her belongings into the car and carried Petra out in her Moses basket.

'Ginger and Fred'd like it too.'

'How do you know that?'

'They like you,' Painter said.

'You mean they like my toes, rather, for lunch!'

'That too. But they respond to your voice. Some voices they tuck their heads in – with you they stick 'em right out, always have. It's the best test.'

Frances didn't ask of what. She drove off waving her hand.

Painter was still standing outside the house when, minutes later, she drove back again.

'Listen,' she said, 'I was thinking – if it'll please Ginger and Fred . . .'

54

There was no longer any pretence of Zahin studying. The sandwich business was up and running: there were the supplies to order for Mrs Michael, deliveries to arrange, the bank manager to be consulted and most of his spare time was spent devising fillings in Bridget's kitchen. He seemed to have wholly forgotten the part he had once played so convincingly for her husband.

One day he came by Bridget's shop. 'Your computer, Bridget, I was wondering, for my cash spreadsheets . . . ?'

Bridget had been turning things over in her mind. 'Sure. I may be able to let you have it outright, soon.'

The new Zahin was matter-of-fact. 'I can give you a good price.'

But Bridget was curious. Taking advantage of the offer of her computer she asked, 'Does your family mind that you're not going to be a chemical engineer?'

'They will mind much more if I tell people I was a prostitute. I have decided to say I will tell, if the family don't let me do as I like.'

So much for his sister's reputation! Bridget thought.

Zahin was not insensitive to the unspoken: there was just a hint of defensiveness when he spoke again. 'Mr Hansome told me to say this if there was any bother.'

'Zahin, why, when you called to see my husband, did you come as a boy – as you are now?'

'Shall I take the computer away with me now then, Bridget?'

The weeks passed and Bridget reached no resolution. Frances had settled in with Painter – and Claris was coming to look after Petra when Frances went back to work part-time at the gallery. Lottie, who had rented the Turnham Green flat, had agreed to fill in some of Frances's hours. It turned out that Lottie's mother's sister had been at school with the sister of Lady Kathleen, this slenderest of connexions being more than enough to endear Lottie to Roy. She had become friendly with Ed Bittle, who was now full of a plan for a sculpture of her – the Virgin post-annunciation, Painter said. A coolness had arisen between Painter and Ed Bittle, but Zahin and Mickey were thick as thieves over Zandwiches Zpecial. I am a cobweb thread, Bridget thought. She saw herself a tiny attenuated wisp, flapping loose in the wind.

The year had moved into October, almost the anniversary of Peter's death. It was nearly two months since Bridget had been to Farings when one morning, as she was on her way to the shop, the phone rang in the hall.

'Yes?'

And at the other end of the line a pause – Stan?

'Bridget?'

'Stan?' A further pause – Stan! 'Stan, are you OK?'

'That's what I rang to ask you, Bridget.'

'I'm OK.' What point was there in saying otherwise.

'You haven't been at Farings.'

'No.'

Another pause.

'That doesn't seem right.'

'Oh, "right" . . . !'

'Well, don't stay away on our account.'

'But what about your wife?' She couldn't bring herself to say the name.

'Gloria's got me. I don't see why you shouldn't be in your house. She'll have to lump it.'

Well, that was a change.

'Look,' said Stan, 'there's something else. About *Antony and Cleopatra* . . .'

'What about them?'

'I was thinking – Antony kills himself because Cleopatra pretends she's dead – she isn't, but he never holds that against her.'

'I see.' She wasn't sure she did.

Was that why the boy had turned up as he did – to blackmail Peter, and show him the 'truth' about who he was?

'Perhaps I do see . . .'

'Probably garbage. Anyway . . .'

'You'd better go, Stan.'

'Yes.' A pause. 'You're unparalleled, Bridget.'

'You too, Stan.'

A week later, passing the estate agents where Mickey had first met Frances, Bridget reached a lightning decision. In a matter of days the house was sold to a cash buyer, an ageing rock star who wanted it for his son – completion to be on October 31st, otherwise, Bridget declared, no sale. Zahin would move in with Mickey

302

where he would be safe for the time being from his family. There wasn't room for any guest there.

Perhaps it was as well that Painter was out when Bridget called at the house in Isleworth. Claris had taken Petra down to the shops and Mrs Painter was at the chiropodist's – so it was just Bridget and Frances. Quite like old times.

'D'you mind if I smoke?'

'Yes, actually.'

'You never did before!'

'I did, but I didn't say. Anyway, there's Petra to think of now.'

Bridget didn't need to say: But she's not here. Frances relented. 'OK, I don't mind that much.'

'I've brought you something,' Bridget handed Frances a small parcel wrapped in lace, 'or Petra, really. I didn't give her a present when she was born.'

'Bridget, you are kind.'

'No I'm not. I'm not kind at all as you will see when you open it. But I'd prefer you wait until I'm gone.'

'Of course.'

'You're happy then?' Bridget drank her coffee – what a relief Frances was back on coffee and no sign of those awful herb teas.

'Very happy, as it happens.'

'"As it happens" is the way to be.'

Frances, conscious that too much 'happiness' could be construed as disloyalty to Peter, said quickly, 'Patrick so adores Petra.'

But Bridget had not only come to deliver the package. There was something she needed to say. A quelling image hovered before her as she summoned her resolution. 'Peter would be glad. He would want Petra to have the best.' At least, she felt, she was now qualified to make this judgement.

Frances looked at Peter's wife. She had been – was – amazingly decent. When you thought how most other women would have behaved . . .

'You've been a real friend, Bridget.'

'I don't know if I've been a friend – but someone – some *thing*,' she corrected herself, 'has shown me that what matters is to be real.' That was what that level ghostly gaze had been meant to show.

'Oh, you're real all right, Bridget!' Frances said.

The house was emptied and the removal van had driven off to take all but a few of Bridget's portable possessions into storage. She watched as it made its way through the bollards which the neighbourhood association had erected at the end of the road. How would the rock star's son get on with Mickey? Well, that wasn't her business any longer – and who could tell, he might turn out to be a friend for Zahin.

'OK, Zahin, I'm packed.'

'I will carry your cases to the car.'

At the car she kissed him and there was a hint of bristle. 'Goodbye for now, Zahin.' Peter must have just missed that emery-board roughness on the soft cheek.

'Goodbye, Bridget. You take care now!'

As the car pulled away the boy – standing outside the house she had shared with him and Peter – put out his hand to wave, and she was held, as if for the first time, by the incredible blue of his eyes. You couldn't blame Peter – that was sheer beauty – that sheen of life: amoral, incomprehensible, and as much part of the scheme of things as lying and faithfulness and forgetfulness and fail-ure – which she had also shared with the pair of them.

The drive seemed to take for ever. Fog had set in making the visibility poor. Bridget, conscious of the three points on her licence, drove, with more care than she had exercised in the past, up the motorway, coming off at the familiar junction.

It was exactly a year and a day since Peter's death: October 31st – Hallowe'en. Tomorrow would be All Saints', the day when, according to the Catholic Church, the disembodied saints mingled democratically with the embodied sinners – but tonight it was the ghosts' turn. Bridget's mind turned to her own ghost, wending his way to whatever destination was to be his. She had believed she had known her husband backwards – but it was forwards you needed to know people. *We know what we are, but know not what we may be*, the mad Ophelia says in her wisdom. How would Peter fare in eternity? What would be his deserts . . . but how could any human measure estimate those? *Use every man after his desert, and who shall 'scape whipping?*

And what of her own deserts? To be sure she hardly deserved to escape whipping! Because she had been reti-cent about her own misery – the wrongs she had been done, as she had seen it – she had secretly thought herself better than her husband, admiring herself for her stoicism and control. But she saw now – or thought she saw – that there was no more good in this way of being than that: she was not a better person than Peter – or Frances. By now, Frances would have unwrapped the 'gift' Bridget had given Peter's daughter, the ring she had found lodged in Zahin's rubber glove the night the milk got spilled –

the sapphire that was the colour of her husband's lover's eyes. Well, no good crying over that! And without all the spilled milk, without Zahin's performance and Peter's blindness, where would they be anyway? Perhaps – no certainly – she and Peter would never have become close after all. They would have gone on, always being polite, never really knowing what they needed to know: to know each other. And Zahin would never have got his sandwich business going – and there would never have been a chance to give Peter's daughter . . . well, but she could have hung on to the ring, couldn't she? Frances, who wasn't so bad herself, would see that.

At the end of the rutted lane light was spilling from Farings' windows, gold on to the receding violet shadow of the garden. Could she have forgotten to turn out the lights before leaving last?

As Bridget opened the front door her heart lurched in hope.

'Who's there . . . ?'

But no one unfolded themselves.

Entering the lighted sitting room Bridget saw – though for the life of her she could not remember leaving it there – a book on the sofa. And between the pages a black feather.

Bridget opened the book, Stanley Godwit's gift, and some flakes of the frail binding fluttered, with the feather, to the floor as she read:

> *I doubt not of my own salvation; and in whom can I have such occasion of doubt as in my Self? When . . .*

I doubt not of my own salvation; and in whom can I have such occasion of doubt as in my Self? When I come to heaven, shall I be able to say to any there, Lord! how got you hither? Was any man less likely to come hither than I?

JOHN DONNE, Sermon VIII, 371

Credits

Visit Salley Vickers'
website at

www.salleyvickers.com

All Fourth Estate books are available from your local bookshop.

For a monthly update on Fourth Estate's latest releases, with interviews, extracts, competitions and special offers visit **www.4thestate.com**

Or visit **www.4thestate.com/readingroom** for the very latest reading guides on our bestselling authors, including Michael Chabon, Annie Proulx, Lorna Sage, Carol Shields.

London · New York

Miss Garnet's Angel

Salley Vickers

'Writes like a haunted angel' *The Times*

When a friend dies, Julia Garnet goes to stay in Venice, where a lifetime of caution is challenged. She encounters the paintings in the local church which tell the story of Tobias and the Angel. The ancient tale of Tobias, who travels to Media unaware he is accompanied by the Archangel Raphael, unfolds alongside Julia Garnet's contemporary journey. As she unravels the story's history, Julia's own life is thrown into question – for, like the shifting sea-light of Venice, nothing here is quite as it seems. Salley Vickers writes with a poise and a wit which belies the novel's deeper themes: love, death and the growth of the human spirit. This many-layered novel truly defies the usual categories.

'Rich, complex and haunting . . . she makes the ancient story as riveting as Miss Garnet's own adventures' *Sunday Times*

'The sort of novel I really enjoy' John Bayley

'A refreshing gentle story'
Anita Brookner, *Spectator Books of the Year*

'A subtle, witty tale'
John de Falbe, *Spectator Books of the Year*

'Delightfully affecting'
Julia Neuberger, *Independent Books of the Year*

'Destined for a long life'
David Sexton, *Evening Standard Books of the Year*

'If you like Penelope Fitzgerald or Barbara Pym, try Salley Vickers'
Sunday Telegraph

'Original and delightful' *Woman's Journal*

'It is a triumph' John Julius Norwich